M.D. LAKE

DEATH CALLS THE TUNE

A Peggy O'Neill Mystery

AVON BOOKS, INC.
1350 Avenue of the Americas
New York, New York 10019

Copyright © 1999 by Allen Simpson
Published by arrangement with the author
Library of Congress Catalog Card Number: 98-91015
ISBN: 0-380-78760-1
www.avonbooks.com/twilight

First Avon Twilight Printing: April 1999

AVON TWILIGHT TRADEMARK REG. U.S. PAT. OFF. AND IN OTHER COUNTRIES, MARCA REGISTRADA, HECHO EN U.S.A.

Printed in the U.S.A.

WCD   10 9 8 7 6 5 4 3 2 1

To Jantje Visscher,
with gratitude for the good things
we did and made together

Prologue

When the phone rang, I was on the porch pretending to read and Gary was outside in the hammock pretending to doze. It was Sunday afternoon and quiet except for the powerboats on the lake and the whine of the mosquitoes trying to get to me through the screen. Gary let the phone ring several times before reaching down to pick it up out of the grass.

He listened, spoke a few words, then pressed the off button and rested the phone on his belly, staring up at the cloudless sky. After a minute, he rolled out of the hammock and came inside, bringing with him the invigorating smell of mosquito repellent.

I was reading Oscar Wilde's essay "The Decay of Lying," a passionate and funny defense of art over nature. I'm very fond of Oscar Wilde. " 'Art,' " I quoted, in an effort to lighten the dark mood that had settled over us that afternoon, " 'is our spirited protest, our gallant attempt to teach Nature her proper place.' "

"So's that," Gary grumbled, gesturing out at the expensive gasoline-powered engines noisily churning up the lake behind him.

"There's nothing spirited or gallant about that," I said. "That's just people with too much money and too few inner resources. You need inner resources to appreciate art. You know that as well as I do."

He shrugged, since it was something he didn't want to know he knew as well as I. "Does the name Evan Turner mean anything to you?" he asked.

"Evan . . . sounds vaguely familiar."

"Dulcie Tyler Farr's grandson."

"Oh, sure." Dulcie Tyler Farr was one of the richest women in the state, if not the richest. I'd met her while trying to solve a murder the previous Christmas and she'd taken a liking to me. I liked her too. "What about him?"

"His body was found a couple of hours ago, washed ashore on Lake Superior. They think he must have fallen from one of the cliffs. That was Kermit on the phone. He wants me to go over there and get the story. You want to come along?"

Kermit was the owner of the *North Country Reader,* a weekly newspaper that served a large area of northern Minnesota. Gary was thinking of buying it, and he'd taken a month's leave of absence from his job on one of the newspapers in Minneapolis to see if he'd like living in a small town and running the paper.

I would have preferred to stay on the porch of the cabin Gary was renting and read Oscar Wilde than follow him around as he gathered the details of a tragic story. But it was the last of the three days I was spending with him at Loon Lake and it would have been unfriendly to let him go off alone, so I said okay, striving for enthusiasm. Lake Superior is about an hour's drive from Loon Lake. Longer if we hit a deer.

Gary's in his late thirties, a few years older than I, with dark, deep-set eyes, a somber face, and a sudden beautiful smile. He'd spent a number of years in Latin America before coming to Minnesota, where I met him. He's written two books about what Western civilization has done to Latin America's indigenous peoples and their cultures, the first of which made the *New York Times* bestseller list. He's been unhappy in the big city as long as I've known him, and dreams of finding a simpler, more natural way of life somewhere else—a somewhere else that always appears just out of reach, like a mirage. It's my belief that he's too complex to live a simple life, but he won't listen to me.

My heart sank when he told me he was considering buying the newspaper at Loon Lake, because I knew that might be a realistic compromise for him between the complex and the simple—at least for a time. I also feared that if he did

buy the paper, it would end our relationship: Loon Lake is a long way from Minneapolis, in more than one sense.

We didn't talk about it as Gary drove the two-lane highway that wound through the forest to Lake Superior. We'd talked about it enough already that weekend. Instead, I asked him what Evan Turner had been doing on Lake Superior.

"Teaching in the summer program the University runs at the conference center there," he answered. "Didn't I meet him at Mrs. Farr's Valentine's Day party?"

"Yeah, and you also met his wife and daughter."

"That's right." After a few moments, he added, "The daughter's name's Annette, isn't it? A nice kid."

I didn't say anything to that. I recalled that Gary had spent most of the evening with her. He likes kids and would like some of his own. That's another interest we don't share.

After a few more minutes of silence, he asked me what I knew about Evan Turner.

"Nothing," I said. "Until we met him at the party, I'd always thought Dulcie had disowned her entire family. He seemed a little boring to me, but his wife was pleasant enough, although I only spoke with her for a couple of minutes."

We came to the lake and turned north. Ahead of us was the Split Rock lighthouse, which stands on a cliff that cuts into the lake like a shovel blade. The U's conference center is a couple of miles north of it.

I thought about how Turner must have died, falling off a cliff like that, and remembered the first time I'd come up to the area and gone hiking, while I was still a student at the U. I'd been surprised by the nakedness of the cliffs, and how straight they fall into the lake. And when I'd hiked in the woods and come out suddenly onto one of the cliffs, I'd been just as surprised at how few guardrails there were. If you were considering suicide, say, you wouldn't even have to climb a fence to get to the edge in a lot of places.

We arrived at the conference center, drove through the open gate, and parked next to a state trooper's car in the lot behind the lodge. The center is built on land donated to

the University by the heirs of one of the wealthy lumber
barons. It's used for conferences during the school year,
but in the summer people come from all over the country
to study there.

A gangly young-old man with an Adam's apple and
scarecrow hair came to meet us. He introduced himself as
Dan McIntyre, a freelance photographer who'd heard about
Turner's death from a state trooper friend and had called
Kermit.

"I got some good quotes," he said enthusiastically as he
followed us to the lodge, "and pictures of them loading the
body into the boat—in a body bag, of course. You couldn't
print pictures of the body itself in a family newspaper like
the *Reader*. It was a real mess."

He pointed down at a row of cabins that lined the lake.
"That's his on the end. The faculty live in the cabins, the
students live in the dorm over there." He gestured to a big
log building half hidden by trees.

A state trooper was lounging next to the lodge's entrance. Gary introduced himself as a reporter for the *North
Country Reader*.

"It appears Turner fell off one of them cliffs up there,"
the trooper said. "He must've been up there taking pictures,
on account of the body was found with a camera wrapped
around the neck by the strap. Tourists, high school kids,
and other idiots are always stepping off the trails to see
how close to the edge of the cliffs they can get. There's
nothing we can do to stop 'em, short of put up high fences,
which would kind of spoil the wilderness, wouldn't it?"

"What makes you think he fell off the cliff?" Gary
asked.

The trooper turned a regulation smile on and off smartly.
"It's too soon to come to any official conclusions, of
course, but according to witnesses, the deceased was in the
habit of hiking around up there, taking pictures. That's one
thing. Another is that there's no way to get to where his
body was found except by boat or by falling, and since he
didn't own a boat and there's no evidence he went off and
rented one, we think it's likely he fell."

A common, garden-variety tourist falling off a cliff on

Lake Superior wouldn't be big news, but Evan Turner wasn't an ordinary tourist. His grandmother was well-known for her philanthropy and her eccentricities, which meant that soon reporters from the larger newspapers would be arriving. We'd got there first, although that didn't mean a great deal, since the *Reader*'s a weekly.

I followed Gary around and listened as he interviewed some of Turner's colleagues, all of whom expressed shock and sorrow at the loss of a valued scholar, teacher, and colleague. When he'd got enough of that, we walked down to the cabins.

We heard music coming from behind them and, curious, went around to see what it was. A woman was sitting on a slab of dark granite on the shore, playing a small harp and singing quietly in a lovely soprano voice. It was a dramatic scene, with the lake lapping at her bare feet and the lighthouse on the cliff in the distance behind her.

We listened a few minutes and then, when she stopped, Gary identified himself and asked her who she was. She told him her name was Fiona McClure and she was the wife of one of the Music School professors. He asked her if she'd known Evan Turner.

She brushed hair away from her face with a long-fingered hand. "Oh, yes. Evan and I go back a long way."

"Could you tell me something about him," Gary asked, "that would give our readers a sense of the man?"

"Perhaps," she replied. She thought a moment, her large, remarkably blue eyes seeming to stare at something far away. "He was a lousy lover, a lousy husband, and a lousy father. His death is no great loss to anybody." She brought her eyes back to Gary. "Will that do?"

Gary, the hard-bitten reporter with a thousand deadlines under his belt, managed to say, "Thank you for your time."

"You didn't write it down," she pointed out.

"No," he said, "I didn't. The *Reader*'s a family newspaper."

She smiled gently. "Well, we wouldn't want to upset families, would we?" She turned back to her harp and resumed playing, something lovely in a minor key.

When we were out of earshot, Gary turned to me. "You know who she is, don't you?"

"Somebody I wouldn't want to stand on the edge of a cliff with," I replied, "if I thought she didn't like me."

"She's a folk musician. Used to be pretty well-known locally—in Minneapolis, I mean. She does recitals and plays at renaissance festivals, and may even have a CD or two still on the shelves. There was a story on her a year or so ago in the *Tribune*," he went on. "She was quite notorious in the seventies."

"How can a harpist be notorious?"

"She once played a recital naked to the waist. Looked sort of like a ship's figurehead, I've been told. The police carted her off to jail, harp and all."

I glanced back at her. "She seems to be sticking to gowns of gauzy material that float lightly in the breeze these days."

Gary stood by our car and stared up at the tree-covered hill leading to the cliffs. "I'd like to go up there and take a look around," he said.

"Of course," I agreed. I didn't mind a pleasant walk in the woods.

The trail climbed gently for a while, then grew steeper as it entered a dense forest of birch, aspens, and maple. The forest floor was covered with spongy moss, fallen trees, and the kinds of flora that are able to grow in low light—I only recognized ferns and poison ivy and a large variety of mushrooms, some of them just as deadly, no doubt, as they were beautiful. It was silent in there too, with only the rustle of birds and small animals busy with their lives. The lake was somewhere to our right, but we couldn't see it.

After about half an hour, blue sky appeared through the trees ahead of us and then the trail opened suddenly into a clearing, with boulders and a few tall pines on hard-packed earth veined with tree roots. The lake lay spread out below us, glittering dully in the afternoon sun like a sheet of rolled lead. The steep granite walls of the cliffs curved away from us on either side, with waves smashing at their bases, and

far out, an ore boat moved with infinite slowness toward the horizon.

I'm not afraid of heights, so I followed Gary to the edge and peered over, holding on to the trunk of a pine tree and experiencing the pleasant hollow sensation in the pit of my stomach that I always get when I put myself in situations like that and imagine what it's like to fall. I could feel the hair rising on my arms and the nape of my neck. We had no way of knowing where Turner had been standing when he fell, but it had to have someplace nearby for his body to have washed ashore where it had been found.

Gary took pictures for the newspaper, then asked if he could take a couple of me. I posed for him leaning against a tree on the edge of the cliff, smiling. Then he set the timer on his camera and placed it on a tree stump, ran over and stood next to me with his arm around my shoulder, and waited for the camera to do its work. I felt his eyes on me, but I looked into the lens.

After that we walked back down to the conference center, with neither of us saying much. Just as we reached Gary's car, another car pulled up beside ours, and a girl jumped out on the passenger side, a look of expectation on her face. I didn't recognize her, but Gary did.

"Annette Turner," he whispered.

I did recognize the woman who got out on the driver's side: Turner's wife. She smiled and nodded to us without recognition—after all, we'd only met once, in February, in quite a different setting.

"Is Dad staying at the lodge," Annette asked her mother, "or does he have one of the cabins?" Before her mother could answer, she went on excitedly, "Oh, look! There's Fiona! Fiona!" she hollered, and ran to Fiona McClure, who was crossing from the lake to one of the cabins, cradling her harp. McClure stopped and put down the harp quickly as the child jumped into her arms, almost knocking her over. They were almost the same height.

I squeezed my eyes shut, then opened them and glanced at Gary—the journalist, the man who was considering leaving the big city and buying a small newspaper on Loon

Lake to escape the confusion of modern civilization—to see if he wanted to interview the widow and her daughter too.

"Let's get out of here," he said quietly, as he slid behind the wheel of his car.

One

We didn't talk much on the way back to Loon Lake and we didn't talk about our future at all the rest of that evening. We made love that night and again the next morning, the greedy and pleasureless kind that people make who know this might be the last time, and then I drove back down to Minneapolis.

That night I was back on campus, walking my beat and keeping an eye on the storm that was moving in from the west.

It had been building since midnight and now, as I hurried across the deserted mall, the thunder and lightning were coming almost simultaneously. I skipped down the steps between the Administration Building and the auditorium and headed across a grassy clearing to the cluster of old buildings that squatted on the bluff above the river. I could choose among them as a place to wait out the storm and I chose the Music School—not only because the late Evan Turner had been a faculty member there, but because the faculty lounge overlooks the river and would give me a fine view of the storm.

I'd almost reached a side door when the sky burst open and the rain came pouring down. I ran the last few yards, used my passkey to slip inside, then pressed the button on my portable radio and told Linehan, the dog watch dispatcher, where I was, and why.

"And haven't I always said Peggy O'Neill knows when to come in out of the rain?" he sang in his fake Irish brogue. "I seem to recall that the Music School lounge is cozy and has a coffee machine."

"Yeah," I retorted, "but the coffee's hideous." I know the quality of the coffee in every building on campus.

"Well, at least the roof doesn't leak," he said glumly. In the heaviest storms, the campus police station's roof does, and it would be leaking tonight. It's an old wooden building that should have been torn down thirty years ago. "Watch out for ghosts," he added, possibly alluding to the death of Evan Turner.

I pushed back the hood on my raincoat and began walking down the hall, whose thick walls, muffling the noise of the storm, were lined with some kind of marble that has what looks like a tree root pattern in it, reenforcing the sense that you're underground—and maybe also reflecting the belief that music comes from deep within the unconscious, who knows? I paused occasionally to peer into the cluttered practice rooms with their music stands and pianos and organs. I imagined I could hear the faint echoes of talented kids practicing their instruments. I'm going to be a concert pianist in my next life, even if it means having to learn *Für Elise* all over again.

Suddenly three dark shapes emerged from the stairs ahead of me, coming down from the second floor. They were each carrying something bulky. The figure in front glanced my way, saw me, and hesitated. The figure behind him, unable to see over his burden, bumped into him Keystone Kop–style, and then one of them shouted, "Run!" and all three turned and disappeared down the stairs to the basement. Not what you'd call normal behavior on the part of people with clear consciences on encountering a cop in the middle of the night.

"Police! Stop!" I called, wasting breath. As I ran down the stairs, I told Linehan I'd interrupted a burglary in progress and was chasing the suspects. With any luck, Lawrence Fitzpatrick, who had the squad car that night, would be somewhere in the vicinity. We only have the one car, since the University is in another of its perennial budget crunches and needs what money it has to purchase a new men's basketball coach.

By the time I reached the basement, the last suspect was just disappearing through the door at the end of the hall.

When I got to it, I shoved it open, ran out into the darkness and rain, plunged down the steps to the sidewalk—and tripped over something on the bottom step.

I landed on my hands and knees, scrambled up whispering horrible curses, retrieved my flashlight, and shone it around. I couldn't see the suspects, or hear them above the earsplitting noises of the storm, which could only mean they'd gone around the side of the building. I went after them, splashing down the path that runs between the Music School and the chain-link fence on the bluff above the river, the rain pouring off my raincoat hood into my face. I almost tripped again over something else the suspects had dropped, but managed to jump over it in time.

My flashlight beam caught dark figures at the fence ahead of me. When I got to them, two had already dropped to the ground on the other side and the third had just reached the top. One of the boxlike things they'd been carrying was lying in the mud at the base of the fence. I dropped my flashlight, jumped onto the box, reached up, and grabbed a foot just before it swung over the fence. He tried to kick himself free, but I hung on, straining to pull him down.

"Don't just stand there, you stupid fuckers—do something!" he screamed at his accomplices on the other side.

I glanced over to see what they might be able to do. One of them, a tall, heavyset male wearing a muscle shirt pasted to his body that made it clear he lifted weights seriously, hesitated a moment, then stooped down and picked something up off the ground—a branch the wind had torn from a tree. He pointed it at my face through the fence and lunged with it, its raw sharp end coming at my eyes.

A lot of things happened then: lightning exploded in the sky above us, throwing the scene into harsh relief, and a woman's voice shouted, "No!" The crack of thunder felt like an earthquake, and one of the figures on the other side of the fence lunged at Muscle Boy. I felt a sharp pain as the end of the branch tore my neck. I let go of the foot I was holding and fell off the box into the mud.

As I scrambled up, I drew my pistol and turned to the fence in time to see the suspect I'd had hold of land on all

fours on the ground on the other side. I had time to note the long jagged tear on the inside of his skinny right arm, which he must have caught on the fence, before he sprang up and clutched it to his side. I caught a quick glimpse of close-set eyes, a bony face, and a skimpy light-brown mustache and goatee as he glanced over his shoulder at me.

"Don't move!" I shouted, pointing my pistol at him.

He turned his back on me and walked to the shrubbery on the edge of the river bluff, said something that sounded like, "C'mon," to the others, then disappeared into the bushes. Muscle Boy let go of the stick and ran after him.

I turned to the remaining suspect, the one who'd saved me from serious harm. It was a woman. Although her face was streaked with mud, I could see her wide mouth and large eyes, and jewelry glittering on her face. A dark-colored T-shirt clung to her breasts.

"Stay where you are," I told her.

She hesitated a moment, her eyes met mine, and then she turned and disappeared into the bushes too.

I wondered if they would have stopped if I'd been a male cop with mean eyes, a broken nose, and a square jaw. I holstered my pistol, told Linehan where they'd gone, then retrieved my flashlight from the mud. I climbed over the fence, my neck throbbing angrily, the raincoat snagging on the top. Uniform shoes that don't dig well into chain-link fences and the equipment on my belt that made it possible for me to enjoy walking around the peaceful University campus in the middle of the night, also put me at a disadvantage in trying to chase suspects wearing only tennis shoes, T-shirts, and jeans. My pistol was useless too, of course, since getting poked in the neck with a sharp stick wasn't serious enough for me to shoot somebody in the back, although the temptation was there.

The ledge on the other side of the fence was about three feet wide, covered in dense shrubbery that concealed the cliff above the river. I approached it cautiously, shining my light on the ground in front of me, then pushed my way through the sodden bushes.

A narrow muddy path angled down to the river on the steep slope. The last of the suspects, the woman, had just

reached the riverbank; the other two had already disappeared. She turned at the bottom and looked back up at me, her facial jewelry glittering dully in the beam of my flashlight. Then she turned and started running upstream after the others.

I watched her go. I had no intention of following them. By the time I got down there, they would have taken one of any number of routes back up to the old warehouse district beyond the University, where they would vanish into the streets and alleys without a trace. The river was also lined in places with thick shrubbery and trees from which they could have ambushed me, if they'd wanted to.

I called Linehan and told him which direction they'd gone, described them as best I could, added that I was returning to the Music School, and then climbed back over the fence. The boxy thing I'd stood on was an amplifier—a black suitcaselike thing with dials and switches. I had no idea how rugged such things were, but I suspected it wouldn't make much difference if I let it sit in the mud and rain awhile longer.

As I rounded the corner, Lawrence came splashing toward me.

"You okay?" he called.

"Never better," I muttered as I sloshed to the front door of the Music School and went in, with him following. He looked me up and down and started to say something. "Don't," I said, holding up a warning hand. I was cold, wet, breathing hard, and mad. I took off my raincoat and let it drop on the floor.

Lawrence peered closely at my neck. "You're bleeding. What happened?" When I told him, he said, "Let me look at it."

"I'll take care of it," I said.

He ignored that too—I was obviously going to have to take a course in assertiveness training or something. He gently pushed my hair away from my neck and peered at the wound, announced that it was a deep gash and that he'd take me to the ER at the University hospital.

I flinched away from him. "It's just a scratch. Do something useful. Find out which faculty member's supposed to

come over here in the middle of the night on occasions like this.'' I turned and marched off to the women's lounge.

"You don't know what was on that stick!" he called after me.

"Probably an obscure South American poison," I snarled. "I'm already starting to feel drowsy—but that could be the conversation.''

I washed the wound, which was more than a scratch but not deep enough that I was in any danger of bleeding to death anytime soon, then covered it with toilet paper. I used paper towels to get the worst of the mud off my trousers, hands, and face.

When I got back to the Music School office, Lawrence had located the number of the faculty member to call in case of an emergency and told him the situation. He said he'd be over in half an hour. I decided I'd done enough for a while and took the opportunity to wait in the faculty lounge with a cup of awful coffee while Lawrence and some other cops prowled around the Music School, trying to find out where the burglars had gotten in and looking for signs of any damage they might have done. I stared morosely out the window at the darkness and rain, pretending I didn't hurt.

"For Pete's sake, Peggy!" Jesse Porter, another cop, exclaimed, peering in the lounge door. "You look like a drowned rat.''

"Skip the sweet talk," I growled. "It doesn't work with me.''

"Go on back to the station," he went on. "Take the squad car.''

"Go away," I said, "I'm on my break." In addition to my throbbing neck, something was giving me a headache. I suspected it was the moon-faced lug standing in the doorway of the lounge, pestering me. Jesse's another good cop, along with Lawrence, but he does tend to mother.

"No signs of a break-in," Lawrence announced, coming back into the lounge in time to interrupt another scintillating conversation. "Must've been students.''

"Or faculty," Jesse, an equal-opportunity accuser, said.

Two

The professor who'd been listed as one of the faculty members to call in an emergency arrived then. His name was David Paul Douglas, a pianist who specialized in accompaniment and also soloed sometimes with the city's symphony orchestra, mostly in summer concerts. I'd heard him accompany singers on a few occasions.

"Well, what'd they get?" he asked as he tossed his open umbrella into a corner next to the entrance. He was a tall, lean man of about forty-five, with dark, sunken eyes, a long nose, and a mustache that, as far as I could see, served only to emphasize how thin his mouth was. He was wearing a light raincoat and a camel beret, and he looked more like an undertaker than a pianist.

I told him about the amplifiers the suspects had dropped as I chased them.

He swore. "Those are kept in the equipment room on the second floor. It's supposed to be kept locked." He shook his head and sighed. "First Evan Turner, now this. What'll it be next? I hope it's not true what they say, that misfortunes come in threes. Well, at least we only lost property this time, and nobody got hurt." He looked at me and flashed a smile full of small white teeth. "Just wet and muddy."

I returned his smile with one of my own that also didn't make it to my eyes.

"Amps are pretty tough," he went on, "so they'll probably be okay, but let's go see what else they got."

Lawrence and I followed him upstairs, stopping at a pair of double doors about halfway down the hall.

"This is where we keep all the expensive stuff," Douglas said. He tried the door, but it was locked. He opened it with a key from his key ring.

The room was filled with audio equipment, only the most obvious of which I recognized: speakers, amplifiers, turntables, microphones, tape recorders. "And that's where the amps are kept," he added, nodding at shelves lining one wall. "Looks like a couple are missing—probably what you found out in the mud." He shook his head disgustedly. "They took the best, so they obviously knew what they were doing." He stood in the middle of the room and looked around.

"Oh, Christ," he exclaimed, and strode over to a large table. "There was a mixing board here this afternoon—twenty-four amps. Not one of the big ones, but big enough." He looked at me. "You didn't see a mixing board out there, did you? You know what they look like?"

I knew what a mixing board looked like. I told him I hadn't seen anything that big out there.

"But how many trips did they make in and out before you interrupted them?" he demanded acidly. "Do you know that?" Without waiting for an answer, he said, "New, that one cost about ten thousand dollars. I'd almost rather the burglars got it than to think of it lying out in the mud."

Lawrence was examining the door. "It doesn't look like it was forced," he said. "They must have had a key."

Douglas explained that only a few people had keys to the equipment room—the director and assistant director, the technicians who set up the audio equipment for concerts—but a lot of people, including graduate students, had keys to the building so they could come in at night and on weekends to work or practice.

He peered more closely at me. "What's that on your neck? You're bleeding. What happened?"

When I'd told him, he said, "So you must have got a good look at the burglars, right?"

"I might recognize them again," I replied, overwhelmed by his sympathy. "One was a woman, the other two were male. One was tall and skinny with long hair and facial

hair, the other was large in all directions—probably a weight lifter—and he'd shaved his head."

"If they were close enough to poke you with a stick, why didn't you use your gun?"

I told him I'd shown them my pistol and ordered them to stop, but they'd ignored me.

"So why didn't you shoot them? Isn't that why you carry a gun, or is it just for show?"

"I only shoot people who pose a clear danger to me or others," I replied, as though I did it on a regular basis. I've actually never shot at anybody.

Douglas started to respond to that, then changed his mind. "Well, I suppose human life is more precious than things," he said grudgingly. "At least, that's what I've been told. Sometimes, though, I wonder if it isn't about time to consider reevaluating that humane notion, to save civilization as we know it."

"Why is 'humane' the first thing to go," I couldn't resist asking, "when we want to save 'civilization as we know it'?"

That seemed to startle him momentarily, but he recovered quickly and threw out his hands in a resigned gesture. "Well, you did scare them off before they cleaned us out, which is obviously what they were planning to do. Thanks for that," he added somewhat lamely.

"You're welcome," I said.

He caught the sarcasm. "I'm sorry. I'm tired. I drove down here yesterday from the Lake Superior conference center for a recital last evening and I'm supposed to be back up there to teach a ten o'clock class this morning. I had a little too much to drink at the party after the recital, so I thought I'd better get a little sleep at home before driving back up north." He gave a short laugh. "My mistake," he added.

Jesse stuck his head in and looked around. He gave a long, low whistle. "Wow!" he exclaimed. "A lot of needy musicians out on the street would love to get in here late at night when nobody's around. It's like a candy store!"

Douglas gave him a suspicious look. "Over the years," he said, "music students have supplemented their incomes

with equipment they've stolen from in here and sold to some of those needy friends of yours out there." He waved his hand in the general direction of Riverside Park, the little community that adjoins the University's New Campus on the west side of the river.

"They're not my friends," Jesse said. "I just know a lot of musicians, and I know what they're like. Not all of 'em, but some. They don't think it's really stealing if you take it from a big public institution like the U."

"I'd like to hear them explain that to a judge," Douglas snapped.

I turned to Jesse, who seemed to be up on the local music scene, and asked him what the burglars would do with equipment they stole.

"Fence it, sell it to friends, or use it. There are hundreds of rock musicians in the Twin Cities and it's a tough business. They get a one-night gig that pays maybe a hundred, hundred and fifty dollars and they have to split it three or four or more ways, depending on how big their band is. And for most venues, the musicians have to bring their own gear. Plus, a lot of 'em want to cut demo—demonstration— tapes too. It's expensive renting studios with the equipment they need. So they need money and equipment both."

"So why do they do it?" Douglas demanded. "Why don't they get real jobs?"

"That's kind of a strange thing for a musician to say," Jesse said mildly, the only way he ever says anything. "Maybe they aren't good enough to be music professors," he added, with an emphasis on "good" so slight it might have been my imagination.

Douglas turned slightly pink. "Well, since you know so much about the struggling rock music scene, maybe you could go undercover to find out if any of these people are using equipment with University serial numbers on it."

"That would take a long time," Jesse answered with a smile. "There're too many musicians, too many bars that have live music, and too many bands. Anyway, musicians don't stay long in one place. Whoever broke in here might be on their way to L.A. or Chicago right now."

Linehan's tinny voice broke in before we could exchange

any more pleasantries. "Peggy, a couple of cops have found a van in the parking lot next to the Music School. It's concealed in the bushes and loaded with electronic stuff and musical instruments."

"Well, thank God for small favors!" Douglas exclaimed, his pale face lighting up as he strode to the door, Lawrence and Jesse at his heels. I felt cold and clammy, but I shrugged into my raincoat and followed them down the stairs and outside.

The rain had stopped, but water still dripped from the trees and rattled noisily down the drainpipes on the side of the building. Without the cops standing around it, the van, nosed into the shrubbery under a large oak, would have been hard to see. It was old and somebody had hand-painted it in black and white zebra stripes. I shone my flashlight into the interior as Jesse and Douglas peered over my shoulder. Jesse whistled again and Douglas gasped at the equipment lying on the torn, dirty carpet inside: stereo speakers, a guitar, a box of microphones, a couple of cases that looked like they held clarinets or some other kind of horn, and the missing mixing board.

"What the hell were they going to do, start a music school of their own?" Douglas whispered in awe.

"They got greedy," Jesse said, a note of sadness in his voice. "If they'd been satisfied with this, they could be halfway to the border by now."

"It's a big truck," Lawrence said, coming up to peer inside too. "Shame to waste all that space on just a few things."

Douglas shot him a hard look.

"That's probably how the burglars thought," Lawrence explained quickly.

Lieutenant Hiller, the duty officer that night, came on the radio. "The van's registered to a Leonard Alvin Nelson, who lives at 477 10th Street, apartment 3A. It's only a few blocks from the Music School. Send Lawrence and Jesse over there to check the place. Maybe they'll catch the suspects still scraping the mud off their shoes. Oh, and Nelson was busted a couple years ago on a narcotics charge—it was a first offense so he got probation—and he's acquired

five parking tickets in the past year, none of which he's paid.''

''A model citizen,'' Professor Douglas muttered sarcastically.

''I'd like to go with Lawrence,'' I told Hiller. ''After all, I can identify the suspects.''

''I'm told you're wet and bloody,'' Hiller's metallic voice objected.

''I'm only damp,'' I said, ''and the scratch stopped bleeding a long time ago.''

''What do you think, Fitzpatrick?''

Lawrence started to say something, saw the look in my eyes. ''She's okay, Lieutenant,'' he replied.

''All right,'' Hiller said, ''but if you bleed to death, Peggy, it's back to sergeant for me.''

I promised I wouldn't bleed to death. Even though he's a lieutenant now, Hiller's still one of the good guys and we need all of those we can get.

The parking tickets he'd mentioned were scattered around on the van's floor in front. Some of them looked as though Nelson had used them to wipe his dipstick. I gathered them up and joined Lawrence in the squad car.

''Please try not to get mud or blood on the seat, would you?'' he said as we drove off.

Three

It was almost five A.M. when we got to Nelson's address, about ten blocks north of the Music School. We parked and walked around the building, a three-story brick square slowly being consumed by the weeds growing up around it and the ivy covering the walls. There was a parking lot in back, next to an alley, with a few old cars in it and an overflowing Dumpster. Two skinny cats slinked away from it as we passed.

There was no security door. We went in and I took the front stairs while Lawrence took the back, checking each floor as we went. The light was dim, the stairwell smelled of disinfectant and old cooking. There was no mud or wet spots to indicate that anybody had entered the building after the rain started. A nice early-to-bed, early-to-rise bunch of tenants—or else they'd removed their shoes before coming in.

After Lawrence had knocked on Nelson's door for half a minute, we heard the thud of feet hitting a bare floor and a moment later the door was thrown open by a tousled-haired man wearing only jockey shorts. He was nobody I'd seen before. He was about my height—I'm five-nine—in his mid-twenties, with heavy, half-closed eyelids that gave his face an expression somewhere between sleepy, bored, and dead.

"Yeah, what?" he asked, leaning out at us, a thin, pasty arm braced against the doorframe, his eyes moving slowly between Lawrence and me. Cops at his door at 5 A.M. didn't appear to upset him greatly. I wondered what would.

"Are you Leonard Nelson?" I asked.

"Lanny. Yeah."

"Can we come in and talk to you?" I fanned out the parking tickets so he could see them.

His eyes opened slightly, apparently an expression of surprise, but he didn't move to let us in. "How'd you get those?" he asked. "You broke into my van? You gotta have a search warrant to do that, don't you?"

"That's what we wanted to talk to you about," Lawrence said. "Your van."

"On account of the tickets?" A smile of disbelief ruffled the placid surface of Nelson's face. "You gotta be kidding! You can't arrest somebody for parking tickets unless you stop 'em for a moving violation."

Great! Just what we needed, a sea lawyer.

He saw the look on my face, laughed. "What time is it anyway? Cops break into my van, then come pounding on my door in the middle of the night! Well, I guess now that you've wiped out all the serious crime in the world, you gotta stay busy somehow."

"Not the tickets, Mr. Nelson," Lawrence said. "We want to talk to you about the van."

"What about it?"

"Where is it?"

Nelson put a puzzled look on his face. "In the parking lot out back." His eyes narrowed even more. "Where else would it be?"

"You sure that's where it is?"

"Well—I'm sure that's where I left it, anyway," he blustered. "Ain't it there?"

"Who'd you loan it to tonight?"

"Loan it to?" He shook his head. "Nobody. You gonna tell me why you're asking these questions sometime before the sun comes up?"

"We found it parked in a faculty parking lot on campus," Lawrence said. "It was used in the commission of a crime."

"You sure you got the right van?"

I pulled out the piece of paper I'd written the license down on and read it to him.

He ran his fingers through his thick reddish brown hair.

"Okay, so that's my van. What kind of a crime are we talking about here?"

"Can we come in?"

"You got a warrant?"

"No, but we're hoping you'll cooperate with us—if you're not involved. What's the problem? You have something to hide?"

He took his time looking me up and down with his sleepy eyes, then shrugged, backed into his room, and gestured us in with his head. "I don't got anything to hide. Make yourselves at home."

It was an efficiency apartment dominated by the bed folded out from the wall. Large water stains gave the ceiling a certain interest, but the walls were bare and cracked in places and the only things of a personal nature were a T-shirt and pair of jeans on the floor at the foot of the bed, a pair of dirty tennis shoes next to them, all drier and cleaner than I. Both the bathroom and a closet door were open and it was obvious nobody was hiding in either.

The only place to sit, other than the bed or the floor, was a rickety-looking butterfly chair with a stained canvas cover, so Lawrence and I remained standing.

"You been mud wrestling or what?" Nelson said to me, looking at my muddy trousers and damp hair.

I asked him who he'd been expecting when he opened the door.

"Me? I wasn't expecting nobody."

I didn't believe him. There was a telephone on the floor next to his bed. The burglars had had plenty of time to get to a phone and warn him they'd had to abandon his van.

"You mind telling us what you've been doing tonight?"

"Besides sleeping, you mean?"

"Besides that, yes."

"I'm a bartender."

"Where?"

"At the Dungeon. You know it?"

I nodded. It was on Hennepin, about a mile north of the campus, in a low-rent student housing area seasoned with bars, X-rated theaters, all-night cafés, and a couple of good

used bookstores. I'd been in the Dungeon a few times, help-ing the city police break up fights late at night, something the campus cops are authorized to do if we're in the squad car nearby and hear the call.

I asked him what hours he worked.

"The night shift. From six to one, when the bar closes on weeknights. I probably got here at, like, one-thirty, one forty-five."

"You didn't hang around afterward and have a couple of beers or anything?" Lawrence asked.

"Uh-uh. The night before, I partied pretty heavy and didn't get any sleep, so by the time I was through this morning, I was too wasted. I came straight home, took a shower, and went to bed—lookin' forward to a good night's sleep," he added with heavy sarcasm.

"If you're telling the truth—" I began.

He threw out his hands in a "What can I say?" gesture.

"—then somebody stole your van and used it to commit a crime."

"I asked you before," he said, "you didn't answer. What kind of crime? Like murder—a drive-by shooting? What?"

"A burglary."

"A burglary, huh? Okay, so go ahead and search the place! Whatever they took, it ain't here. If you found my van over at the U, it was stolen and I don't know nothing about it. Only an idiot would use his own van to commit a crime."

"Only an idiot would leave his keys in his van in this neighborhood," Lawrence put in.

"Yeah, there's that," Nelson admitted good-naturedly. "But hey, I told you, I was wasted and my brain wasn't working too good."

Apparently feeling on safer ground now, he went on, "Besides, a lot of people in this building know me and my schedule, so why don't you go door to door waking every-body up and asking 'em if you can come in and search their apartments without a warrant? Or it could've been somebody just passing by, lookin' in cars to see if they had

keys in 'em. You have any idea what they looked like?" he added, a little too casually, I thought.

I described the suspects to him.

"Jeez!" He laughed. "That really narrows it down, don't it? A gal with jewelry all over her face, a big bald guy, and a tall skinny guy with a mustache and goatee! Maybe they escaped from a circus." He laughed, except for his lidded, watchful eyes.

"We can take you to the police station and go over your story in more detail there," Lawrence said calmly. "Would you like that?"

"No sense of humor, huh?" Then, seeing the look on Lawrence's face, Nelson added quickly, "No, I wouldn't like that. But would you? I've told you everything I know. You got rubber hoses down there or what? You think torture's gonna make me confess to something I didn't do?"

"Mr. Nelson," I said, "whoever took your van was involved in committing a felony. We're going to catch them, because they aren't very bright. And one of them's going to cut a deal with us by telling us how they got the use of your van. It would be best for you if you decided to help us now, before one of them does."

He stood in the middle of his shabby room, skinny and pasty, and watched me with his sleepy-lidded eyes, keeping his face just straight enough so we wouldn't decide to arrest him on probable cause. When I was finished, he said, "I told you, I don't know nothing about it. I'm sorry I left my keys in my van. I'm sorry somebody stole it and used it to rob the U. But I don't know nothing about it. Okay?"

We locked eyes. I gave in first, turned and looked at Lawrence. We both knew that taking Nelson in would be a waste of everybody's time. We knew it and he knew we did.

I asked him if he'd ever been a student at the U.

"Who hasn't? I almost got a degree in accounting, but I got bored with it and dropped out. Now, when do I get my van back?"

I told him he'd have to call the campus police about that and that the van would be taken to the city's impound lot, where it would be fingerprinted.

I tried again. "You're going to be without wheels for a while, Mr. Nelson, thanks to some inconsiderate friends of yours."

He sighed elaborately. "I told you. They ain't friends of mine. How come you don't believe me?"

"Because you're not a very good liar," I replied. That wasn't quite true. Lanny Nelson had the kind of face that would make you doubt him if he told you it was dark at midnight. Faces like that seem to be all the rage now.

I tossed the parking tickets on his bed. "You might want to take care of these before you come looking for your van too," I said, then turned and headed for the door. Not a great exit line, but given the circumstances, the best I could do.

"I'm not inviting him to my birthday party," Lawrence grumbled as we drove away.

Back at the station, Lieutenant Hiller stopped me. "Let me see that gash on your neck, O'Neill." He only called me O'Neill when he was angry.

"Scratch," I said. "It's a scratch. You should've seen the other guy," I added, remembering the gash on one of the suspects' arms.

He gave me an exasperated look, turned to Lawrence, and gave him one too. "Take her over to the ER, Fitzpatrick. You should have done it an hour ago." Back to me: "I'm surprised you turned your head instead of taking it in the eye to show how tough you are."

"I probably would have taken it in the eye," I said, "but the female suspect saved me from it."

"I hope you get a chance to thank her for that someday."

"I do too." I plodded back out to the squad car with Lawrence at my heels. At the ER room they gave me a tetanus shot, washed the wound, and put in a couple of stitches.

We wrote up our reports when we got back to the station, then said good-night and I headed out the door. I wasn't looking forward to the long bike ride home with a sore neck, and now an even sorer butt, courtesy of the ER nurse's hypodermic.

Jesse caught up with me as I was gritting my teeth, about

to swing onto my bike. Even in uniform, he somehow manages to look like he's wearing baggy pants with holes in the knees and a baseball cap on backward. "We can stash that old thing in the back of my truck," he said, "and I'll give you a ride home."

"Deal, Jesse. Thanks."

I didn't say much on the way, just sat hunched in the passenger seat staring out at the new, mostly cloudless day.

"Lucky for you one of the suspects was in a good mood," Jesse said after a while. "You could've been blinded."

"Yeah," I expostulated at length.

"You know what I think?"

I thought about shaking my head to indicate that I didn't, but figured it wouldn't be necessary.

"They're probably local musicians."

"Oh?"

"Who else would know where to come, and take only high-quality stuff? Like I said to Professor Douglas, there's lots of bands out there would kill for stuff like that."

"How come you know so much about it?"

"Lyn and I still get out to hear rock bands sometimes, even though it's not easy when you've got young kids. And when I was in school, before I decided to become a cop, I played in bands around town."

"You did? Were you any good?"

He thought about it a moment. "I dunno. But then Lyn and me got married and I had to get serious about my life, you know?"

"You miss it?"

"What?"

"Making music."

"Nah." Pause. "Oh, a little, I guess. But I haven't given it up completely—I make up songs for the kids. I'm even thinkin' of trying to record some of 'em." He laughed, embarrassed.

I turned and looked at him, wished I hadn't, but managed a smile anyway. "I hope you do," I said. "So, what I have to do is go around and listen to all the rock bands in town until I find a young woman whose face looks like a jewelry

box and a couple of guys straight out of a slacker movie, is that right?"

Sweet guys don't get irony. Jesse chuckled at my ignorance. "That would take a very long time. Besides, these kids might not be far enough along to get gigs yet. There's only so many places they can play and there's a lot of 'em wanting to do it."

He pulled up in front of my place and I got out and thanked him for the ride. I dragged myself and my bike up the walk to my apartment, the lower half of a duplex. My landlady, Mrs. Hammer, lives in the upper half. She was standing on the front stoop, holding her newspaper and watching me approach.

"Hard day at the office?" she inquired.

I laughed in spite of myself, told her it had been one of those nights.

"You want to come up—when you've showered and changed, of course—and tell me about it?"

"No, thanks, Mrs. Hammer. It's a bubblebath and bed kind of morning for me."

I soaked for a long time in the hot bubblebath, something I only do when I'm miserable and need to regress for a while. With my butt aching from the tetanus shot, my neck throbbing from the stitches, and the memory of that stick coming at my face through the chain-link fence, I found myself wishing I could live with a nice guy like Gary at someplace called Loon Lake, happily ever after, as in a fairy tale.

Four

The rest of the week passed uneventfully. One night I broke up a fight outside the Student Union between a couple of nonstudents, other nights I accompanied women who'd worked or studied late to their cars and waited until they'd driven away. I walked along the river below the Old Campus, checking for cars illegally parked there and shooing them away, once I'd assured myself that the women inside were there voluntarily.

Thoughts of Gary drifted in and out of my mind like the stray clouds trailing across the moon and I wondered what he was doing in the evening to keep busy at Loon Lake. And in the night. With a dull stab of jealousy that surprised me, I thought of the woman who wrote the society column for the *North Country Reader*. She was about my age, widowed, and with a five-year-old son. She'd seemed nice and she had a big warm smile. I remembered the thoughtful look she'd given me when Gary introduced us, like a slalom skier assessing the obstacles on the course.

The biggest excitement of the week was when a drunk business professor decided to take a shortcut from his office across the Mall in his shiny red convertible just as I was coming out of a nearby building. I managed to reach in and switch off the engine as he was about to try to drive up the stairs in front of the auditorium. I got him out of the car and handcuffed him and when Lawrence arrived in the squad car we took him to detox downtown, ignoring his threats to have us fired. "Do you have any idea how much grant money I bring into this goddamned place through my

contacts in the business community?'' he screamed. "I'll have your fucking badges!''

I took my breaks, sometimes alone, sometimes with another dog watch cop, either on the bank of the Mississippi below the Old Campus where we could watch the barges float by like ghosts, or in one of the all-night coffee shops on the fringes of the campus. I watched the sun come up and, then, a little before seven A.M., strolled back to the station, filled out my report, and rode home on my bike in the fresh morning air, as the rest of the world was heading off to work. This is what a campus cop's life is usually like in the middle of the night: nine-tenths quiet and one-tenth excitement. It's better than most jobs I could get and it suits me just fine.

I'd only been asleep a couple of hours Friday morning when the phone rang. I let my answering machine take it. It started ringing again a minute later, which was unusual.

I lifted my head from the pillow and contemplated the extension phone on my bedside table. Telemarketers aren't usually that pesky, and friends and what I have in the way of family don't make social calls during the day unless it's an emergency or bad news that couldn't wait. So I reached out and said "Hello" warily, expecting to hear something unpleasant.

"Miss O'Neill?" The voice was soft and unctuous.

"Yes?" I said, drawing it out like a snake hissing.

"This is Butler. I'm calling on Dulcie's behalf."

"Oh." Snappy repartee isn't my strong suit on only a couple of hours' sleep.

"I'm sorry if I awakened you," he went on.

"I don't believe you, Butler. You know I work nights."

"Dulcie insisted," he said with a hint of remorse in his voice.

I liked Butler, so I modulated my tone of voice from annoyed to cool and said, "Why?"

"She wonders if you would be free this afternoon for tea—around four, perhaps?"

"Tea at four, perhaps!" I exclaimed. "How delightful! What's the occasion? The queen's dropping by and Dulcie's short a guest?"

"Ah, Miss O'Neill," he said with a moist chuckle. "Ever the persifleur! May I tell her you'll come?"

Then the coin dropped. "Is this about the death of her grandson?" The funeral for Evan Turner had been the day before.

"Dulcie would prefer to discuss it with you herself," he said. "This afternoon, if that's convenient."

Turner's death had been ruled an accident. When I'd read that, I'd wondered briefly if Dulcie had used her considerable influence to cover up suicide, but rejected the idea. She wouldn't hide something like that, since she's indifferent to what other people think.

"Tell me what's going on, Butler," I demanded.

He lowered his already soft voice. "Your speculation that this concerns the late Evan Turner was most astute, Miss O'Neill. Dulcie is not happy about her grandson's death."

"I should hope not," I said, with a longing glance at my pillow.

"She suspects foul play," he continued, "and wants you to investigate."

"Foul play? Why?"

"She would prefer to tell you that herself."

"Why me? She can afford the best private detectives in the country—in the world, for that matter."

"That's true, of course, but Dulcie believes your knowledge of the University would give you an 'edge,' as I believe they call it in the cruder sorts of crime fiction, over a private operative. She was greatly impressed with your tenacity and shrewdness in solving the murder of the unfortunate Professor Bell last Christmas, when the police were so sure the culprit was that García—"

"Sánchez—and how do you know they call it an 'edge' in the cruder sorts of crime fiction, Butler?"

"Unfortunately," he replied, "Dulcie's addicted to that form of literature and I am sometimes asked to read aloud to her. Be that as it may, she hopes to persuade you to apply the same tenacity and shrewdness—and insight into the mysteries of the academic mind, if I may so put it—to

investigating her grandson's death that you showed on that occasion.''

"I nearly got myself killed on account of my tenacity and shrewdness on that occasion,'' I reminded him. "I'm sorry, Butler, but the answer's no.''

"Dulcie will be distressed to hear that,'' he said sadly.

"That's too bad,'' I replied, and after a few insincere pleasantries, we hung up.

I went back to bed and lay there a few minutes thinking grumpily over the conversation. Who did Dulcie think I was, Mike Hammer? As I fell asleep, I heard again Butler's voice saying, "Dulcie will be distressed to hear that.'' His tone should have reminded me that Dulcie doesn't take distress well, and "no'' not at all.

At a little after two that afternoon, showered and dressed, I was sitting on my deck overlooking the backyard, drinking my first cup of coffee of the day and skimming the newspaper. I was looking forward to a racquetball match at the U with a faculty member who'd been threatening my position on the ladder for several months, a swim at Lake Eleanor afterward, just down the hill from my place, and then fixing dinner for my friend Ginny Raines, who was going to tell me all about her Italian vacation and show me her photographs before I had to go to work that night.

The phone rang. It was Pam Fielding, the midwatch dispatcher. "Captain DiPrima wants to see you in his office as soon as you can get here,'' she said.

My first reaction—it always is—was to wonder what I'd done now, but I couldn't think of anything. The intoxicated business professor had been too embarrassed to follow through on his threat to file charges against me for brutality—it's hard to explain why your expensive convertible is parked on a flight of steps—so it couldn't have been that.

Then I remembered the phone call from Butler that morning. I'd thought it was a dream.

"Okay,'' I sighed.

"When?''

"Four-thirty.'' My racquetball game was scheduled for three.

"You couldn't make it sooner, could you?"

"You know I can't."

After the match, which I won handily, I showered and dressed, then rode across campus in the afternoon heat, dodging summer school students paying no attention to where they walked, locked my bike, and went into the police station. It's a two-story wooden box on the edge of the Old Campus that was put up at the end of World War II as a temporary classroom to handle the influx of GIs, and given to the campus cops when the students and faculty complained of the inhuman conditions.

As I walked down the hall to Captain DiPrima's office, I paused at Ginny's open door, knocked, and peered in. She's my oldest friend on the force, a lieutenant now, the first woman to make that rank. She's short, dark, and sturdily built, with a small upturned nose, big eyes, and a beautiful smile.

"*Ciao,*" I greeted her, since this was her first day back from her vacation. "What's 'Welcome back' in Italian?" Ginny had taken a quickie course in Italian before leaving.

She looked up from her computer. "Beats me."

"Are you sure? That doesn't sound particularly Italian to me. How was Italy? That tower still leaning?"

"Yes, and Italy was *fantastico*! But you haven't really got the full flavor of it, Peggy, until you've been in Venice and watched flotillas of gondolas glide past in the night, loaded to the gills with Japanese tourists singing 'O solo mio.' Did you get my postcards?"

"One of them."

"You'll be getting more. What're you doing here so early?"

"I've been summoned by DiPrima."

"Oh." She didn't ask why. "Well, in that—"

"C'mon, O'Neill!" Lieutenant Bixler said as he stomped past me down the hall. "Chief's waiting. Shake a leg."

"Do *what*?" I called after him.

"You heard me."

"Don't do it, Peggy!" Ginny whispered, as I was about to lift one leg and shake it. I followed Bixler down to

DiPrima's office. Bixler's a pompous rooster of a man who seems to think that if he parts his hair across the nape of his neck and combs it forward, the resulting absurdity will hide the fact that he's going bald. What it does is make him look as though he's being pursued by a high wind. We've never gotten along, largely because, after five years in the Navy, people like Bixler don't terrify me, and it shows.

DiPrima's door was open. I was a little surprised that Dulcie Farr and Butler weren't there too, but it was just DiPrima, Bixler, and me.

As administrators go, Captain DiPrima's not too bad. He's fairly competent and knows it, so he isn't always trying to prove something to himself or others. He's a tidy-looking man with an olive complexion and short-cropped hair going gray, and the whitest real teeth I've ever seen, which makes his smallest smile dazzling.

He favored me with that smile now and told me to sit down. "Coffee?" he asked. "Mine's better than what you get out in the squad room."

"No, thanks." Just because it was better than what we got in the squad room didn't make it drinkable. Also, I don't like fraternizing with administrators. It makes them think they've won me over. I put an expectant look on my face, hoping to hurry this along.

"Apparently you're a close friend of Dulcie Tyler Farr," he began.

"Not a close friend," I replied, "but a friend."

The look on his face told me he was wondering how a mere patrol officer could have a friend that rich and powerful, but he was too proud to ask.

"Did you also know her grandson, Professor Turner?"

"No, I only met him once, at a party at Duls—Mrs. Farr's home."

" 'Duls—!' " Bixler exclaimed in disgust. "My guess is, you went to *Duls—Mrs. Farr*—and asked her if you could investigate her grandson's death. Am I right?" He pointed a fat finger in my direction.

"No," I said. I didn't bother adding that I'd tried to turn down her request to investigate Turner's death. I learned a

long time ago that getting defensive with bullies just feeds their habit.

DiPrima tapped his pen impatiently on his desk. "Mrs. Farr isn't satisfied with the way her grandson's death was investigated by the police up north," he said, "and so she wants us to conduct our own investigation. However, she doesn't seem to think we will do a conscientious job of it. The only one she trusts is you."

He flashed me his bright, white smile. "The way you solved Professor Bell's murder last year seems to have impressed her greatly—as it did all of us," he added smoothly. "She communicated her concerns and desires to President Hightower, who communicated them to me. Needless to say, I'm going to do all I can to satisfy her. And I hope you will too."

DiPrima had been agitating for a new building for the campus police ever since he arrived here, and turning down the president, or botching the job for Dulcie, wouldn't help his cause. Dulcie has given a great deal of money to the University over the years, and the University hopes for a lot more.

"I don't have much choice, do I?" I asked.

"None of us does," he replied. "I'm sure you know the proverb, 'Who pays the piper calls the tune.' Well, these days money always calls the tune around here."

He leaned back in his chair and clasped his hands behind his head. "Actually, I don't know what you can do, Officer O'Neill. I've looked at the report of the police up there and it seems obvious the man's death was an accident—or, just as likely, suicide. But Mrs. Farr won't believe it until she hears it from you. I very much hope that you can lay her concerns to rest—while upsetting as few people as possible."

"There's no reason to put faculty through a grinder just to please a rich old lady," Bixler stuck in, translating DiPrima's words into the vernacular to make sure he'd understood them.

"Please keep in mind," DiPrima went on, "that we are not calling Evan Turner's death a murder. We're simply conducting our own investigation to satisfy ourselves that

nothing has been overlooked." He waited for me to nod, then added, "You'll report to Lieutenant Bixler."

"I'd rather report to Lieutenant Raines," I said.

Bixler's face mottled and DiPrima's eyes—none too warm at the best of times—went chilly. "Lieutenant Raines has just returned from vacation," he said, "and she has a lot of work to catch up on. You'll report to Lieutenant Bixler." He also knew Ginny and I were good friends.

"Yes, sir," I said, for I know when to quit.

He picked a fat manila envelope up off his desk and held it out to me. "This is your copy of the police report. Mrs. Farr also wants to see you this evening at her place at seven-thirty—for coffee and dessert, I believe."

"I have a dinner date," I said.

He gave me a slightly baffled look, as though he didn't understand the relevance of my words. "I've assured her you'll be there," he said. "That's all. Good luck."

Bixler and I went back out into the hall. Neither of us was happy. "Coffee and dessert at Dulcie's," he muttered in disbelief. Dulcie wouldn't let Bixler cut her grass, not unless he were tethered like a goat.

"Now that I'm a detective," I asked him, "do I get an office of my own?"

"In your dreams. And you're not a detective, O'Neill, you're on special assignment. Temporary. And remember, you work for us. When you're through jumping through hoops for 'Dulcie,' you're gonna have to come back here—unless you expect her to mention you in her will," he added with a phlegmy guffaw. "So don't go stepping on any toes while you're enjoying a vacation on our time. And don't forget, I want a daily report waiting for me on my desk every morning when I come in."

"Sometime before noon, then?" I asked. As long as I had Dulcie behind me, I might as well make the most of it.

His stoat's eyes bulged out of his fat head and he started to say something, then changed his mind and stomped down the hall to his office.

I went into Ginny's office, pulled a chair up to her desk, and cleared a space for the report DiPrima had given me.

"Sit down," she said. "Make yourself at home. You

look like you want to commit a murder. Do I get to guess who the victim might be?''

I told her why I'd been called in, then began reading through the police report on Turner's death, with Ginny reading over my shoulder, chewing noisily on a stalk of celery.

Turner had been the outgoing director of the Music school. At the time he'd fallen or jumped—or been thrown—off the cliff into Lake Superior, he'd been at the conference center a week. He was last seen after classes were over on Friday afternoon, by a couple of students who claimed they'd spotted him walking up the trail into the woods, carrying his tripod and camera bag.

Hikers found the camera bag on the cliff above where his body had been found. His camera was discovered around his neck and the film inside it was ruined.

It was assumed that he'd decided to spend that weekend at the center rather than drive down here, something a lot of the faculty and students did, since it's an easy three-hour drive, and two straight weeks in the woods without a break is asking a lot of anybody except the hardiest of pioneers— at least in my opinion. Nobody could recall seeing him that weekend, however, after he'd disappeared into the woods Friday afternoon.

''Isn't that a little odd?'' Ginny asked. ''Nobody wondering where he was that weekend?''

The medical examiner's report appeared to answer that question. Faculty and students came and went on the weekends and nobody had noticed that Turner's car was in the parking lot the whole time. Furthermore, the cabins had kitchens and people either fixed their own meals or drove to one of the nearby restaurants, since the lodge dining hall was closed on the weekends.

The medical examiner estimated that Turner had been dead at least twenty-four hours, probably longer, when his body had been found. There were no signs of foul play that couldn't as easily be explained by the fall and the time the body had spent in the water being battered around on the rocky shore by the waves, which can get pretty fierce in a high wind. There was no evidence that he'd been drinking

or under the influence of drugs, and no water in his lungs, which meant either that the fall had killed him instantly or that he'd been dead when he hit the water.

He'd been forty-eight when he died, with one child. He and his wife were divorced. I hadn't known that until I read the obituary in the paper.

The report included summaries of interviews with the faculty who'd been at the conference center with Turner, none of whom could shed any light on his death other than what seemed obvious, that he'd got too close to the edge of a cliff in search of a good photograph and fallen over. He'd seemed more preoccupied than usual, according to some of the people who saw him regularly, and even a little depressed, probably due to the breakup of his marriage. According to his wife, he'd asked her for a reconciliation a few days before leaving for Lake Superior, but she'd turned him down.

"Reading between the lines," Ginny said, tapping the report with the celery stalk, now badly chewed, "it sounds as though the police up there wouldn't be terribly surprised if Turner had committed suicide."

"Neither would I," I said, "if Dulcie hadn't pulled strings to get me to look into his death." I snatched the celery stump out of her hand and popped it into my own mouth, since I like celery, even when it's slightly used.

"Are you going to have to drive up there and interview everybody?" she asked.

"I hope not. The session ended today, so the Music School faculty should all be coming back down here sometime this weekend."

"Too bad about the film," she said. "It might've answered the important question, like the black box in an airplane. Maybe it would've shown a deer rearing up on its hind legs, about to kick Turner off the cliff—or a bear. I've been up there a few times, and it's a dangerous place if you're not looking where you're going. One minute you're strolling happily along a path, the next you're standing at a breath-sucking drop of a couple hundred feet straight down to the lake."

She rooted around in a plastic bag for something else to

chew on. "It would kill me to fall off a cliff like that," she went on, contemplating a radish. "Getting kicked in the head by a deer before falling would be better than just falling, in my opinion—more merciful. Or knocked over by a charging moose. The pain might take your mind off what was about to happen to you."

She popped the radish in her mouth, chewed it and swallowed it, then leaned back in her chair and stared thoughtfully out into space. "I wonder if the human brain can process what's happening as the ground rushes up at you. It probably can—the brain just doesn't know when to quit."

Lieutenant Bixler strode past Ginny's door, glared in at us.

"There are exceptions, of course," she added.

The medical examiner's conclusion was that Turner's death had been an accident.

"You're supposed to prove he was murdered, huh?" Ginny asked.

"Or convince his grandmother he wasn't. That's what DiPrima really wants me to do, of course."

"Well, it's easier to prove a positive than a negative," she said, "so you'd better prove it was murder."

She tapped her teeth with a pencil, probably because she knows it annoys me. "Maybe his death and the Music School burglary are connected, since the one followed the other so fast. The burglars might've killed Turner, taken his University keys, and planned to clean the school out—until our feisty Peggy O'Neill, sensing something amiss, went in to investigate."

I ignored that, sat back and stared at her messy bulletin board a moment, then stuffed the report back in its envelope and got up. "I've been ordered to attend upon Dulcie at the mansion tonight," I said, "so dinner's off. How about tomorrow night?"

"Tomorrow's fine," she said. "Just no pasta, okay? I'm off pasta for a while."

"I wasn't planning to cook Italian," I said. "I'll microwave a couple of pieces of chicken and stir them into one of those premixed salads. It makes a tasty, nutritious, and low-fat dish."

"Don't go to too much trouble," she said.

I drove home to get ready for coffee and dessert with Dulcie Tyler Farr at seven, which was marginally better than tea at four.

Five

I got out my evening-at-the-mansion outfit—pearl slacks and jacket that cost me a fraction of what the original owner must have paid for the outfit, a green silk blouse that matches my eyes and complements my red hair—and at the appointed time drove across town to Summit, a wide street paved with money so old it no longer stinks. Dulcie's mansion is the one at the very top, with a view of the entire city.

She's never made a secret of the fact that she met her late husband, Maurice D. Farr III, in the whorehouse where she worked as the pianist. "Three," as she called him, was heir to one of the largest fortunes in the state, and their wedding—sometime around the Second World War—was the event of the decade. Dulcie insisted on wearing a white gown since, as she'd pointed out, she'd only provided the music in the whorehouse, she hadn't danced to it, unlike the bridegroom and many of the male guests present.

When Three died, Dulcie set out to use her immense fortune to redress the damage that the patriarch, One, had inflicted on the world in earning it, through the Dulcie Tyler Farr Foundation.

While I was trying to solve a murder that involved one of her paintings, she'd taken a liking to me, and since then she's invited me to lunch, tea, and dinner occasionally, and also to the occasional soiree. Valentine's Day was the only holiday she celebrated with any enthusiasm, and it was at the last one that Gary and I had met the late Evan Turner and his wife and daughter.

I drove through the open gates and up the wide, curved

driveway, parked and walked up to the massive front door, and rang the bell. It was opened a minute later by Butler.

"Good evening, Miss O'Neill," he oozed. "How nice that you could come."

"Yes, isn't it?" I replied churlishly. I could hear piano music coming from the living room.

He gave me his smile, composed of long snaggly teeth and amused old eyes. Dulcie's ninety or close to it and Butler can't be far behind. He's tall, cadaverous, and gray, with a long nose and a jutting, bony chin. I have no idea if Butler is his first name, last name, or occupation, but I do know that he's been with Dulcie at least since her husband died some forty years ago and that he spent much of his early life in the theater.

As I followed him down the hall, the music grew louder: Chopin's "Funeral March." Across the dark, cluttered living room, her back to me, Dulcie was playing the battered old upright piano that she'd liberated from the whorehouse where she'd met her husband. Butler held up a hand to warn me not to disturb her.

I would have been too awed to disturb her in any case. Her hands moved ceremoniously over the keys, her body swaying like a slow metronome as she played a piece of music that I didn't suppose had been much requested during the years she played professionally.

When the last lugubrious notes died away, she held her hands on the keys a minute longer, then swung around on the bench, pointed a long, bony finger at me, and cried, "Vengeance!"

"Caffeinated or decaffeinated, Miss O'Neill?" Butler asked.

"Caffeinated," I told him.

He nodded solemnly and vanished in the direction of the kitchen.

I crossed the room and sank into a sofa under a wild abstraction painted by a young artist who'd attracted Dulcie's attention. Dulcie got up from the piano, came over, and sat down next to me, almost disappearing into the sofa. She's a tiny woman with sharp birdlike features, dark eyes

that tend to glow, and an enormous, messy pile of silvery hair, possibly real.

"Thank you for coming, my dear," she said, patting my hand. She leaned closer, peered at the bandage on my neck. "How did you do that?"

"The Music School burglary." I explained how it happened.

She shook her head in disgust. "I hope they catch them! We don't want people like that running around loose, do we?"

I agreed with her, then got down to business. "The police have called your grandson's death an accident."

She made a disgusted noise. "The police! They may be good at catching men in wool shirts who've caught more than their limit of fish or moose, but they're hopeless when faced with real crime. Now tell me, Peggy: how'd you happen to be at the conference center when they found Evan's body?"

When I'd explained, she nodded. "I'm glad you were there, and that you mentioned it in your note of sympathy. Otherwise, I might not have thought of you for this task."

Next time, I promised myself, I'd send a ready-made card with a one-size-fits-all expression of sympathy, and leave it at that.

Butler wheeled in a cart of rich desserts and a silver coffee service. I took a piece of chocolate praline cheesecake and a cup of coffee, and Butler poured Dulcie a cup of tea.

After we'd eaten and drunk for a few minutes, she said, "You remember Evan, of course, from my little Valentine's Day get-together."

I nodded. Her "little Valentine's Day get-together" had included a number of scantily dressed cherubs, a Cupid, a vulgar Dionysus, and a string quartet, as well as many of the more prominent people in town in evening dress. I had only a vague recollection of Evan Turner as a man of average build, slightly overweight, with brown hair beginning to gray at the temples and a pleasant smile. Not somebody you'd think could inspire murder.

"And you met his wife too," she added, her lips thinning

in disapproval. "Marcy. They were still together in February." Her eyes glittered maliciously. "Although she was cheating on him at the time."

Butler, hovering, coughed discreetly, probably the only way he was capable of coughing. "Those were not Evan's precise words," he said.

"Close enough!" she snapped, glaring at him.

"Since I'm supposed to play sleuth," I said, "I'd like to hear how Butler recalls him expressing it."

"He said he *suspected* there was another man," Butler said.

"He must have had his reasons!" Dulcie flared.

Butler pursed his lips. They engaged in a brief stare fight that ended in a tie, as these contests usually did.

"But he didn't give any reasons?" I asked.

"No," she answered. "But why else would she throw him out, if she hadn't found somebody else?"

I found Dulcie's obtuseness unlike her. "Because *he'd* found somebody else?" I ventured.

"I asked him if that was the case and he assured me it was not," she said.

I looked at Butler, who gazed back at me with a look of serenity that spoke several slim volumes. "I take it you think Evan was murdered," I said to Dulcie, "and that Marcy was responsible."

"I'm keeping an open mind about it," she replied virtuously, "but I'm not satisfied that Evan just fell off that cliff. I don't know of anybody who had a motive for wanting him dead besides Marcy. That's something else for you to look into—whether Evan had enemies."

"And what was Marcy's motive?"

"Money, of course—the classic motive! Evan's insurance." She shook her head in disbelief. "They were divorced, Marcy had been cheating on him, and yet he hadn't changed his will at the time he died! It's my belief he still loved her, and hoped they could patch things up somehow. Men are such fools where women are concerned. Marcy, you realize, is French," she added, giving me a knowing look.

"Her parents were French," Butler amended. "She's as American as you are, Dulcie."

She glared at him. He glared back.

"How much money are we talking about here?" I asked, to break the impasse.

"Half a million dollars."

"Where'd he get that kind of money? From you?"

"When Marcy was pregnant with Annette," she said, "I took out a life insurance policy on Evan that's payable to Marcy. Once Evan was promoted to full professor, he took over the payments. It's worth a quarter of a million dollars—double that for accidental death. So you see, my grandson was worth nothing to Marcy alive, but he was worth more than half a million to her dead. Oh, I don't believe she pushed him over that cliff herself—necessarily. But find out who her lover is, Peggy, and where he was that weekend! Or find out who had a better motive, if such a person exists. Then, perhaps, I can rest more easily, knowing Marcy and her—her Casanova are in their love nest, squandering the money I intended for poor Annette."

After a moment, I sat back and looked from the one to the other. Butler's gaze met mine with complete equanimity. Dulcie's did not.

"So Evan falls off a cliff while out taking photographs, and you think it was murder," I said to Dulcie. "Why?"

"I've told you. I'm not satisfied it was an accident."

"Why?"

"Marcy—!"

"I know, she's French. Not good enough."

Butler cleared his throat. She shot him a look. He folded his hands in his lap. She pressed her lips together. I waited.

"Evan had vertigo," she said finally.

"How do you know?"

"I know. Trust me, he would not have gone near enough to a cliff to fall over it."

"I trust you," I replied, not entirely truthfully, "but I'd like to know how you know."

"That's not important." She gave me a look that told me that subject was closed.

"All right," I said. "So he may have had vertigo at one time, but grown out of it."

"I thought of that," she replied. "I spoke with a very distinguished psychologist about it, and he assures me that would be most unlikely. Most unlikely."

"You can find a very distinguished psychologist to tell you anything you want to hear," I pointed out. "Just ask any trial lawyer."

"You're much too cynical, Peggy. Cynicism ages a woman's skin. Vertigo's very real to the people who have it, but it's like allergies, people who don't have them don't believe they really exist."

I asked her when she'd last seen her grandson.

"A week or so before he left to go up to Lake Superior. We had him over for dinner. He seemed in good spirits."

I asked her if Turner had enemies. She threw out her hands in a helpless gesture. "I suppose he must have stepped on a few toes in his capacity as director of the Music School, but I don't know anything about his professional life, other than that he was glad his term as director was up this spring, and he was looking forward to doing other, more creative things."

"Do you have any idea how he was taking the breakup of his marriage?"

"My impression," Butler put in, "was that he was indifferent to it. Wouldn't you agree, Dulcie?"

She didn't say anything, just nodded.

"Do you know why?"

They both shook their heads, said nothing, watched me like two decrepit birds.

"So you don't really know very much about Evan, do you?" I said.

Dulcie looked down at her hands. Butler looked at her, concern in his face. "No," she said finally, "I saw very little of Evan in recent years. I suppose he was busy. I'm old, after all, and he's still a relatively young man. . . ." Her voice trailed off. This kind of pathetic comment was unlike the Dulcie I thought I knew.

Butler came over and poured me more coffee. "We do see Dulcie's great-granddaughter, however," he said,

something glittering in his eyes that I couldn't define. "Annette. She's thirteen. She's old enough now to take the bus, and for the past year she's visited us regularly. She's a very sweet girl."

Is Dad staying at the lodge, she'd asked as she jumped out of her mother's car at Lake Superior, *or does he have one of the cabins?*

I asked Dulcie if she knew what Turner's wife and daughter had been doing up there at the time his body was found.

"According to Annette, they'd been staying at a friend's summer place somewhere north of the conference center," she answered. "They were on their way down here, and she wanted to stop in and say hello to her father if he was there."

"Why didn't Turner invite her to spend some time with him there, especially if she was so close by?"

"I don't know," Dulcie said, looking uncomfortable. "I'm sure he was busy, with teaching and such."

"Taking photographs," Butler murmured, the first time I'd ever heard anybody murmur something acidly. Dulcie attempted to demolish him with a look, but he pretended to busy himself with the coffee things.

I asked her why she cared what happened to Evan Turner.

"Why?" she flared, as though the question were insane. "What do you mean, why? He was my grandson!"

"I mean, you didn't like your children. You paid them off, sent them away. Why this concern for your grandson? It can't be the half a million dollars—that's nothing to you. It can't be some abstract idea you have of justice. Why?"

"Because she loved him," Butler said.

"Because I raised him," she said, suddenly looking as old as her years. "And because he was the only member of my family who amounted to anything."

"*You* raised him?"

She nodded, then didn't say anything for a minute, just stared out her big picture window at the city in the distance glowing in the sunset.

"Evan," she went on after a while, "was the result of

a brief and, I'm sure, sweaty bout of lovemaking between my daughter and a member of the high school baseball team in the backseat of a car. She claimed she had no idea which player it was, and I believe her.''

"Lucy was quite the wild teenager," Butler observed mildly.

"Once she'd had the baby," Dulcie continued, "she abandoned him to me and ran away, after which she has devoted her life to marrying and divorcing worthless men. During one of her early marriages, Evan went out to California and lived with his mother for a few years. Her husband—a man named Turner—adopted him. When Lucy divorced Turner, Evan returned here to us. As far as I know, he's never seen his mother since."

"That's a horrible story!" I exclaimed.

She nodded. "Yes, it is. But his stepfather introduced him to the guitar and Evan proved quite proficient at it. He graduated from high school with grades good enough to get him into the University and, with a little prodding from me, he actually graduated. Then, however, instead of going out and getting a job, he spent a couple of years playing his guitar in little coffeehouses over in Riverside. He'd started doing that in high school to supplement the allowance I gave him. He inherited his musical talent from me, of course."

"It's quite a change," I said, "from street musician to university professor."

Dulcie frowned. "Too big a change, in my opinion. He had talent as a musician and songwriter and I hoped he'd make a success of that. Instead, he suddenly gave it up and returned to school."

"Did he tell you why?"

She made a face. "He said he didn't think he was good enough to make a real living as a performer and songwriter."

I sat back in the big, soft couch with my coffee cup and thought about it for a minute.

"All right," I said finally. "Thanks to your clout with the University president, I've been shanghied into looking

into your grandson's death. But why me? You could hire the best private detectives in the country.''

Dulcie opened her mouth to say something, then closed it again and looked helplessly at Butler. This was not characteristic of the woman.

''Dulcie feels,'' Butler interjected smoothly, ''that if Evan's wife is not the guilty party, then the culprit must be somebody at the University. Your knowledge of the institution, Miss O'Neill, and your contacts there, would give you a great advantage over any private detective, no matter how skilled, Dulcie could hire.''

Dulcie gave him a grateful look. ''After all, Peggy,'' she said, ''you have a B.A. in English, so you can put professors at ease and get them talking. You've also been around the University a long time, so you're experienced at detecting the bullshit through their big words. And if you agree to do this, I can rely on you to do it well, not just go through the motions to pacify a rich old lady. Admit it— that's the assignment your chief gave you, isn't it?''

DiPrima had come close to telling me that, but he hadn't said it outright. He was too shrewd for that.

I asked her if she'd spoken with Marcy since her grandson's death.

''We sat together at the funeral, which I'm sure Marcy attended only for Annette's sake. Marcy is having a birthday party tonight, by the way,'' she added, her eyes flashing angrily, ''only a week after Evan's death and a day after his funeral.''

''How do you know?''

Her eyes met mine, darted away. ''Annette happened to mention it to me—at the funeral.''

We talked a bit longer, but now that she'd got what she wanted, Dulcie suddenly seemed tired. As I got up to leave, I asked them if Marcy Turner was in the phone book. Butler tiptoed away, returning a few minutes later with the address on a piece of paper, then led the way through the mansion to the front door.

''I'm sure it did not escape your notice,'' he said, ''that Dulcie loved her grandson.''

"I noticed. I also noticed that you don't share her feelings for the man."

"Regretfully, no," he admitted. "While Evan was an adequate guitar player, I'm sure, he was a virtuoso when it came to playing his grandmother. He was a very moody child who, I believe, never got over his mother's neglect, or not knowing who his father was. I'm afraid that Dulcie, for all of her feigned hardness, spoiled him as a child. I think she blames herself for the way he turned out, since she bore the daughter who produced him."

"It's not like Dulcie to blame herself for what others do," I said.

"No," he replied. "I'm worried about her."

Six

I drove away with the feeling that I'd missed something, that both Dulcie and Butler were keeping something from me.

It was only a little after nine. If I were still on the dog watch, Ginny and I would be at my place, eating raspberries we'd picked in my backyard with ice cream and she'd be telling me about Italy until it was time for me to leave for the U. But I wouldn't be on the dog watch until further notice, and it was much too early to go to bed. So instead of going straight home, I decided to drive down Marcy Turner's street. Dulcie had mentioned she was having a birthday party that night—the day after her ex-husband's funeral. Annette, her daughter, had told Dulcie that. That was odd too.

The Turner home, white stucco and two-story, was in a pleasant middle-class neighborhood a couple of miles southwest of the University. Light in the front windows threw the large birch tree on the lawn in silhouette.

One of the important lessons I've learned is that it doesn't hurt to be told to leave, so I found a parking place five or six houses down the street from the Turners' and walked back. It was a lovely summer night, warm and humid but not unbearably so, with a half moon floating in a cloudless sky and crickets chirping in the hedges that separated one house from another. It was way too nice a night, I thought, to spend snooping into the lives of people who might have killed somebody. I'd rather be strolling around campus.

As I passed an old VW Microbus from the seventies—

I'd noticed it because you don't see many of them anymore in states with a harsh winter climate; they rust away— movement inside the cab caught my eye. I glanced in and saw the silhouette of two people in a passionate embrace, as though they were expecting the world to end soon and they had to *carpe diem* and anything else they could get their hands on while there was still time. One of the figures seemed to push the other away and I heard a tormented male protest and a woman's soft laugh.

I sighed at the memory of moments like that and tried to tell myself I was glad those days were past. My life's a lot more comfortable now, but there's something to be said for desperate passion unleashed in a car—although the back of a Microbus, properly equipped with a futon or air mattress, was much more comfortable, I recalled, than the cab.

The front door of the house was open, so I tried the screen, found it unlocked, walked in, and looked around.

"Hey, Red," a man called from the dining room. He was standing at a table littered with bowls of finger food, paper plates, plastic glasses, and the wreckage of a birthday cake. Cheerful Mylar balloons bounced around on the ceiling, moved by any slight breeze coming through the open windows.

"Hey, yourself," I said, flashing him my party smile.

"You missed the blowing-out-of-the-candles and the 'Happy birthday, dear Marcy,' " he said, "but there's still some frosting left. Help yourself. Ice cream's melting in the kitchen sink, beer and soft drinks on the deck."

"Thanks," I said. "Where's Mrs. Turner?"

"The birthday girl? Marcy?"

"That's the one."

He looked at the front door. "She went out to say good-night to somebody. Didn't you see her on the sidewalk?"

I told him that no, I hadn't.

"Oh, well," he said, "maybe she found a livelier party down the street and ditched her own. More likely, though, she went around the side of the house to the backyard instead of coming through here. I'm Randy, by the way— that's my name, not my condition," he added, with a chuckle that implied there was a lot more humor where that

came from, we'd only just scratched the surface. "Who're you?"

"Red," I said, and began loading a plate with veggies and dip by way of camouflage. "You got it in one."

"Yeah?" He seemed pleased. "I live across the street. Me and the missus have known the Turners as long as they've lived here. Terrible thing, what happened to Evan, but hey—life goes on, right? To tell you the truth, I didn't know him well, except to talk to at neighborhood get-togethers—the block parties and such. It's the wives who're friends, on account of the kids."

I gave him a wave and escaped through the kitchen onto the deck in the backyard. There were about fifteen people scattered around on the lawn. Those bad-smelling torches that are supposed to keep the mosquitoes away but don't were smoldering here and there, and the fence around the deck was threaded with strings of bright lights. Sitting in a swing in the far corner of the deck were a cluster of what looked like teenagers, whispering together, a transistor radio at their feet playing rock music softly.

I stood at the deck railing and looked around, didn't see Marcy Turner anywhere. I wasn't surprised. I hesitated, thinking maybe I should quit while I was still ahead—or at least go back around to the front and get the license of the bus—when I saw a woman break away from a little cluster of people and come toward me. It took a moment before I recognized her: Fiona McClure, the harpist Gary had talked to briefly—very briefly—at Lake Superior. It was too late for retreat now, so I went down the stairs and met her at the bottom.

"I know you from somewhere," she said, looking up at me with her large blue eyes. She was a small, slender woman with thick hair that fell to her waist and glowed silver in the moonlight and she was wearing a diaphanous gown similar to the one she'd been wearing the last time I'd seen her. "Where?" she persisted.

I didn't see much point in lying, since Fiona McClure had to be pretty high on my list of people to talk to about Evan Turner's death, so I told her I'd been with the reporter who'd talked to her briefly about Turner at the conference

center the afternoon his body had been found. "You have a good memory for faces," I added.

"Not your face," she said. "Your face is okay, but it's your hair I remember. You have beautiful hair, but you should let it grow. What are you, a reporter too—looking for more sensation on the widow's birthday?"

"No, I'm a campus cop. I do want to talk to Mrs. Turner about her husband's death, but I can see that this is a bad time. I'll leave now, give her a call tomorrow."

"Her husband's death? What about—"

"What's going on, Fiona?" a voice behind me asked. It was Marcy Turner, coming down the stairs from the deck.

"That's what I'd like to know," McClure said. "She says she's a campus cop and wants to talk to you about Evan's death. But she was with some kind of reporter at the conference center right after Evan's body was found, so I'd ask for some identification if I were you."

I got my ID out of my purse and handed it to Mrs. Turner. "We've met before," I told her, "at Dulcie Farr's Valentine's Day party in February. I just came from talking to Mrs. Farr, and she gave me your address. She's asked me to find out what I can about her grandson's death. I thought you might be willing to help."

Fiona McClure laughed brightly. "Find out—! What's to find out? How fast he was moving before he hit the rocks? You can get that from a physics textbook, or—"

"Fiona," Marcy Turner said quietly. She turned back to me. "Fiona does have a point, though, doesn't she? Falling off a cliff seems pretty cut-and-dried to me. Doesn't it to Dulcie?"

"Mrs. Farr wants to be sure her grandson's death really was an accident. I've been assigned to look into it."

"Dear God!" Fiona McClure exclaimed. "And you've already learned that Marcy is celebrating her birthday with poor Evan barely in the ground!"

Marcy gave her a look that said she wished she'd shut up, then turned back to me, studying me with her dark eyes. "I guess I'm not surprised," she said after a moment. "The only surprising thing is that Dulcie hasn't ordered the entire

University police force to look into it. Or has she?"

McClure laughed, too loudly. I was beginning to realize she was a little drunk.

"No," I replied with a smile, "I'm it. But you're right, she probably could mobilize all of us if she wanted to."

"Maybe we could hold a séance," McClure said. "Summon Evan to tell us—"

"Let's get to the point," Marcy cut her off impatiently. "Dulcie thinks Evan was murdered and I'm her prime suspect, aren't I? I did it for the big insurance policy she took out on Evan's life. Does that pretty much cover it?"

"That's pretty close," I admitted. "But I think there's more to it than that. Dulcie's a pretty complex woman."

Marcy Turner gave me a cold stare. "My ex-husband's death came as a shock to me and I was sorry he died. I didn't like Evan anymore, but I'd loved him once, and he was Annette's father. A few days ago I realized I didn't want to celebrate my birthday alone, with just Annette, so I called some friends and neighbors and they rallied around. I hope that doesn't make me seem like a monster to you."

I shook my head. "There aren't any rules for how to deal with a tragedy," I said. I thought of the Microbus and a man's urgent voice and a woman's soft laugh. I've heard of people who handle tragedy that way too. I don't know the rules for how long you mourn an ex-husband.

"Evan's death wasn't a tragedy," she snapped. "It was a news item. From all indications, he was pursuing his hobby when he fell. As a nurse, I can tell you there are a lot of worse ways to die. Now that you know what's going on here, how about leaving? I'd hoped I wouldn't have to think about Evan tonight."

"His death was probably just another of his attention-getting devices," McClure stuck in.

"Bad career move, if so," a man said, joining us. "This is the first time I've heard Evan's name mentioned all evening."

He'd been standing nearby with a bottle of beer, gazing out over the backyard but obviously eavesdropping on us. He came over and dropped an arm negligently around Fiona

McClure's shoulder and looked at me curiously. "What's going on over here?"

It was David Paul Douglas, whom I'd met at the Music School the night of the burglary.

"This is some kind of detective friend of Dulcie Farr's, David," McClure said with a toss of her head in my direction. "Mrs. Farr doesn't think Evan's death was an accident. She thinks Marcy pushed him off that cliff for his insurance, the way they do in very, very old detective novels."

"Mrs. Farr only wants to be sure her grandson's death *was* an accident," I said.

"Well, of course," Douglas said with a little smile on his thin lips, "there's a third alternative, isn't there?"

Since I didn't suppose he was implying that Turner had died of natural causes, I said, "You mean suicide?"

He nodded. "I wouldn't put it past him. In fact, I rather supposed it was suicide, at the time, and took for granted that Mrs. Farr had used her influence to have it called an accident. But if she's bought herself a detective . . ."

"Evan wouldn't commit suicide," Fiona McClure said. "He wasn't the type. So if it wasn't an accident, then somebody had to have thrown him off that cliff." She looked sternly at Douglas. "It wasn't you, David, was it?"

"No, dear," he said absently, staring at me. "I've seen you before. Where?"

"At the Music School last Tuesday morning," I said, wondering if all musicians had such good visual memories. "I was the campus cop who interrupted the burglary."

Douglas explained to the others what we were talking about. "She could have shot the burglars," he added, "but decided summary execution's too harsh for bread thieves. Isn't that right?"

"That's right," I agreed.

His eyes narrowed. "You think there might be some connection between the burglary and Evan's death?"

"I don't know. I've only just begun looking into it." I turned back to Mrs. Turner. "If your husband was murdered, would you want his killer caught?"

"Careful, Marcy," McClure warned. "I know a trick question when I hear one."

Mrs. Turner was about to answer me when suddenly one of the girls from the swing on the deck came over to us. Annette. Instead of going to her mother, though, she slid up to Fiona McClure and took her hand and held it.

"Where'd Ben go?" she asked truculently.

"He had to leave, honey," her mother said. "He's on call tonight. And you look like you need to get to bed."

She ignored that, the way kids do. "Who're you?" she asked, looking me up and down.

It was one of those rare moments when I didn't know what to say. Before I could come up with a plausible answer, Fiona McClure said quickly, "She's a friend of Grandma Dulcie's, Annette."

Something resembling interest flickered on the child's face. "Oh, yeah? Why are you here?"

I started to stammer something, but before I could, her mother said, "Let's talk about it tomorrow, shall we?"

As though in on some secret, the child smiled knowingly and said, "Yeah, sure." She gave me a long, assessing look, then turned and went back to her friends on the deck.

Marcy Turner sighed as she followed her with worried eyes, then turned back to me and said, "You asked me if Evan was murdered, would I want his killer caught. Yes, of course I would. But I don't believe he was murdered."

"I'd like to talk to you anyway," I said. "Dulcie loves her great-granddaughter and Annette loves her too. It would be a shame if anything got in the way of that love."

"That's emotional blackmail!" Fiona McClure exclaimed.

Marcy Turner gave me a smile. "Fiona's right, of course, but then, so are you." She thought a moment. "I'll talk to you, but not tonight. Tomorrow's Saturday and I'm working the day shift at the University hospital. There's a little park across the street. Do you know it?" When I told her I did, she said, "I'll meet you there at noon."

Douglas said, "I suppose you're going to want to talk to everybody who was at the conference center who had any-

thing to do with Evan, so I'd better start rehearsing my story.''

I gave him a polite smile and then something occurred to me. ''Wasn't today the last day of the summer session up at Lake Superior?''

He nodded. ''Uh-huh. It ended at noon with a big party—dampened somewhat by the memory of what happend to Evan last weekend, plus having to come down here for the funeral, which some of us did. I wouldn't have minded staying up there a few more days without the stress of teaching and the constant badgering of students, but Fiona couldn't wait to get back here. She doesn't care for nature.''

''I don't care for horseflies,'' she corrected him. ''Besides, I wanted to get back for Marcy's birthday party.'' She turned to Marcy Turner, went on with a grin, ''I give you my permission to tell the snoop here everything you know about Evan and me. She won't have to beat it out of you.''

Back to me, she went on, ''But you're wasting your time, Nancy Drew. Nobody could feel strongly enough about Evan Turner that they'd shove him off a cliff. Nobody!''

Wondering why she felt so strongly about that, I said, ''If that's the case, I shouldn't have any trouble getting his friends and colleagues—and former lovers—to answer my questions.''

''No, I'm sure it'll be quite easy,'' she agreed, ''especially since Dulcie Farr's got a lot of money and the Music School's hoping to get more of it than it already has. After all, that's how Evan—''

''Fiona, please,'' Douglas said sharply.

''How about you?'' I asked her. ''Will you talk to me too?''

''Sure! Nothing I'd enjoy more than talking to you about Evan Turner—at taxpayers' expense!''

Feeling unwelcome, but pleased that I'd learned more than I'd expected to, I apologized insincerely for crashing the party and left, following the path around the side of the house.

As I started down the street to my car, I glanced at the

place where the VW bus had been parked, with Marcy Turner inside making out with somebody I suspected was named Ben and who was on call that night. Soft running steps behind me made me spin around in time to see a shadowy figure duck behind a tree in the yard next door to Marcy Turner's. I'm pretty good at self-defense, even when I'm not armed with a pistol, nightstick, and portable radio, so I wasn't frightened. I'd also seen enough of the figure to believe I didn't have anything to be afraid of.

"Allee-allee-all-in-free!" I called out.

Annette Turner stepped out from behind the tree, hesitated, then came slowly toward me. In the moonlight, she looked a lot like her mother—French, Dulcie would probably say—with big dark eyes under curly dark hair.

"Hi," I said. "What can I do for you?"

"Did Grandma Dulcie hire you to find out who murdered my dad?"

"No, she got the University to assign me to look into his death. I'm a campus cop."

"Oh." She sounded disappointed. "I was thinking, like, maybe she'd hire a private eye, you know? She could afford one."

"She thinks I'm better than a private eye," I said. "Was your dad murdered?"

She stood there wide-eyed, stiff and pale, like a young animal trapped in the headlights of an onrushing car. "I don't know!" she whispered. "I don't know!"

"What makes you think he might have been?" I suspected the answer, but wanted to hear it from her.

"I have my reasons."

"Not good enough. I need to know what they are if I'm to help."

Her face was torn with indecision; her body wanted to turn and flee but couldn't, as in a nightmare.

Finally she said, "My dad was afraid of heights."

"How do you know?"

" 'Cause last year, when he took me to the State Fair, we went on the Ferris wheel and he was so scared, I thought he was gonna die. He was holding on to *me* for dear life, like I could save him, and he was swearing under his breath

and praying at the same time. When we finally got off, he told me he'd had a real panic attack. It was scary for me too—*he* was, I mean, not the ride, which wasn't scary. But it was like he was having a heart attack and I didn't know what to do.''

''He'd never acted like that before?''

She shook her head. ''He said it had gotten worse as he got older, but he hoped he could, like, overcome it with willpower and go on the Ferris wheel with me. But he couldn't. He was totally ashamed and asked me not to tell anybody, so I didn't until I told Grandma Dulcie after he died. When he told me he was going up to Lake Superior to teach, I asked him if he was planning on going near any cliffs. I mean, I've been up there a few times and they're scary even for me. He told me no way he'd go near those cliffs. So you see, he wouldn't have fallen off by accident. And he wouldn't have jumped either!'' she added, her voice rising. ''He was too scared of heights to go close enough to jump! If he was going to commit suicide, he would've bought a gun and shot himself, or swallowed poison, or something. So what else is there, except murder?''

''He may have got lost in the woods in the dark or something,'' I said, ''and come to the edge of the cliff without realizing it. Or maybe he was trying to overcome his fear, the way he did with you at the fair.''

She thought about it a moment, looking uncertain, then shook her head from side to side, making her hair fly.

''Who do you think might've killed him?''

''I don't know.''

''You haven't told your mother about this, have you?''

She didn't answer for a few seconds, then started crying, spun around, and ran back to her house.

Seven

As I drove away, I thought that it's one thing to suspect your father was murdered because you knew he had vertigo; it's another thing to suspect your mother killed him. Surely Dulcie hadn't put that thought in Annette's head! But if she hadn't, who or what had? Well, at least I had one question answered: why Dulcie had been so uncharacteristically evasive with me.

Considering that I'd slept until almost two that afternoon, expecting to be on patrol that night, it was much too early to go home and go to bed, so I drove back to campus and across the bridge over the Mississippi to Riverside, the little community on the University's west side. There's an all-night coffeehouse there called the Boardinghouse where I sometimes take my breaks when I'm on patrol. The coffee's good and I can usually find a night owl friend or acquaintance to shoot the breeze with. I parked around the corner and walked back.

The Boardinghouse started life as a home in a pleasant neighborhood sometime around the First World War. When the University expanded into that area, it became a boardinghouse offering cheap meals to students from the country, and when the fast-food joints took away that business, it adapted to the new times and became an all-night coffeehouse and also a place to perform for writers and musicians. A sign on the podium on the little raised platform that serves as a stage says, WE DO NOT WANT TO HEAR ABOUT YOUR VICTIMIZATION, which Stilwell, the owner, claims keeps down the number of local poets who want to read there.

It was a little after ten when I walked in. Five or six people were sitting around a table off to one side who seemed to be discussing the coming end of the world in soft, urgent voices, drawing diagrams on the table with foam from their coffee. A retired faculty member I know slightly was reading a French journal in a corner of the room under a floor lamp. He looked up and gave me a nod, then ducked his beret-clad old head back down into his journal, signaling he didn't want my company that night. Under a bad reproduction of a painting from Picasso's "blue period," a pair of gaunt chess players contemplated their next move.

I saw some people I knew at a round table near the front windows: Sam Allen, a theater professor, Christian Donnelly, the U football team's starting quarterback, Pia Austin, a graduate student in English, and her boyfriend, Andy Blake.

Sam, of course, seemed to be expounding on something of great importance to himself when I took my coffee over to them. He broke off when he spotted me, and looked me up and down. "If you're working undercover here tonight, Peggy," he said, "don't you think you're a little over-dressed?"

Andy jumped up and got a chair from another table, brought it over for me. "Thanks," I said, and sat down, making sure there was nothing spilled on the seat first.

Sam Allen's big, about six-two, and solidly built. The first time I laid eyes on him, I thought he'd make a great Falstaff, which turned out to be a role he'd played many times. He's got a lush head of dark hair and a beard to match, and his eyes, nose, and mouth seem to be trying to work their way out of the thicket. Christian, his lover, looks like a Greek god. In spite of that—and in spite of being a football player—he's a nice guy.

"What're you doing here so late, if you're not on duty?" Pia asked me.

"I just got transferred to days," I replied, "and it's upset my sleeping schedule. I thought I'd stop in and see what the beautiful people were up to." I turned to Sam. "You taught up at Lake Superior last summer, didn't you?"

He nodded, "Indeed, yes. The experience reminded me of the years I spent eking out a living in summer theater." He shuddered. "The students were worse than the mosquitoes, since you're allowed to squash mosquitoes. They were forever buzzing around with questions. Not that I blamed them, of course—they'd paid a lot of money for the privilege of being up there rubbing shoulders with us geniuses, and they didn't want to leave shortchanged."

"I spent a couple of days up there with Sam," Christian stuck in. "It was rough. People recognized me and wondered what a football player was doing in a theater camp. We had no privacy." It goes without saying that Sam and Christian are deep in the closet, and hope to stay that way until Christian is named MVP after winning the Super Bowl.

"You'd think people trying to improve themselves culturally wouldn't recognize a football player," Sam said. Sam isn't happy with Christian's career choice. He thinks he'd make a great actor instead.

"Instead of sharing a cabin with Sam," Christian went on, "I had to get a room in a motel down the road. Felt sleazy."

"Had an evocative name, though," Sam said, reminiscing. "The Dew Drop Inn, with a little café next door called Granny's Kitchen. The *spécialité d'maison* was sautéed whitefish liver, melted butter, and boiled potatoes. Granny's got a lot on her conscience."

"What's your interest in Lake Superior?" Andy asked me. "Wasn't the focus on music this year?" Andy's a theater major. Although he's scrawny and nondescript, he has a deep rich voice and, properly costumed, can play just about any role convincingly.

I explained what I was doing. When I'd finished, Sam shook his head and said, "My, my—Dulcie Farr buys herself a campus cop! I read about Turner falling off the cliff last week. A spectacular way to go. It's a very long way down."

"Did you know him?"

"I think I met him once, at a committee meeting or something."

"I took a music history course from him when I was a freshman," Pia said, "a survey course he taught in a big auditorium. It was popular because he never changed his lectures, so you didn't have to attend class if you were willing to buy the lecture notes from one of those places that sells them."

"A lot of the football players take that course," Christian said.

"Did you?" Sam demanded.

Christian looked away. Sam groaned and put his head in his hands.

"I took it," Pia said with a laugh, "because I needed a quick three credits in art or music and it fit my schedule. I sat through the lectures for a week, then bought the notes and never went back except to take the final. Turner had obviously been teaching the same material for years and years, and now all he was doing was trying to put style into it—like polishing an old piece of furniture, you know? I'd rather spend my time with teachers who are still excited by discovery, not actors reading lines."

"It would depend on the actor, of course," Sam murmured.

"What's left to learn about the history of music anyway?" Christian asked.

Pia glared at him. "A lot! History isn't dead, you know, Christian. It has to be rewritten for every new generation. Stuff that was ignored in one generation becomes important in the next—the roles of women, for example, and Afro-Americans—and gays," she added pointedly.

"It's a scary thought," Andy stuck in, "that history is only written by the winners. Unless you lull yourself to sleep at night believing only the good guys win."

"Somebody should write a book on the future of the past," Sam mused. "I could do it, of course, but I'm too busy at the moment. By the time I got it written, it would be history itself."

We paused a moment to consider that and sip our various coffee drinks, the quiet drone of other no doubt equally profound late-night discussions filling the air around us.

I asked Sam what he knew about the Music School.

"Not much. Just that it's small, lacks luster, and the faculty isn't very distinguished anymore. Most of the good people have retired or gone elsewhere. I suppose Scott Hall's the best they've got left. He's enjoying something of a revival, now that melody's back in vogue. For a long time, Hall was shunned as old-fashioned because he wrote stuff you could actually leave the concert hall humming."

He frowned. "There was some sort of commotion over there a few years back, though. They had a visiting musicologist—a woman. The younger faculty wanted her hired permanently, but it didn't happen."

"Why not?" Pia demanded, suddenly interested. "Were the old white hetero European males scared she'd rewrite *their* history of music?"

Sam gave her his gentlest smile. "Precisely. She'd written a book on Beethoven in which she argued that women can't listen to his symphonies because they feature powerful masculine themes tormenting weak feminine ones until, in a violent climax, the male themes rape the female ones and then murder them."

"You're kidding, aren't you?" Andy said, appalled.

"Unfortunately, no," Sam replied. "I stood in the University bookstore and skimmed the thing to be sure the reviewers had got it right. They had."

"Well," Pia said huffily, "men write stuff just as ridiculous, and *they* get hired and promoted. Penis envy!" she added fiercely.

"What?" Christian said, giving her a startled look.

"Penis envy," she repeated. "If women had been equally represented in the field of psychology a hundred years ago, Freud would be ranked right down there with the phrenologists and the Flat Earthers!"

Sam glanced up from his cappuccino. "He isn't?"

"Back to the Music School," I said, rapping the table with my cup.

"Right," Sam said. "This woman's theories aroused a certain amount of hysteria on the part of the guys, as you can imagine."

"Did she explain how she could speak for all women on the subject of Beethoven's music?" Andy asked.

"Of course not. Now that nobody outside the ivy tower gives a damn about what goes on inside it—at least in the humanities—you don't have to *prove* anything you say. You may notice that the number of Beethoven performances has not declined noticeably since the publication of that woman's book. I can't even recall her name."

"So what happened to her?" Andy asked.

Sam shrugged, sipped coffee, wiped foam off his mustache. "The traditionalists prevailed and she was cast out. Angry letters were published in the *Daily*, the music majors protested, one or more of the younger faculty resigned in protest—once they'd assured themselves of better jobs elsewhere, of course—and then it was business as usual, as usual."

Stilwell, the Boardinghouse's owner, had been wiping off a table next to us during the last part of this discussion. I'd wondered why he was spending so much time on it, considering how many other tables there were that needed his attention, and had for years, until I remembered that he adored women—like Pia—with small, heart-shaped mouths and large, soulful eyes.

Since Dulcie had told me that her grandson had been a musician before he'd decided to become an academic, and had played in bars and coffeehouses around here, I asked him if the name Evan Turner meant anything to him.

"Yeah, I knew him," he said, then started to beat a retreat, not wanting to set a precedent for *gemütlichkeit*.

"Come back, Stilwell," Pia said sweetly. "We need you."

He turned reluctantly.

"How well did you know him?" she demanded.

"Pretty well," he replied, gazing at her deeply with his close-set rodent's eyes. "But I haven't seen him in years. He used to play here regularly, until he decided to clean up his act and become a professor." He started to walk away again.

"What do you mean," she called after him, "clean up his act and become a professor?"

"Perfesser," Sam said. "According to Stilwell, he decided to become a perfesser."

"He played guitar for a living," Stilwell said, coming back, "and he taught guitar at that music school down by the river that's gone now—the Riverside Music Academy, they called it. He played in here a lot, for tips, too. He knew how to work a crowd, I'll say that for him—a lot more than some of the other musicians did back then, anyway."

"That's how he taught too," Pia muttered.

"He had a following," Stilwell went on, "mostly on account of he came off the way a street musician's supposed to—y'know, beard, beret, boots. But he wasn't real. He was just pretending."

"What do you mean, just pretending?" Pia asked.

"He had a rich grandma—Dulcie Tyler La-De-Da." Stilwell blew air through his nose, his equivalent of a hearty belly laugh. "He probably would've killed to keep it a secret!"

"I can understand that," Sam said. "It wouldn't give a street musician much credibility if something like that got out. After all—" He broke off and said, "Stilwell, why do you have that soulful look on your face? Dyspepsia?"

Stilwell's eyes seemed to have gone out of focus and there was a little smile on his sad rat's face that made him look almost soulful.

"I was just remembering somethin'," he said.

"What?" Pia asked.

"Turner's girlfriend back then. She was really something else. A lovely little gal with long gold hair, eyes big as headlights and blue as Windex. She played the harp."

"How could she not?" wondered Sam in an awed whisper.

"Fiona McClure," I said. It was still a pretty fair description of her, except that her hair was silver now.

Stilwell nodded, his eyes flicking to me and back to Pia again. "Yeah, Fiona McClure," he said. "And for a while there, they were pretty serious, but then another musician stole her away from him."

He smiled at the memory. "Turner took it kinda hard. He even wrote a song about her, but it wasn't any good. John Denverish." He glanced over at the little stage. "I

can still see him playin' it, but I can't remember how it went.''

''I had the same problem with John Denver,'' Sam murmured.

I asked Stilwell how serious Turner had been about Fiona McClure.

''Who knows? They was together a long time, and they played together sometimes—harp and guitar—stuff that Turner adapted from other people's music, some that he made up himself.''

''I heard Fiona McClure play at the Renaissance Fair several summers ago,'' Sam said. ''She wore a garland of flowers in her hair and sang ballads that featured maidens who kept crying 'prithee, Lord Spencer' or, in darker moments, feeding faithless lovers poisoned eels.'' Catching the look on Stilwell's face, he threw up his hands as if to defend himself and added hastily, ''They were lovely tunes!''

''The guy who stole her away from Turner,'' I said. ''Was it David Paul Douglas?''

''Dave Douglas?'' Stilwell snorted. ''Maybe in his dreams! I heard she married him a couple years ago, but back then she wouldn't've given ol' Dave the time of day.''

''So what happened to the guy who stole her away from Turner?'' Pia asked.

''Dead,'' he replied solemnly. ''A long time dead.''

A couple of customers had come in and were waiting patiently at the counter for service. Stilwell finally deigned to notice them and slouched off, pausing to give empty tables a swipe with his rag as he went, to indicate he wouldn't be hurried, he didn't need customers.

''How?'' Pia called after him.

He paused and turned. ''How what?''

''How'd he die? Was he murdered?''

''Murdered?'' He gave a chuckle that was raspy from disuse. ''Uh-uh. He choked on a carrot. Right about where I'm standin' now.'' Stilwell was standing in front of the stage. ''By the time the fire department got here, he was brain-dead. It broke Fiona's heart,'' he added as he turned and went off to deal with his customers.

''Well,'' Sam said after a few moments, ''who would

have thought Stilwell was such a romantic! 'A lovely little gal with eyes as big as headlights and blue as Windex,' indeed! It's disappointing, though. I always hope that people like Stilwell arrive at their hard-bitten cynicism through reflection and close observation of humanity, as I have, instead of through such trivial events in their pasts as unrequited love for a harpist. But it never seems to turn out that way.''

He sighed, buried his bearded face in his latté a moment or two, then suddenly looked up at me. "Speaking of cynics, Peggy O'Neill, what's the situation with you and Gary? I haven't seen you since you got back from whatever that funny little town is he's considering moving to."

"Nothing new to report," I said.

"Do you think he's going to move up there permanently?" Pia asked.

"I dunno," I said.

Before I could change the subject, Andy said, "Loon Lake's not that far away. I've known commuter relationships separated by greater distances."

Andy and Pia like Gary. Everybody likes Gary except me. I love him, whatever that means.

"Peggy and Gary are separated by more than distance," Sam said. "Much more."

Startled, I looked at him.

"Gary's a nice guy," he said, an amused gleam in his round button eyes, "if you like the moody, introspective type. But even if he didn't move to a small godforsaken village in a forest, he needs things Peggy can't give him. It's time for Peggy to let him go."

"Sam!" Pia exclaimed.

He ignored her, kept his eyes on me. "He wants to get married. There's nothing wrong with that, of course— Christian and I probably would if we could. And he wants to live in a small town and run a newspaper—at least for now. Maybe it's an enthusiasm that'll last, maybe not—I wouldn't know. But one thing I do know is that Peggy O'Neill could never live happily forever after in the woods! I just can't see her in a Pendleton shirt, for one thing."

"They itch," I said, attempting a smile.

"He also wants kids," Sam went on. "But Peggy's unnatural. Despite having the necessary equipment—the God-given plumbing—she doesn't want them. Right, Peggy?"

"Right."

"So let him go, before one or the other of you commits psychic suicide."

"Commits what?" Andy asked.

Sam turned his big bushy face to Andy. "It's where you kill your individuality in order to conform to somebody else's idea of what you are—your mom's, your dad's, your church's, your society's. Most people do it sooner or later, of course, since it's easier to get ahead in the world that way."

Nobody said anything for a minute and there were just the quiet sounds of the coffeehouse, a car honking outside somewhere. I had to clear my throat before I could say, "Thanks for your input, Sam."

"Ask to see his therapist's license," Christian put in dryly, "before you take him too seriously."

We drank coffee and talked about other, less profound things for another half hour or so and then Pia and Andy left, holding hands, and a few minutes later Sam and Christian followed, keeping their distance even in the Boarding-house, where they were unlikely to meet football fans or people who use moral outrage as an excuse to sniff around in the private lives of others. Before stepping out the door, Sam turned back and winked at me.

I took my time finishing my coffee in the dark and shabby coffeehouse, almost empty now. The chess players were still at their table in the corner, motionless under the Picasso. A middle-aged couple—a man and a woman— were talking quietly at another table, their heads almost touching. The woman giggled suddenly and the man laughed.

I thought about what Sam had said. I'd never loved a man more than Gary, and we had a lot in common. We both loved skiing, hiking, sailing, and a lot of the same music and books. We never seemed to run out of things to talk about—but neither of us minded long periods of si-

lence either. We were very compatible sexually, and we even liked a lot of each other's friends.

But he wanted to get married, have kids, and live in a small town, and I don't. Well, he's known for a long time that I don't, yet he sticks around—or has until now. *It's time to let him go*, Sam said.

That's not for me to do. If he wants to split up, let him be the one to do it.

I thought of him up at Loon Lake, and the widow who worked for the paper. She'd followed her husband when he moved there to get away from the crime and violence in Chicago. And then he'd drowned while fishing. He'd never learned to swim and wasn't wearing a life vest when he fell out of the boat. She was a little overweight, her teeth a little too regular for my taste, but she'd seemed nice enough.

I smiled at my catttiness. Maybe she was just what he wanted.

Let him go—and then what? A kind of chill went through me and I saw the faces of all the people over the years—relatives, mostly—who have asked me, "When are you gonna get married?" and "When are you gonna have babies?" and—more recently—"Aren't you afraid you'll be too old to have babies, if you don't start soon?"

I looked around and noticed a woman sitting by herself, nursing a cup of coffee and staring across the room at me. It took me a couple of seconds to realize it was me, reflected in a dirty mirror. I made a face at her, got up quickly and slipped out into the warm night, found my car, drove home, and went to bed.

I had trouble getting to sleep, as images passed through my head of Gary's dark eyes and beautiful smile, a child standing in the moonlight who was afraid her mother had killed her father, a woman I didn't recognize sitting alone in a coffeehouse in the middle of the night, and then that same woman diving off a cliff in a wedding gown. I woke up sweating.

Eight

I called Dulcie in the morning. Early. When Butler answered, I skipped the preliminaries. "Dulcie didn't put the idea into Annette's head that her mother killed her father, did she?"

There was a long pause. "If anything, it was the other way around," he said.

"Why?"

"A few nights before Evan left for Lake Superior, he came over to the house after Annette was in bed. She overheard her father say he wanted a reconciliation. Her mother refused."

"So? That's no reason for Annette to think her mother had anything to do with his death."

Butler hesitated a moment, then sighed. "She said her father threatened to resign from the University and go back to being a street musician. He taunted Marcy by asking her how much she thought she could get out of him in child support if he did."

"Why didn't Dulcie tell me this to begin with?" I asked.

"Annette made her promise not to tell anybody," he said. "I told her she'd have to tell you, but she refused. She said you'd find out on your own if there was anything in it."

"Is there anything else she knows that I'm expected to find out on my own if there's anything in it?" I asked.

"I think that's all, Miss O'Neill," he said.

Great! I thought as I hung up. What if I discovered that Annette's mother was, in fact, a murderer—or an accessory to murder?

I mangled a banana onto cold cereal and spooned the resultant mess into my mouth, washing it down with coffee as I scanned the morning paper, looking for something relevant to my life. Nothing, as usual.

I looked up Geraldine Asher, the new director of the Music School, in my staff directory and called her at her home, hoping she'd have returned from Lake Superior now that the summer session was over.

She answered on the first ring. "This is an official investigation?" she asked, when I'd told her who I was and what I wanted.

"Yes."

"How very strange! It never occurred to me there might be anything suspicious about Professor Turner's death." There was another pause, and then, "Is this urgent?"

"The sooner the better, in cases like this," I replied vaguely.

"Well." She thought some more. "I was just leaving for the campus when you called. Could you come to my office at the Music School in the next hour or two?"

We agreed to meet at ten-thirty, which would give me plenty of time to bike to the U and talk to her, then get across campus to the hospital for my meeting with Marcy Turner at noon.

As I was locking my bike into the rack next to the entrance to the Music School, another bike slid to a stop beside me. The rider, a woman wearing shorts and a T-shirt, dismounted and removed the bike's front wheel with a couple of deft clicks. I could see why, since it was a very expensive bike. I don't have to worry much about mine, and I only use a lock to discourage the impulse thief.

"Professor Asher?" It seemed a reasonable assumption. She was in her mid-forties, I guessed, tall, tanned, and with her pure white hair cut short, perhaps to emphasize the length and slenderness of her neck and the shapeliness of her head. She was a well-known concert violinist, at least in this area, although I'd never heard her play. The violin's an instrument I haven't acquired much of a taste for yet.

She nodded and led the way briskly and without speaking into the building and down the hall to her office, where

she deposited her wheel and helmet inside the door. She wasn't even sweating, a tribute either to her fitness or her bike's.

As she went over to a coffeepot on a table beneath a window, she gestured imperiously to an uncomfortable-looking chair in front of a large desk. Since I never take a chair in front of a desk if I don't have to—the position reminds me too much of involuntary visits to the mother superior in junior high—I walked over to a window through which the sun was shining brightly and stood with my back to it.

"I got back in town from Lake Superior yesterday evening," she said as she plugged in the pot. "I'm behind in my work." She returned to her desk, glanced over at me, blinked.

"Oh, for God's sake," she exclaimed with an annoyed laugh, "go sit on the couch over there! I'm not going to sit here squinting at you. What do you think this is, an interrogation room in a B movie?" I grinned and went over and made myself comfortable on the couch, her big desk no longer between us.

"Have the Lake Superior police found evidence to suggest Turner's death wasn't an accident?" she asked.

"No, it's just that the University wants to conduct its own investigation."

She frowned. "Frankly, that doesn't make any sense. What could you possibly—" She broke off as something occurred to her. "Oh, of course! His grandmother's behind this, isn't she? Mrs. Farr?"

I didn't see any point in denying it. "She thinks the police up there were too quick to conclude it was an accident. She wants more assurance that that's all it was."

"Well, it seems like a waste of time to me, but I suppose it's understandable. She must have loved her grandson very much," she added, as though not finding that particularly understandable. She glanced at her watch. "I have no objection to helping you, but I really am swamped here, playing catch-up. I've only just taken over as director of the school, and now I have to find a replacement for Turner before the fall semester begins. So what do you want from

me, other than a full confession?'' She got up and went over to the coffeepot, which couldn't have had enough time to come to a boil. ''Would you like coffee or tea?''

I declined both, watched in horror as she poured water into a large mug and then picked up an obviously used tea bag and dropped it in.

Returning to her desk bearing the mug like a chalice, she said, ''Do you know the area around the conference center, Officer?''

''A little,'' I said. ''I've been up there a few times.''

''Then you know that you don't have to stray far off the path to find yourself on the edge of one of the cliffs.''

''But according to somebody who knew him,'' I said, ''Turner had vertigo.''

''Oh?'' She frowned, looked down at her mug, and used a pen to swirl the tea bag around in it. ''I didn't know that. But people with vertigo fall off cliffs too, don't they? Accidents happen.'' Using her fingers to squeeze liquid out of the tea bag into her cup, she tossed the bag into her wastebasket, where it landed with a dull metallic thump. She took a sip of the horrid brew and seemed to find it good. ''Now, how can I help you?''

''I know what the summer program's about,'' I said, ''but could you tell me who among the faculty were up there and what they did?''

''Well, I was there, of course. I taught a master class in violin to a small group of advanced students. David Paul Douglas was there too. He taught piano. Scott Hall taught a music theory and composition course. Gordon Hart taught voice and chorus classes and Natalie Kruger taught flute. Both Hart and Kruger are out of the country for the rest of the summer, so you'll have to wait if you want to talk to them. There were also a few visiting faculty from other parts of the country. They've probably all returned to their own institutions now, of course, but if you need it, I can get you a list of their names and addresses. They are just as likely—and just as unlikely—to have pushed Turner over a cliff as any of us.''

''Were any of them friends of his?''

''I wouldn't know. I also—to forestall the question—

don't know if any of them were his enemies. Evan Turner and I weren't close, and I know nothing about his personal life. You'll want to talk to Professor Hall, of course. He knew Turner far longer than I did and was probably the closest thing to a friend Turner had in the school. He was here when Turner enrolled in our graduate program as a student some twenty years ago, and he gave a warm eulogy at the funeral. Professor Douglas was here back then too. I believe he was a friend of Turner's even before Turner joined the faculty.''

"Is Professor Hall back from Lake Superior yet, do you know?"

She nodded. "Oh, yes, all the faculty returned here Friday afternoon, after the farewell party. We have a faculty meeting bright and early Monday to discuss the problems facing us in the coming year, and we all need this weekend to recharge our batteries. Two weeks of interaction with students, in a place where you can't get away from them night or day, can be a little exhausting. And a faculty member's tragic death besides," she added, almost as an afterthought.

"What about Douglas's wife, Fiona McClure?" I asked. "Did she teach up there too?"

She shook her head. "Fiona's not on the faculty. For her it was just a vacation, although she didn't seem to be enjoying herself much. But she made sure everybody knew she was there. She could often be found on the lakeshore with her harp, keening Celtic ballads. I'm told she was especially effective in high winds."

"Maybe she was trying to lure sailors to their deaths," I said.

"Perhaps," she replied, "but Evan Turner was no sailor."

"She's quite open about not being too unhappy about his death," I said, "or about having been his lover twenty years ago."

"Fiona's something of a free spirit, isn't she?" Geraldine Asher said, giving me a frosty smile. "You no doubt hear a lot of gossip and rumor in your line of work. The

challenge must be in trying to separate the relevant from the merely titillating.''

I admire people who can express themselves so succinctly, although I sometimes wonder if it doesn't parch them inside. ''And what did Turner teach up there?''

''A music survey course. After his death, I took it over.'' She glanced at her watch again, then took a sip of her tea and waited for me to continue.

I said I supposed the faculty had a lot of free time while they were up there, and she answered, ''Of course. I'm told Turner spent much of his roaming the woods with his camera.''

''How about you? Did you roam the woods too?''

''Oh, yes, I spent some of my free time hiking around.'' She gave me a patronizing smile. ''I even carry a rather sturdy walking stick, although I didn't use it on Professor Turner. It's a big, dense woods, easy to get lost in, and I never met him in it. Mostly, however, I stayed in my cabin, alone with my laptop, writing a book.''

''On what?''

''Why?'' she asked with a puzzled frown. ''Do you think it could be relevant?''

''I should hope so!''

She laughed in spite of herself. ''It's a study of the relationship between women and musical instruments. Do you play an instrument, Officer O'Neill?''

I told her I'd taken piano lessons when I was a kid.

She nodded. ''I thought so. Do you know anything about the history of music?''

''Not much.''

''Then you've probably never wondered *why* you took piano lessons, or why there have been many well-known women pianists right from the time the piano became popular, but, until recently, very few violinists and cellists.''

I composed myself for a lecture, for I recognized the signs. I hadn't realized there were that many women pianists in the past. I thought I took piano lessons because my father played the piano and we had one in the house.

''To play the cello or viola,'' she said, ''you have to

spread your legs, which isn't becoming for a lady. And to play the violin, as I do, you have to stand above the audience in an assertive way, which is not only unbecoming in a woman, it's threatening—like women with guitars today who want to play in rock bands, or like women conductors. And adding to that, you have to move your arms and sway with your body to the music—almost dance. You'd never get a respectable man that way!"

Her eyes glittered and she laughed sarcastically. "Ah, but the piano! You keep your legs together, your posture straight—and you're turned modestly away from the audience too. What could be less threatening? What more could a 'lady' want in a musical instrument—or a man want in a lady? Did you know that a man once invented a combination piano and sewing machine?"

"No!" I said, and laughed in spite of myself.

"It's not particularly funny," she said coldly.

"You didn't like Evan Turner much, did you?" I said, deciding the lecture was over.

"No, I didn't."

"Why?"

She tapped her teeth with a pen, seeming to consider something. "Because, as director, he was providing no leadership, only maintaining the status quo, which, in the present academic environment, meant he was letting the ship sink. He was not publishing anything of a substantive nature—an occasional piddling article or review, nothing more than that. So you're right. I didn't like Evan Turner."

She smiled suddenly, a beautiful smile. "But since I managed to win the directorship from him in the election this past spring, I hardly needed to throw him off a cliff to get his job, did I?"

"You won the directorship from him?" I recalled Dulcie telling me he was happy his term was up.

"Yes," she said. "He was quite upset about that. He wanted a second term. He liked the prestige and perhaps the salary augmentation too. The trouble is, he didn't seem to think he had to do anything to earn it."

"Did you have any reason to think he might have been considering resigning from the U?"

She thought about that a moment, frowning, her lips pursed. "He might have considered it, but I'd be very surprised if he'd actually done anything so drastic. Some time ago—around the time of the breakup of his marriage, I think it was—I happened to share a table with him at the faculty club. We made small talk, and I took the opportunity to try to learn a little about him. I wanted to see if he was doing any kind of meaningful research.

"You see, I'm very concerned about the future of the school, Officer. I want to see it return to the standing it had in the music community in this country twenty, thirty years ago—it's my dream to restore it to that level of distinction! So I asked Turner what research project he was working on. And do you know what his response was? 'I'm working on finding myself,' he said!"

She laughed incredulously, as though she still couldn't believe it. "I thought he was being facetious, but he was quite serious. He added that he was going to spend some time trying to discover what to do with the rest of his life. I said, 'But Professor Turner, that's not what the University *pays* you to do!'

"He replied that he earned his salary by being director of the school, teaching his courses, and publishing enough to get by. He claimed he was an excellent teacher, and that was all he owed the University. So you see, Officer O'Neill, he had no intention of resigning from the University. Why should he? He could spend as much time as he wanted, on University money, 'finding himself!' " She spit the last words out, sat back in her chair, and glared at me, waiting for me to say something to that.

I thought she was probably right. The threat Annette Turner had overheard her father make, to quit the U and go back to being a street musician, was probably only something he'd said to scare his wife. But what might it have scared her into doing?

I thanked Professor Asher for her time and got up to go. At the door, I said, "I've heard there was a lot of bitterness in the Music School sometime ago when some of the younger faculty members wanted to hire a feminist scholar."

Her face turned stony. "That's no secret. The students and some of the faculty made quite a fuss about it. The fuss died down, as it always does," she said, sounding tired.

"Were you a part of the fuss?"

"You could say I was *behind* the fuss," she replied with a grim smile, "but I had a lot of support."

"Where'd Turner stand on the issue?"

"Where do you suppose he stood? He was opposed to her, of course, for although she was still a relatively young woman, she had a longer list of publications than he did." She laughed angrily. "If somebody killed him because he opposed the hiring of Marilyn Schaeffer, then there are other old men in the school who had better be careful about walking near cliffs too."

"Well," I said, "with Turner gone, you've now got a vacancy in the school—and one less vote against her."

She laughed harshly. "So by pushing Turner off that cliff somebody might have killed two birds with one stone, is that it?"

"Something like that. You could try to get her hired again now, couldn't you?"

Geraldine Asher stood up and glared at me. "When we couldn't hire her, Marilyn applied to Oberlin College, which has one of the best music schools in the country, and they snapped her up. She would no longer be interested in coming here."

"I understand some other faculty members left when she did," I said, "in protest."

"That's right. Are you sure this line of questioning is relevant to your investigation?"

"I'm just trying to get an idea of what the Music School was like during the years Turner was its director," I said, wondering what button I'd pushed to turn her so hostile.

Smiling coldly, she said, "I'm sure you'll find no shortage of people in the Music School who can help you with that. People with more time than I have. Good day, Officer O'Neill."

Nine

I bought a sandwich, an apple, and a can of Coke from the sub shop on the edge of campus, then biked over to the park tucked on a side street between two wings of the University hospital. Because it was the weekend, not many people were around, just a couple of mothers pushing baby carriages and strollers, a few nurses, and what looked like patients from the hospital at picnic tables. I found an unoccupied table under an oak and a few minutes later Marcy Turner came across the lawn, looking crisp and cool in the white uniform that emphasized her dark complexion and hair, and slipped onto the bench opposite me.

"Fiona said you were at the conference center with a newspaper reporter the afternoon Evan's body was discovered," she began as she tore open her lunch sack. "Why?"

I explained, then asked her why she and Annette had been there at the time.

"You think I was visiting the scene of the crime—and bringing my daughter with me? Nothing so sinister. We were driving back from a long weekend with a friend on a lake farther north. Annette knew we had to pass the conference center, and asked if we could stop and say hello to her dad if he was there."

"Didn't she get to spend time with him while he was up there?"

She laughed derisively. "Evan had no time for his daughter when we were a family. Why would he want her underfoot up there?"

"And yet she loved him."

She nodded. "Yes, she loved her father, with that des-

perate love kids have for parents who neglect them. She refused to talk to me about our splitting up. I tried to get her to see a therapist with me, but she did that rolling-of-eyes thing teenagers do so well and said she was fine, she didn't need therapy. She reminded me of her father at that moment, I'm sorry to say!"

"How's she taking his death?"

Marcy stared off into the distance, squinting into the sunlight. "She won't talk to me about that either." She shook her head. "She acts like she thinks it's my fault. When I suggested we see a therapist about that, she flew into a rage and ran out of the house. I can't make her get therapy, can I, or make her talk about it?"

"No, you can't."

"What makes Dulcie think Evan's death wasn't an accident?" she asked. "Can't she accept the fact that her little golden boy could trip on a tree root and fall off a cliff?"

"She doesn't think he would have gone near enough to a high cliff to fall over it," I said.

"Why not?"

"She claims he had vertigo."

"You're kidding!" She gave me a startled look. "*Evan?* He wasn't afraid of heights when we first got together. We didn't do a lot of nature-type stuff, but we did some. And we went on Ferris wheels and roller coasters."

"Do you remember the last time he did anything like that?"

She thought a moment, then shook her head. "No," she said, a note of sadness in her voice. "No, we hadn't done anything like that in a long time. But I remember him telling me that one summer, before we got together, he worked part-time in construction. He even showed me some of the buildings he worked on—tall buildings. He was quite proud of it."

She smiled suddenly. I asked her what she was smiling at.

"Evan," she answered, the smile disappearing. "Evan as I imagine he was back then, climbing around on scaffolding, high above the ground. Not the Evan I knew, the stuffy, discontented academic," she added bitterly.

She looked up at me suddenly. "Maybe that's why he fell from the cliff—he was trying to recapture what he'd been when he was a kid! And he got dizzy and fell."

"He was a guitarist when he was young, wasn't he? He played in the coffeehouses and bars in Riverside."

"Yes, he was part of a group of late-blooming hippies, I guess you'd call them, who performed over there. Fiona McClure was also a part of that group, and her husband, David Douglas—you met him last night too. They all taught at the Riverside Music Academy that used to be over by the New Campus. Evan taught guitar, David piano, and Fiona taught harp."

"Were Douglas and your husband friends back then?"

She shook her head. "No, but they knew each other. David was on the University faculty by then, you see. He only taught piano at the Riverside school to supplement his assistant professor's salary. But he never performed in the coffeehouses. That would've been undignified for a professor. That's what Fiona says, anyway."

"Mrs. Farr told me she was disappointed when Evan abandoned performance and went back to school. What made him do it?"

"He told me it was because he wasn't good enough to ever make a real living at it." She stared off into the distance for a minute, watching a young man and a woman, who'd just entered the park with a dog, playing catch with a Frisbee.

"I used to hear Evan play sometimes," she said after a minute. "I loved to watch his hands on the guitar, loved his voice. I thought he was good enough to make something of himself as a performer, but what did I know? I was just a nursing student in from the country who hung out with friends in smoky coffeehouses and bars."

She tipped back her head and drank some of her milk. "Evan was a skinny guy with a crooked smile, long hair, and a droopy mustache back then. Very outlawish."

There were still a few like that around, playing guitar on street corners for spare change. That might have been what Turner feared he'd end up doing. I couldn't imagine the

Evan Turner I'd met at Dulcie's Valentine's Day party in that role.

"That's when he was with Fiona McClure?"

She laughed. "I guess Fiona gave me permission last night to tell you everything, didn't she? I don't know very much, since I wasn't a part of that crowd, and Evan never talked about it. Yes, Evan and Fiona were lovers back then, but that was before I knew him."

"The way I heard it," I said, "she dumped him for another man, and yet she seems quite bitter about him. Shouldn't it be the other way around?"

"Oh, you mustn't take everything Fiona says at face value. She's a very emotional woman. Maybe she never forgave Evan for never forgiving her, but I don't think Evan hated her. It was just that she'd hurt him so badly that he didn't want to see her again."

"She dumped him for somebody who's dead now," I said, echoing Stilwell from the Boardinghouse the night before, "a long time dead."

She looked at me in surprise. "How—" Then she recovered. "My, you've been busy!"

"His death apparently broke Fiona's heart," I said, "just as her dumping Evan broke his."

She laughed. "I should work in cardiology, shouldn't I? A husband and a best friend with broken hearts—and a daughter too. You obviously know as much about it as I do."

I asked her how she'd become friends with a woman who'd dumped her husband for another man.

"Well, after a series of love affairs that all seem to have ended miserably and two ghastly marriages, Fiona married Douglas four or five years ago. Apparently he'd been waiting in the wings for her a long time. After that, I kept meeting her at school parties, and we hit it off."

"Must've been a little awkward for your husband."

"He was quite unhappy about it. He even ordered me not to see her, which of course I refused to do. That may be one of the reasons I like having Fiona as a friend so much—it upset Evan. He even made me promise not to talk to her about him—as though I would!"

"And it didn't bother you that she'd been so important in your husband's life?"

She thought about it a moment before answering, then shook her head. "No, it just made me sad that a man who'd been interesting enough to attract Fiona's attention, however temporarily, could turn out to be such a—a disappointment!" She paused to take a deep breath. "And maybe it annoyed me a little," she added more softly, "that Fiona had been clever enough to drop him, whereas I married him."

"So after Evan and Fiona split up, you got together with him."

"Yes, I got him on the rebound. I didn't know it at the time, of course. I pieced it together from little things he said over the first few years we were married."

She smiled sadly. "I didn't think Evan even knew who I was until one night after he was through playing he came over to my table—I was sitting with a couple of other nurses—and asked me out. We dated for only about four months when he asked me to marry him."

"Did you know who his grandmother was before you married him?"

"That wasn't very subtle!" she said with a laugh. "It wasn't until I'd agreed to marry him that he told me about his rich grandmother. You can believe that or not, but it's true. I don't suppose Dulcie believes it."

"You agreed to marry him assuming he was going to continue to be a musician?"

"That's right!"

"So when did he give up that idea and decide to go back to school?"

"It wasn't long after he asked me to marry him. A month or two after, I guess. I was surprised. I told him I'd be willing to support him for as long as necessary. I didn't need a lot of money, and I didn't think he did, either."

She lowered her voice. "But I was wrong about that. It turned out he needed more than what I could earn as a nurse and he could earn performing. In the end, I wasn't sure what he needed, what he wanted. I don't understand it. He

rushed to get married and join the middle class and then, after a few years, it lost all its attraction for him. *Why?*''

When I didn't try to answer that, she went on, ''It was Evan who wanted kids too. So we had Annette. And you know what? He never had any time for her!'' She shook her head, as though still finding it hard to believe. ''He traded a life of creativity and risk for respectability and security and then, according to you, he ended up with vertigo!''

She laughed suddenly, a bitter laugh. ''Or maybe his Pegasus wanted to fly too high for him and he fell off.''

''His Pegasus?''

''Yeah. You know who Pegasus is, don't you?''

''A mythological horse with wings.''

''Right. Creative people are supposed to be flying on Pegasus when they're inspired. Fiona told me that. You see, a few nights after Evan moved out, she dropped· over—I guess she thought I needed consoling. We got a little drunk together and started talking about Evan and the past. I figured my promise not to discuss him with Fiona no longer applied. And at some point during the night, when we were talking about Evan's need to be creative, she said his Pegasus wasn't a horse, it was a donkey. I had to ask her what a Pegasus was, I hadn't heard of it.''

A horn beeped in the street and Marcy glanced up.

''Excuse me a sec, will you?'' She got up quickly and went around the picnic table. I turned to watch as she crossed the lawn to the street. A car—an old VW Microbus, actually—was at the curb, a man leaning across the passenger seat, his head framed in the window, his sunglasses aimed our way. Marcy went up to the bus and talked to him for a few minutes, then backed off, waved, and came back to me.

''Sorry,'' she said, slightly pink, perhaps from the exertion and the heat, ''where were we?''

''You were telling me about how Evan decided to become respectable and fell off his Pegasus.'' I watched the Microbus disappear into the hospital parking lot. I couldn't make out the license number.

''I used to think Fiona's dumping him had a lot to do

with his giving up music and going back to school," she said. "Fiona's beautiful now, of course, but she was both young and beautiful back then. But she told me she thought what made him decide to become respectable was Chris's death—Chris was the guy she dumped Evan for. According to her, Evan had worshiped Chris. So his sudden death came as a terrible shock to Evan."

"I would have thought a man like Evan would be pleased to hear that somebody who'd stolen his lover from him had died," I said.

"I don't know. He never said a word to me about Chris. Maybe Fiona was just projecting, you know? *She's* never been able to get Chris out of her system, so maybe she assumes Evan wasn't able to either."

After a moment she added, "I suppose it's terrible when a lover dies before you discover he's just a man, not a god. Unfortunately, I wouldn't know."

I was beginning to feel like a classical music buff struggling through a thicket of country-western lyrics. "Chris what?" I asked.

She screwed up her face in thought, finally shook her head. "I don't remember—something Greek. But his death was an accident, so don't waste your time trying to make it murder too."

I didn't say anything to that, just wondered how much better off I'd be if I took advice like that.

"It's funny," she said after a minute. "Some people, when somebody they know dies unexpectedly, would take that as a sign to live life for all it's worth and to hell with the consequences—but not Evan. When the wake-up call arrived, he went out and got a wife, a kid, a haircut, went back to school, became a college professor—and lived to regret it. And so did I."

"Did he ever tell you he regretted it?"

"Evan? Talk to me about anything important? Never! But he didn't have to tell me. He acted it out, through neglecting me, Annette, and—according to Fiona, who got it from her husband—his duties as director. Do you know about his hobbies?"

"Besides photography, you mean?"

"Photography was only the latest. His first hobby was pottery. He even bought an expensive potter's wheel and threw pots in the basement. We had his pots all over the house—vases, cups, bowls, you name it! He got pretty good at it, actually, and I'm still using some of the things he made. But then he lost interest after a couple of years, sold his wheel, and went back to doing scholarship again, but obviously without finding any pleasure in it.

"Then he bought one of those electronic keyboards you hook up to a computer, and tried to compose music on it. I was happy about that at first because I thought he was going back to creating music the way he'd done when I first met him. But he wasn't interested in that kind of music anymore. He was trying to write 'classical' music."

"Did you hear any of it?"

"Oh, yes, he asked me to listen to it. I thought it was kind of boring, but I didn't say so, of course—Evan didn't take criticism well. He finally worked up the courage to ask Scott Hall to listen to some of it. We'd been pretty good friends with Hall and his wife back when Evan was new on the faculty, and we still got together occasionally for cards."

She smiled sadly. "Evan never told me Hall's reaction to his music, but soon afterward he lost interest in that too and the keyboard sat in a corner of Evan's study, untouched, until he moved out. And we didn't see anything of the Halls socially after that either."

"What came next?"

"Photography, about a year ago. He plunged into it with the same enthusiasm he'd shown when he took up pottery and music. He bought himself an expensive camera, took a night course at a community college, built himself a darkroom in the basement—even entered a few photographs in local art shows." She laughed suddenly. "It's too bad he didn't go up to Lake Superior next year instead of this. By then he would probably have had some new hobby, one that wouldn't have taken him near a cliff."

I asked her if he'd ever talked to her about leaving the University and going back to being a street musician.

She darted a look at me, as though wondering where I'd

got that idea. I'd got it from Butler, of course, who'd got it from Annette, but it was a reasonable question to ask anyway, given Turner's dissatisfaction with his life as a professor.

She shrugged. "Yeah, when he was especially depressed he sometimes talked about doing that, but I never took him seriously. He didn't have the guts. He couldn't go back. Sometimes," she added, speaking so low I could barely hear her, "I feel sorry for him. He clipped his own wings, then spent the rest of his life struggling to get back into the air."

She dug an orange out of her lunch sack and stared at it a moment, as though wondering what to do with it. Then she began peeling it, her eyes on her hands.

"Why," I asked, "after putting up with so many years of neglect, did you suddenly decide you'd had enough and ask for a divorce?"

"It wasn't sudden. First I told him I wanted us to see a marriage counselor. He was shocked, or pretended to be. He refused, but he did start spending more time at home and doing more things with Annette and me. But then, in the spring sometime, he began to backslide, spending as little time with us as possible, burying himself either in his study or his darkroom."

I asked her if she thought he might have been having an affair.

"I don't know," she answered, "but I doubt it. As I say, he'd been neglecting us for years, but I never saw any of the obvious signs of cheating—and I really don't think he was clever enough to keep something like that from me. Not for long, anyway. But I finally decided it was hopeless and told him I wanted a divorce. And when I saw the look on his face when I told him that, I realized that was exactly what he wanted! He didn't have the guts to leave himself, he wanted me to throw him out."

She offered me a piece of her orange and plopped one in her mouth, chewed a moment, and swallowed. As she got up from the picnic table, she said, "So I did him that small service."

Ten

As I followed her across the lawn and back to the hospital, I asked her when she'd last seen her husband.

"The night before he left for Lake Superior," she answered. "He showed up at the house that night after Annette was in bed and asked if he could come in and talk. He said he realized he'd made a mistake not working harder to save the marriage and he'd like to go to counseling with me, see if we could put it back together. He sounded panicky, like somebody who realizes winter's coming on and doesn't know what to do about it. I told him it was too late."

"How'd he take that?"

With her hand on the big glass entrance door to the hospital, she paused, then said, "Not very well. I had to remind him that Annette was in bed and his yelling might wake her up. He left, and that was the last I ever saw of him."

"And your husband didn't change his insurance policies before he died."

Something glittered in her eyes. "No, he didn't. I made sure, of course, in the divorce settlement, that he was required to keep Annette as his beneficiary on his University insurance policy until she graduates from high school. And the policy Dulcie took out on his life, with me as beneficiary, was still in force at the time he died too—as you apparently know."

"If he *had* had the guts to quit the U and go back to playing guitar over in Riverside," I said, "you would have lost child support and the insurance."

She looked at me steadily. "Believe me, he would never

have done that. But so what if he had? I make a pretty good salary—not enough to maintain the house, maybe, but Annette and I would survive. Women have survived on a lot less.''

The ghost of a smile flitted across her face. "It was lucky for Annette and me that Evan was never very good with details and he tended to put things off. He never changed his will either, so I'm entitled to the contents of his apartment. He took some things with him I'd like to have back. His stereo and CD player are better than the ones I bought to replace them, and his computer's better than mine too. And Annette might want the keyboard.''

"I'd like to look the apartment over," I said. "Would you mind?"

"Why should I mind? It's your time and Dulcie's money. But I don't have the key with me.''

"Maybe you could write a note I could show the caretaker," I said.

"Sure, why not? If you're that eager.''

Once she'd disappeared into the hospital, I went around the corner to the parking ramp and walked through it to the staff lot, looking for the Microbus the man she'd talked to had been driving. It wasn't hard to find, a large green and tan box with rust accents, parked between two sleek new convertibles. I wrote down the license number, then went into the hospital, found a directory on a wall, and looked for somebody whose first name was Ben.

There weren't any Bens. I found a pay phone in the lobby, called Ginny at the police station, and asked her to run the license number through her computer.

It took less than thirty seconds. "Ben Anderson. No middle name.''

"He works at the U hospital," I told her, "but I don't know as what. He drives a rusty old VW bus, so he's probably not a doctor.''

"Don't be so sure," she replied. "With managed care, a lot of doctors are driving beaters to work these days. But I'll see what I can find out. I know some people at the hospital.''

"See what you can find out about Marcy Turner too, while you're at it. She's a nurse there."

"You don't mean to tell me sex is rearing its ugly head!"

"Could be," I said. "Are we still on for dinner tonight?"

"Sure. How're your raspberries coming along?"

"The birds'll probably leave enough for us, but we'd better hurry."

"I'll pick up some ice cream on the way. *Gelato*, we call it in Italy."

I knew that.

I went out, got my bike, and rode over to Evan Turner's apartment, thinking about what my life would be like if Ginny ever quit the campus police, something she's talked about doing for a long time. Would being a campus cop give me as much satisfaction without her? I had other friends, sure, but none as much fun to be with as she was. I wondered why that was. Maybe because she wasn't married either, or in a relationship, although she'd like to be.

Evan Turner had spent the last months of his life in an old three-story apartment building. It took up most of a block in a neighborhood just far enough from the university to escape the blight it brings with it wherever it expands, but close enough to attract transient faculty and the occasional well-heeled student. It was surrounded by oaks and a few elms that had somehow escaped the plague that had swept most of them away.

According to the directory, the caretaker's name was Ethel Wynn and her apartment was in the basement. I waited for her to buzz me in, then walked down into the basement's chill gloom and knocked on her door. After a minute or so, it opened a crack and a slice of middle-aged woman with a tiny nose and small eyes like currants in a bowl of pudding peered up at me over a piece of chain. She gave me the look all caretakers give people who come to the door, the one that's expecting to hear news of overflowing toilets, leaky faucets, broken air-conditioning. A television set was on in the background, some kind of talk show, from the sound of it: angry voices, whining.

I slipped her the note Marcy Turner had written for me.
"I'd like to take a look around Evan Turner's apartment,"
I said. "His ex-wife has given me permission. She said I
could get a key from you."

She took the note, put on a pair of glasses, and read it.
"She claims she inherits it all," she said, pushing the note
back at me. "Lucky her! What's your name?"

When I told her, she said, "Peggy O'Neill, huh? I like
that. Wasn't there a song about somebody with that name?"
She thought a moment, then hummed a snatch of "Peg O'
My Heart."

"Different Peggy," I said, and hummed a snatch of the
correct one.

"Oh, sure," she said, joining in. When we'd finished—it
didn't take long—she went on, "Now, anybody could've
written that note, but you've got an honest Irish face—we
won't say nothin' about your singing voice—so I'm gonna
let you go in."

"Thanks," I said as she went to get the key. She didn't
ask why I wanted to look around Turner's apartment. She
was a lousy music critic but a detective's dream.

She slipped the key through the crack in the door and I
took it and headed back down the hall to the stairs. Turner
lived in the middle wing of the building, on the second
floor in back. The hallway and stairs were carpeted, quiet,
and cool. I unlocked Turner's door, pushed it open, stepped
in.

The venetian blinds were closed against the afternoon
sun, leaving the room in semidarkness, which emphasized
its dreariness and impersonality. An archway separated the
living room from a small dining room and, beyond that,
the kitchen. The place had the forlorn look of an empty
stage set. It also smelled faintly of cigarettes, which surprised me. I wouldn't have thought Evan Turner smoked,
but figured that maybe the previous tenant had smoked and
left the stink behind, or Turner had had guests who smoked.

I closed the door behind me and crossed the living room
to the dining room. I intended to start at the back of the
apartment and work my way to the front. I'd got halfway

across the dining room before I noticed another smell—
marijuana. I froze because, although faint, it seemed too
strong to have been left behind by Turner, who'd died the
week before and hadn't been in the apartment for a week
before that.

A man suddenly filled the hall door in front of me—a
huge man in jeans and sleeveless T-shirt. He didn't hesitate,
just rushed me before I had a chance to react, shoved me
back against the dining room table, and pressed me there
with his heavy body, his slablike arms around me, pinning
my arms to my sides.

"Who are you?" he growled. His eyes were small and
red-rimmed, he was panting slightly, and his breath was
foul.

The table moved slightly behind me under our combined
weights. I didn't hesitate; I smashed him in the nose with
my forehead and shoved backward with my legs and, as he
stumbled forward with a howl, I knocked one arm loose
and ducked away. I knew I couldn't get out the front door
before he regained his balance and came after me, so I
dodged around the table, putting it between me and him.
He wiped his nose with the back of his hand, looked down
at the blood on it, and then up at me, his face a mask of
rage.

I know a number of ugly ways to incapacitate a man, but
even if they worked on this monster, the chances of my
getting hurt too were good, so I thought I'd save that for a
last resort.

Luckily, I can talk. I said, "I'm with the movers and
they're on the way up the stairs now. Who are you?
What're you doing in Evan Turner's apartment?"

He blinked. "The movers?"

"Yeah, movers," I said, sounding annoyed. "The owner
of this apartment's dead, didn't you know? He doesn't need
it anymore."

"Shit!" he said. His eyes flitted around the room, as
though looking for the answer to a difficult problem. They
came back to me.

I wanted him to leave before he started wondering where

the movers were and why, if they were on the way, I'd closed the front door. But I also wanted to know what he was doing here. "Who are you?" I asked again.

"Turner's a friend of mine," he answered. "Was, I mean. He let me crash here sometimes, okay?" His mouth twisted into a grin of sorts that didn't reach his eyes. "Sorry to jump you like that—I was asleep when I heard you come in. I thought you were a burglar or somethin'. Hope I didn't hurt you," he added, bleeding.

He lied without conviction, stupidly, the way bullies do because they can't or don't have to work as hard at it as the rest of us, since people don't usually confront them about their lies. He was about twenty-five, with a shaved head and the bulky arms of a weight lifter, and I was sure I'd seen him before: he was one of the Music School burglars, the one who'd tried to stab me in the face with the tree branch.

"I'm a friend of Turner's wife," I said. "She asked me to help clean out his apartment. You a friend of hers too?"

"Never met the lady," he replied. "No hard feelings, okay?" He held out his hand across the table.

"No hard feelings," I said, keeping my hands where they were.

His face hardened. "So where are the movers?"

I pulled my cell phone out of my shoulder bag and as I punched in 911 said, "You might be able to hurt me, but I can hurt you too. Why don't you just leave?" Judging from our last encounter, I didn't think I'd be helping myself any by telling him I was a cop.

He shoved the table into the wall, blocking my escape, then started around the other side toward me. I jumped onto the table as the 911 operator came on the line. I said, "I'm being assaulted. Middle wing, second floor in back." She'd have the address on her monitor.

Muscle Boy gripped the table with both hands, started to heave it up. I kicked at his bleeding nose. He flinched away, grabbed for my foot with one hand, missed and let the table fall. He glared up at me, his eyes filled with hate, and then swearing softly, impotently, turned and ran into the kitchen,

flung open the back door, and I heard him running down the outside stairs.

I got to the top of the stairs in time to see him jump on an old bike lying in the weeds in the alley and start pedalling away. He glanced back at me over his shoulder—I noticed that his nose was still bleeding—then turned into the street. As I went down the stairs, I told the 911 operator what had happened and where I was, then waited in the alley for the squad car. When it arrived, we wasted ten minutes driving around the area looking for the suspect while I told them who I was and who I thought he was, and then we returned to Turner's apartment.

Except for the bedroom, where it was obvious the intruder had taken up residence, the place looked untouched. The bedroom reeked of marijuana, an ashtray next to the unmade bed was overflowing with cigarette butts, and there were empty beer cans, crushed, littering the floor.

"You're sure he was one of the Music School burglars?" one of the cops asked me.

I said it had been dark and raining heavily, but I was pretty sure.

"And he told you he was a friend of Turner's, huh? Do you believe him?"

"I don't know what to believe. But that might explain how they got into the Music School, if they had a key to this place. When they heard Turner was dead, they might've come in here and taken his University keys. There wasn't any sign of a break-in at the school."

"You wonder how a guy like Turner, a music professor and all, could have friends like that, though, don't you?" the cop went on.

"There's no sign of a break-in here either," the other cop said, coming into the room from a search of the apartment. "And there's no way for us to determine if the place was burgled, since we don't know what was supposed to be in here. You think his ex-wife'll know?"

"She told me he had a good stereo, a computer, and a keyboard," I told her. "They're not here."

They said they'd report it as a possible burglary and trespassing, and get in touch with Marcy Turner so she could

come over and try to establish what was taken. I said I'd have a University detective come over and get fingerprints to compare with those taken from the van used in the Music School burglary.

Then they went off to tell the caretaker what had happened, leaving me alone in the place to do what I'd come there to do.

Eleven

It was a furnished apartment in which everything managed to look used without having acquired character. I opened the blinds in the living room to let in some light, then went over to the phone and picked it up, to call Ginny at the station and tell her what I'd encountered in Turner's apartment. Instead of a dial tone, though, I got the signal that told me Turner had voice-mail messages. That was nice, except I didn't have the code necessary to retrieve them.

I called Ginny and explained where I was and what I was up to, and asked her how long it would take her to get the access code.

"Minutes," she said.

"I'll still be here in minutes," I told her, gave her Turner's number, then described my encounter with Muscle Boy.

"Interesting," she said. "I'll send a detective over to get prints. You don't have to wait, he'll get a key from the landlady."

I started with the bedroom, careful not to touch anything that might destroy prints. Apparently Muscle Boy hadn't been interested in Turner's wardrobe. That was no surprise, since there wasn't much of Turner's that would have fit him. I went through the pockets of his shirts, jackets, and trousers—even shook his shoes, in case he'd hidden something in them—and came up with nothing.

I found a photographic enlarger on a table in the bathroom, a safe light, a black curtain that could be pulled over the window, and the smell of photographic chemicals. The chemicals and trays and other things of use to somebody

who develops and prints his own photographs were in a closet in the hall outside the bathroom, along with some large portfolios.

I brought them out and went through them carefully. They contained black and white photographs, the subject matter ranging from picturesque old buildings to moody scenes along the Mississippi. The quality was pretty good but I'd seen the subject matter a million times before. There were also a few pictures of Turner's daughter Annette. She'd clearly enjoyed posing for her dad.

There were envelopes full of negative strips in glassine sleeves. I held each strip up to the light, but couldn't see anything out of the ordinary in any of them, and no people except Annette.

In the kitchen, the refrigerator contained a half gallon of milk, a can of ground coffee, and a couple of microwavable frozen dinners of the kind I eat too, so at least Turner and I had something in common. I emptied the milk and coffee into the sink, in the best detective tradition, but found nothing.

It occurred to me that Muscle Boy couldn't have been staying at Turner's place long, since the only signs of his occupancy were in the bedroom. If he had been staying there more than a day or so, he was a very neat intruder, relatively speaking.

I arrived back at the living room, began with the couch, where I found a nickel and a couple of pennies under the pillows. I kept them, for my pains.

The bookcase contained a number of books on music, including Turner's own, a social history of the guitar, which looked almost interesting, a few works of fiction, and a stack of photography magazines. I went through them all, just to try to cover all the bases, even though I had no idea what I was looking for.

There were also a large number of CDs, mostly jazz, folk, and classical, which meant that if the burglars had taken Turner's stereo, they didn't share his taste in music.

Ginny called with the numbers I wanted. I thanked her and said I'd see her at six and tell her all about it. Then I dialed into Turner's voice mail. He only had three mes-

sages, of which two were hang-ups and one, from the previous Monday, was a picture-framing shop telling him that his photographs were ready and he could come in and pick them up anytime.

I glanced around his apartment, noticed there weren't any pictures on the walls, although there was a hole in the wall over the couch where one had once hung. Maybe Turner had planned to do something about that with some of his own creations. Because the message on his voice mail was the only thing the burglars wouldn't have been able to get their hands on, and because I was on a wild goose chase in which anything could be important, I decided I wanted to know a little more about Turner's taste in art, so I noted the name of the frame shop, went through Turner's apartment one more time, then walked back down to the caretaker's apartment.

Ethel Wynn greeted me through the crack in her door with, "Had a little trouble up there, huh? The cops were here and told me about a guy living in Turner's apartment rent free. He do any damage?"

When I told her I didn't think so, she looked me up and down curiously. "They said you're a campus cop. What's all the excitement about? Turner fell off a cliff, didn't he? I heard it was an accident."

"It's just routine," I said. "There are a few things about his life we're looking into, to assure his family that we've done all we can to explain his death. I wonder if I could come in and talk to you for a few minutes."

"Don't see why not," she said. She shut the door in my face to undo the chain, then opened it again to let me in.

"Pick a chair," she said, "any chair."

She wasn't kidding. The room—and from what I could see, the entire apartment—was furnished with whatever the tenants had left behind for the last thirty years, and they'd left behind a lot. The place looked and smelled like the home furnishings room at the Salvation Army, a smell I remembered well from my student days. Floor lamps and dirty windows high in a wall provided what light there was in the room.

I settled cautiously onto the edge of a couch. She picked up a clicker, pointed it at the television, and the sound went off, which meant I'd never learn why the three indignant-looking women with big hair were confronting the sobbing little man with the toupee. "It's a Saturday rerun," she told me. "I've seen it before. You wouldn't believe what that man expected them to do for him!"

She plunked herself back into her recliner and said, "I'll tell you right now, I don't know nothing about Turner. He was quiet, didn't complain about nothing and nobody complained about him."

Ethel Wynn picked up a long-toothed comb and began picking at her hair with it. She was a short round middle-aged woman with a black beehive hairdo, dark little eyes, and a chin that poked out of her round soft face like a chubby baby's fist. She was wearing pink polyester slacks, a matching sweatshirt, and slippers in some silvery material.

"Terrible thing, him falling off a cliff like that," she went on. "I was up there to Duluth a few times when Earl, my first husband, was alive—he'd go for the smelt, you know—and I even been up in the lighthouse once, before my rheumatism got so bad. I'm telling you, that cliff's way the hell up there, you should excuse my French, and to fall off it like he did, straight down—boom!" She shuddered, thrilled with the image she'd conjured up with her narrative gift. "What can I do for you?"

I asked her if Turner had any friends in the building. She said she didn't know, but she doubted it, he hadn't been there long enough.

"Did you see him, or anybody else, moving stuff out of his apartment: stereo speakers or a computer, for example, a keyboard?"

"Uh-uh. Why?"

"His wife told me he'd taken those things with him when he moved out, but they aren't there now."

"Most likely whoever took 'em, took 'em out through the back door and down the stairs into the parking lot. I

wouldn't've seen it. Probably that intruder you surprised took it all, don't you think?''

"I guess so," I agreed. "How about visitors?"

"Visitors?" she repeated, as though the word were foreign to her. Her eyes strafed my face, and she picked more furiously at her hair with the comb. "I don't spy on the tenants," she said, raising her little chin righteously.

"I'm sure you don't," I assured her. "But Turner did have a visitor who struck you as a little out of the ordinary, didn't he?"

She chuckled. "My second husband, Harold, always said I couldn't keep anything from anybody and I never could play poker either. Yeah, Turner had a visitor I suppose you could say was a little unusual. A girl. I only seen her a couple times—once coming in with Turner and once standing outside his apartment door waiting for him to let her in. At first I figured she was his daughter. But when I heard her call him by his first name, I wasn't so sure, although kids do that sometimes these days. A kid of mine might try that kind of shit once, but only once.''

"But you don't think it was his daughter."

"Uh-uh."

"Could she have been a student?"

The effort to think pushed her lips out, like Nero Wolfe. "That's what I thought too, at first, on account of students come in all sizes and shapes these days. But a professor who invites a student to his apartment—especially a divorced professor living alone—oughtta have his head examined. But I ain't Big Brother, you realize. Live and let live is my motto and a man's home is his castle. What the tenants do in their own places ain't none of my business, just so long as they don't bother anybody else or flaunt it— and Mr. Turner wasn't doin' neither.'' She picked vigorously at her hair with her comb.

"Describe her for me, will you?"

"Like I say, she was young, eighteen, nineteen. Couldn't've been much older than that, but maybe younger—who knows anymore? Not too skinny, not too fat. Shorter'n you, taller'n me—five-six, maybe. She had curly brown hair and rings dangling from one eyebrow and

glass and rings in her ears and a stud of red glass—or maybe it was a ruby, I wouldn't know—in one of her nostrils. Wasn't as bad as some of the gals you see running around loose these days, with faces you could stick refrigerator magnets on. Guys too, for that matter.''

The image of the woman who'd deflected Muscle Boy's aim with the tree branch at the Music School burglary came into my mind. ''You don't happen to know her name, do you?'' I asked.

''Elli,'' she replied. ''Either that or Helen.''

''Elli or Helen?''

''Yeah. The time I heard her knockin' on his door, I happened to be passing in the hall and when he opened up, he said 'Come on in, Helen,' and she said, 'It's Elli. You know that.' Very stern, like she'd had to remind him of it before. She had a kind of a deep voice. A little on the hoarse side, I remember.''

''Do you remember when you saw her here?''

She examined her comb thoughtfully. ''Not really. June, maybe. Sometime in early summer anyway.''

''Night or day?''

''I only saw her in the day. I'm pretty sure they wasn't shacked up, if that's what you're gettin' at, but that don't mean they weren't gettin' it off during the day.''

She laughed contemptuously. ''We get a lot of professors living here, and most of 'em never seem to have much to do over at the U. Course, when you bring the subject up— you know, make a joke about the hours they keep—they get all defensive and say they do a lot of their work at home. And maybe they do. You don't need a laboratory with a lot of fancy equipment to read twelve books just so you can write a thirteenth, do you? Harold used to say the profs keep parsons' hours, except they don't do funerals and weddings.''

She chuckled, remembering Harold and his sense of humor, and I joined in to keep her company.

''But I did wonder what Turner was 'working on at home' that he needed this gal's help with it,'' she went on. ''She didn't look like somebody who took dictation, but

she could've been his cleaning lady, I suppose. A lot of kids earn money that way these days.''

I asked her when she'd last seen the girl. She used her comb to scratch an itch on the side of her face. ''I think I seen her comin' out of his apartment the day before he left to go up to that summer school thing where he died.''

I wrote down my name and phone number and asked her to call me if she ever saw Elli, or Helen, again, or could think of anything else that might be helpful. She was turning up the sound on her television set, so I wasn't sure she heard me.

Twelve

The frame shop was in a little strip mall about a mile from Turner's apartment. I got there at a few minutes after four, chained my bike to a parking meter, and went up to the door. A sign on it said it closed at four on Saturday, but the lights were still on inside and a young woman was standing behind the counter, doing something at the cash register. I dug out my shield and held it up where she could see it and rapped on the glass in the door. She looked up with a frown, saw the shield but probably couldn't make it out, shook her head, and returned to her work. I rapped on the glass again, more loudly, and when she looked up again, I pointed at my shield. She rolled her eyes and came over, peered at it, looked at me, then opened the door and let me in.

"What's the problem?" she asked. She was about twenty, tall and thin, with brush-cut rainbow-hued hair, a small gold ring in one nostril, and a bewildering array of colorful studs in her prominent ears.

I told her who I was and what I wanted.

"What's he done?" she asked, chewing gum and looking me up and down.

"He fell off a cliff."

"Way!" she said, not exactly overwhelmed, then disappeared into a back room and reappeared a few minutes later with a stack of framed photographs wrapped in butcher paper. She started to unwrap them, then stopped and looked up at me. "We always ask the customers to inspect them before they leave the store, to make sure

everything's okay, but I don't guess that's necessary in this case, is it?''

"Let's do it anyway," I said.

There were three eleven-by-seventeen black and white photographs, nicely matted and framed. The first was of a lake somewhere, with an old boathouse, a dock, a half-sunken rowboat, and trees reflected in the water.

The woman squinted at it with a critical eye. "Needs some ducks or geese," she said. "Or perhaps a stag. Stags are always good in pictures like this, with a huge rack of antlers and a thoughtful expression."

She popped her chewing gum and unwrapped another photograph, this one of an abandoned cabin in a woods, surrounded by weeds, the windows boarded up, holes in the roof and walls. "Ah!" she exclaimed. "The old 'abandoned-cabin-in-the-woods' photograph. Second in popularity only to 'Old Red Barn' among the amateurs."

She unwrapped the last photograph, studied it a moment, then said, "Well!" and turned it so I could see it too.

It was completely unlike the other two. This one was of a young woman standing cranelike on one leg in front of a couch and pulling off the boot on the opposite foot. She seemed to have been caught off guard by the photographer and was giving him a look composed of equal parts scorn and amusement as he took the picture.

She had dark curly hair cut short, a high forehead, dark eyes under heavy brows, and a wide full mouth, and light from the flash flickered in thin rings hanging from one eyebrow and flared from a stud on the side of her nose.

It was the woman from the Music School burglary.

I recognized the couch behind her as the one in Turner's apartment, and on the wall above it, where I'd seen a nail hole for a picture, another photograph hung, this one a softly lit nude of a young woman, her body in profile, her arms hugging her drawn-up knees. She stared incuriously out at the woman taking off her boot in front of her.

"It's the same woman in both pictures," the saleswoman said.

I asked her how she could tell.

She lay a long, elaborately decorated fingernail on the

photograph. "The bracelet, there and there. It's the same pattern."

I took a closer look. It was clearest on the wrist of the woman in the foreground pulling off her boot, but once it had been pointed out to me, I could see a piece of it on the wrist of the nude on the wall too.

"It's called the 'Greek key' pattern," the saleswoman went on. "Also known as the 'meander' pattern. Meander was the name of a river that twisted and turned a lot. I majored in design," she added, by way of explanation.

She studied the picture some more. "It's pretty cool," she said grudgingly, "but not because of any talent Turner had. I mean, a guy who'd think these other pictures were worth paying good money to frame, he couldn't actually compose a picture like this, could he? Even the nude on the wall behind her is boring. No, this was just a lucky shot."

I agreed that the other photographs could have been done by any Sunday photographer, whereas this one was powerful because of the life in the woman in the foreground, and her contrast with the conventional photograph on the wall behind her.

"Maybe he jumped off that cliff," the saleswoman said, "when he realized he was doomed to take photographs like millions of others."

"Well, at least he must have recognized how good this one was," I said, "considering he brought it in to be framed."

She wrinkled her nose at the logic of that. I removed the photograph from its frame, paid the bill and got a receipt, told the saleswoman to keep the other photographs in case Turner's family wanted them, then biked back to Turner's apartment building and roused Ethel Wynn from her Saturday television stupor and showed her the photograph—just to make sure Turner hadn't had a slew of young women with facial jewelry as models for his photography.

"Yep," she said, "that's her all right. Helen to him. Elli to her."

*   *   *

I biked home, took a glass of iced tea and my cordless phone out onto my deck, and called Marcy Turner at home. Annette answered and I asked to talk to her mother. When she came on the phone, I told her about the photograph I'd found and what I'd learned from Ethel Wynn about the woman in it.

"The bastard," she said, keeping her voice low. "I suppose I should have guessed there was a woman involved—but a woman that young, with facial jewelry and an attitude? I wouldn't have thought he'd have it in him—or be that dumb! Do you think she was living with him?"

"There weren't any signs of it in the apartment," I answered, "but she and her friends had plenty of time to remove any evidence after his death—along with his computer, keyboard, and stereo."

The city police had already contacted her about the intruder in Turner's apartment. "It's very bizarre," she said, "Evan hanging around with people like that. He had better taste in friends in the old days, back when I first knew him. I guess I'd like to see that photograph sometime, see what she has that I don't—aside, of course, from the youth and vitality I had when we first met."

Ginny arrived at my place at a little after six, put the ice cream in my fridge, and opened one of the cans of beer she'd brought for herself.

I stirred two packages of microwaved chicken—you cool it first—into the packaged salad and served it with crusty French bread, with iced tea for me and beer for Ginny. I can't imagine why anybody has a stove anymore, considering how well you can dine with just a refrigerator, a microwave oven, and a good bread shop nearby. Not to speak of all the great takeout you can get nowadays at your local supermarket.

We ate on the deck and I filled her in on the Music School burglary, since that had taken place while she was away, and described my encounter with Muscle Boy at Evan Turner's apartment.

She paused with a forkful of food at her mouth. "Some relationships are just doomed from the start, aren't they?

You think he was telling the truth and Turner really had given him permission to be in there?"

I said I didn't know. I slid the photograph of Elli or Helen across the table to her and related what I knew about her as Ginny studied it, prodding it this way and that with her fork.

"Pretty good picture," she said finally. "It sounds like your Evan Turner had some unusual friends. You think he could have been involved with the burglars in some bizarre plot to loot the Music School?"

"It's possible," I said, "but why would he? I imagine he made a pretty good salary at the U. He didn't need to earn extra money, especially doing something as risky as that."

"How do you know? He might've had a drug or gambling problem. For that matter, this Elli or one of her friends might have had some kind of hold on him."

That was possible too, of course.

"Or," Ginny continued, "this mysterious woman could have gone up with him to Lake Superior for a romantic vacation. They could have quarreled on the edge of the cliff, and she threw him over—or killed him, took his keys, and then threw him over. A little melodramatic, of course, but then going over that cliff was pretty dramatic even if he just tripped and fell."

"If she was up there with him," I said, "she couldn't have been living in his cabin. Somebody would have noticed that." But I supposed she could have been staying at a motel down the road, as Christian had when Sam taught up there. I made a note to myself to call the Lake Superior police and see if there'd been keys found with Turner's body.

"Another scenario," Ginny went on, "is that Turner was simply undergoing a common, garden-variety midlife crisis and Elli or Helen played the all-too-conventional role of Girlfriend Young Enough to Be His Daughter. When she learned he was dead, she rounded up a couple of unsavory friends and they broke into his place to burgle it, found the keys to the Music School, and decided to burgle it too."

"Which doesn't explain Muscle Boy being in the apartment," I pointed out.

"You can't always explain why losers do what they do," she replied. "Turner was dead, so he didn't need the apartment anymore. Muscle Boy did."

She stared into her beer can, found it empty, went inside and got another. When she returned, she asked me what I'd found out about Turner so far.

"Well, one thing that fits with the midlife crisis theory is that, according to one of his colleagues, he wasn't planning to do any more serious scholarship for a while, he was going to spend some time trying to 'find himself.' "

"Find himself!" Ginny scoffed. "Isn't that something people did in the eighties—and ended up in the chubby arms of their 'inner brat'? Maybe Turner went looking for himself in the arms of this Helen or Elli and got more than he bargained for."

"His wife thinks he was trying to make up for having betrayed his 'real calling,' which was composing and performing music instead of teaching about it. He even tried his hand at composing 'classical' music."

"What happened to it?"

"Apparently he showed some of it to Scott Hall, the composer," I said. "Hall must not have thought much of it, because shortly afterward Turner decided to try his hand at photography."

"Maybe it was such a wonderful piece of music," Ginny said, "that Hall killed Turner and stole it."

Ginny has a lurid imagination. "I still think a moose did it," she continued. "Or a bear. Turner was standing at the edge of a cliff, focusing through his camera lens, and—"

"There's something else," I said. "Annette Turner, his daughter."

"What about her?"

"She thinks her dad was murdered."

"Oh? Why?" Ginny was no longer being flippant. She likes kids.

"According to her, he had vertigo."

"Hm. And who does she think killed him?"

"Her mother."

"For the insurance, huh? That's certainly a motive, but does she have anything else? Opportunity, for example? Or has she just been reading too many thrillers?"

"She and her mother were up in the area at the time Turner died. I'd like to know more about that. I also want to know more about Marcy Turner's boyfriend before I consider sitting down with Annette for a little heart-to-heart. I don't suppose you've heard anything from your spies at the hospital yet?"

"No, but it's Saturday and even my spies need time off. So who else is on your suspect list?"

"Geraldine Asher, the woman who just took over as director from Turner, couldn't hide from me her anger at Turner because he'd helped block the appointment of a feminist scholar to the Music School."

"Well, people have been killed for less than that," Ginny said, "but since she's now the school's director, she wouldn't have to risk her career by pushing Turner off a cliff over something so small, would she?"

I didn't know. I just remembered her suppressed anger when she'd told me about it, and wondered what she'd do if she came upon Turner near a cliff with that walking stick she'd mentioned. He wouldn't have had to be close to the cliff—Geraldine Asher looked fit enough to drag an unconscious man a long way. It would have been the perfect crime—at least if she got rid of the hair and blood on the stick.

Ginny asked me if I had any other suspects. I asked her if she'd ever heard of a harpist named Fiona McClure.

She burst out laughing. "No, but what a great name for a harpist! You couldn't get away with naming a harpist Fiona McClure in a book, because nobody'd believe it. What's her connection to Turner?"

"She was Turner's lover once, but she dumped him for somebody else. Turner took it hard. Now she's a close friend of Marcy Turner's and married to a pianist who used to be a friend of Turner's. Both she and her husband were at Lake Superior the same time Turner was. Gary spoke to her for a few minutes and she made no secret of the fact

that she wasn't sorry Turner was dead. She seemed quite pleased about it, in fact.''

Ginny peered morosely into her beer can. "Do you sometimes suspect other people live more interesting lives than we do?" she asked.

"It's the music they're around," I said, "day in, day out, stirring the passions."

We cleared away the plates and walked down into the backyard and began picking raspberries from the bushes on the fence. It was a good year for raspberries.

"So what's new on the Gary front?" Ginny asked casually. She likes Gary. She comes from a small farming community herself, and talks of moving back there someday, and she doesn't understand why I don't jump at the chance to marry him.

"He still hasn't made up his mind whether or not to buy the paper."

"Why not? It's perfect for him." Her mouth was full of berries.

I shrugged. "I don't know. It's a pretty drastic step. He'd have to sink all his savings into it."

"And lose you."

"I doubt that'll be a factor in his decision."

She turned and stared at me, then laughed shortly and went back to picking and eating berries. After a minute she asked, "Don't you ever get tired of living in a big city, Peggy, with all the crime and noise, people always in a hurry, which makes them rude, angry, and dangerous? Don't you ever want to get away from it, live someplace where it's quiet and the air's clean and the people friendly?"

I shook my head. "No," I said. "I belong in the city."

"Why? Because you can hide here?"

Not too many people can say that to me and get away with it. I didn't respond for a moment, just went on picking berries. "You don't *have to* hide in a big city," I said finally, "because nobody's looking for you—nobody's looking *at* you. It's in small towns like Loon Lake that you have to hide, that you have to pretend to be what you're not."

"*If* you're not."

"Exactly. And I'm not."

We started walking back to the house. "My life's here, Ginny," I went on. "That's the bottom line. I don't need to live with somebody or be married to him, just because I love him. I don't even need to live in the same town with him—just close enough to see him fairly often. Loon Lake's only a three-hour drive. I've known people who've lived happy lives together who've been separated by greater distances than that. I've told Gary that—I told him that again last weekend."

"What did he say?"

"That you can't raise kids that way."

"And what did you say to that?"

"Nothing." The "nothing" was, in fact, the silence that had grown between us when the phone rang to tell Gary about Evan Turner's death.

While I dished up the berries and scooped ice cream on top of them, Ginny made cappuccino in my espresso machine and we carried it all into my living room, where she showed me her Italian photographs and some of the souvenirs she'd brought back, and described the trip. I found it ironic that she was especially enthusiastic about Italian Renaissance art and architecture, considering that's where our modern questioning of all received truths began. She gave me an expensive coffee table book of Italian art.

When it was time for her to leave, she popped the last raspberry into her mouth and chewed it thoughtfully, squeezing every last bit of summer out of it, for our winters are long. Then she picked up the photograph of Elli again and looked at it. " 'Elli' is just a variation of 'Helen,' isn't it?" she said after a minute.

"I suppose so," I replied. I hadn't thought of that.

"Both Helen and Elli are in this photograph," she went on. "Helen's in the picture on the wall—bathed in soft light and nicely dressed in classical nudity. And Elli's in front of her, looking like she wants to give the photographer the finger."

"What's your point?" I asked, for it sounded as though she might have one.

"I think you're lucky Helen was there with Elli the night of the burglary," she said.

Thirteen

I sat in my living room a while after Ginny left and stared at the photograph. Ginny was right. It seemed to contain two sides of a single woman. In the one—the nude on the wall—the face didn't look all that different from the faces you see in high school yearbook photographs, in which photographers who specialize in graduation pictures manage to remove, along with the zits, almost everything of interest. In the other, the woman seemed to be showing her contempt for the kind of artist who would hang such a picture on his wall. I wondered if Evan Turner had seen the ironic contrast and realized that he'd produced a real work of art, at least for anybody who appreciates irony, which I do.

After a few minutes, when the photograph began to dissolve into the chemical grain it was composed of, I put it aside, got up, and went to bed, but I couldn't sleep. I thought about Gary. If I were working my regular job, this would be the last night of my six days on duty—we work a six on/three off rotation—and I could drive up to Loon Lake tomorrow morning and spend three days with him. We hadn't talked about it, but I knew he'd like it if I did— or I thought he would, anyway. But, remembering the tension between us the previous weekend, I suddenly wasn't sure.

I wondered if I could talk him into giving up the idea of moving to Loon Lake and buying the newspaper. What had Sam called it? Psychic suicide. I wondered if I could get Gary to commit psychic suicide for me. Men get women to do it all the time. And women get men to do it. And

most people do it to themselves, according to Sam. It sounded to me as though Evan Turner had done it too, back when he'd given up his music, decided to join the respectable middle class, got himself a wife, a kid, and a job with tenure.

Had my father done it too? I quickly erased that thought.

I tried to get to sleep by pretending I was pitching a softball game—it works better than counting sheep for me. I know that if I'm still awake after striking out the side in the first inning, I might as well get up and read.

Instead of reaching for a book, I lay there thinking about the Helen who wanted to be called Elli. The image of her throwing herself at Muscle Boy to keep me from getting hurt gave way to her eyes in her muddy face staring at me through the chain-link fence before she turned slowly and disappeared down the river bluff, and then that face disappeared too, replaced by the Helen of the nude and then the Elli who was laughing at the photographer, at Turner.

Who was she and how was she involved in Evan Turner's life? Could she have been involved in his death, or was she, as Ginny had suggested, just the other woman in a rather ordinary man's midlife crisis?

I sat up suddenly, glanced over at the clock on my bedside table. It was a few minutes after midnight. I got out my phone book and looked up the number of the Dungeon, the bar where Lanny Nelson, the owner of the van used in the Music School burglary, worked, and dialed it. It rang a long time, then somebody picked up the phone and hollered, "Hello," over the noise of a band playing in the background. It was a male voice, but I couldn't identify it.

"Lanny in tonight?"

"Yeah. Hold on a sec."

I hung up, dressed quickly, went out to my car, and drove over there. Because it was a Saturday night—Sunday morning, actually—the area was still alive with people, so it was hard to find a place to park, but I managed to find one a couple of blocks away.

The Dungeon's on a corner, with a theaterlike marquee above the door that lists the featured bands which, that weekend, were Stone Pucker, the Loafers, and the head-

liner, Gacy's Diner. The names were tame compared to some I'd seen, many of them apparently chosen so they can't be printed in family newspapers, mentioned on television, or advertised in any publication where a child's eye might fall on them and be corrupted.

As I pulled open the door and stepped in, a wave of sound and the hot stench of cigarettes, booze, and bodies almost blew me back out again. The room was jammed with people, with waitresses cruising the place like barracudas, balancing trays of drinks. On the small stage at the end of the room, bathed in garish lights, a band was churning out rock music, a young-old kid in front with long pipestem legs, hair in his face, and a guitar jutting from his crotch screaming angrily into the microphone, as though haranguing the dancers on the floor beneath him for their dissolute ways—a real clash of values, I thought. Occasionally he did a pirouette on his scuffed boots and played to the three band members behind him. On the back of his leather jacket, a human arm on a dinner plate was painted in garish colors, suggesting that this was Gacy's Diner and not, say, the Loafers.

I slipped in among a mob of people milling around near the door and let my eyes run over the crowd, looking for a face I recognized. There were a lot of young dark-haired women with jewelry who could have been Elli, but there was no way I could be sure in a room so smoky and full of people in constant motion. I didn't see any man big enough to be Muscle Boy, but I spotted Lanny Nelson behind the crowded bar, one of three bartenders, a bandanna wrapped around his forehead to catch his sweat in the overheated room.

I kept moving, hoping not to attract the attention of any of the single men or the cruising waitresses. One song ended and, with almost no transition, another began. I couldn't tell how it differed from the song before it, but apparently that wasn't important to the dancers, and anyway I wasn't listening that hard myself. Jesse Porter, the night of the Music School burglary, had suggested the burglars might be musicians, so I studied the band members to see if I recognized any of them. I didn't. In jumping over

the fence behind the school, one of the burglars—the one I thought had to be the leader—had gashed his arm. There was no evidence of that on the skinny arms of any of these men.

After about fifteen minutes, the din, the smoke, and the stench began to get to me, so I figured it was time to do what I'd come there for. I made my way to the bar and found a place to stand close to where Nelson was working.

"What can I get you?" he asked after a few minutes. His heavy-lidded eyes showed no interest in me at all.

"A Coke," I said. He moved down the bar to scoop chipped ice into a glass and spray Coke over it from a hose.

The guy next to me, his forearms resting on the bar and bracketing a bottle of beer protectively, caught my eye in the mirror. "What are you, a teetotaler?" he asked, smiling a filmy, fly-specked smile.

"The designated driver," I said.

Lanny came back with my Coke. As he set it down, I asked him if Elli had been in tonight.

"Elli?" he said. "She—" Then he took a second look at me, a puzzled look on his face. "I don't know no Elli," he said, and moved quickly down the bar.

The man next to me caught my eye in the mirror and winked. "Yeah, and the Pope don't know mass, right?"

Those were my sentiments too, but I followed Nelson down the bar and said, raising my voice to be heard over the music, "I want to thank her for saving me from serious injury a week or so ago. I'm not interested in the Music School burglary, I'm interested in Evan Turner."

Again he darted me a glance, his eyelids fluttering. "I don't know what you're talking about, lady." He moved down the bar with the glass of beer.

I went after him again, said between two drinkers, "C'mon, Lanny, it's important! I only want to know what her relationship with Turner was." I was conscious that my tone of voice was pleading, almost wheedling—far different from the officious cop's voice I'd used on him the last time we'd met.

He noticed the difference too, and enjoyed the power

shift. His heavy eyelids sank to half cover his eyes again and his face became a sleepy blank.

"A cop asking me a favor!" he said in a loud hoarse voice, as though trying to speak over the crowd noise and music. "Ain't that a gas! One week she's kickin' in my door in the middle of the night like some kind of Nazi, callin' me a thief and a liar, the next she's comin' around begging for favors."

A drunk some way down the bar leaned around some of the other customers to give me a blurry *How could you?* look and then returned to his drink as another customer came up to the bar next to me. I didn't pay any attention to him, just noticed in the mirror that he was thin and pale, with a hard, angular face and short hair.

"Would you at least give her my name and phone number and tell her I'd like to hear from her?" I said to Lanny. "Let her decide if she wants to talk to me? She saved me from serious harm the night of the burglary. Tell her that, and tell her I'm grateful."

"You must be deaf," he said, sounding incredulous, "or stupider than you look."

I scribbled my name and both my cell phone and home phone number on a piece of paper, and tried to hand it to him. He just stared at me, so I pushed it across the bar, avoiding the wet spots. "Tell her a child's involved too, will you?"

I dropped a couple of bills on the bar to pay for the Coke I hadn't touched and then turned to leave. At the door, I glanced back to see what Lanny was doing with the note.

He was talking to the thin man, whose eyes were still watching me steadily in the mirror. I looked down at his arms, but I was too far away to see anything. It had only been five days, so a wound that had bled as much as his had wouldn't be healed yet—the one on my neck certainly wasn't, anyway. The leader of the burglars had had a mustache and goatee and this man was clean-shaven, but that didn't have to mean anything.

I threaded my way back through the crowd to the bar. The man watched me come and so did Lanny. When I stood next to him, I said, "This isn't about the Music School

burglary. It's something more important than that."

He turned and looked at me, his pale eyes expressionless. "Lady," he said, "I don't even know what language you're speaking."

"I'd appreciate it if one of you would give Elli the note," I said. "Let her decide if she wants to speak to me."

He said nothing, just went on staring at me, as Lanny moved down the bar. I glanced down at his arms, but they were resting flat on the bar, so I couldn't see the underside. He followed my eyes and then, with an insolent smile, turned one thin white arm over. The gash ran down the inside of it about a foot, still livid and puffy in places, as though he hadn't taken very good care of it.

"I cut myself on a fence," he said, "tryin' to get away from a broad who was chasin' me. What happened to you?" he added, looking at my neck, where I still wore a bandage to keep my shirt from rubbing the wound.

I thought of punching him in the face, but that wouldn't have done me any good. So I said, "Let her decide," again, then turned and left the bar. I stood a moment outside in the fresh, early morning air to clear my lungs, then walked back to my car, glancing over my shoulder regularly to make sure I wasn't being followed.

Fourteen

A Catholic childhood takes the pleasure out of Sunday. Add to that a father who drank heavily Saturday night and worked off his hangover on his family the next day, and you can understand why it wouldn't bother me if they removed Sunday from the week. I stayed in bed with coffee and the paper, surrounded by Mendelssohn's piano trios and then his two piano concertos, some of the happiest music ever written.

I half expected Gary to call that morning just to say hello, but he didn't. Well, I could have called him too.

I mowed the lawn and edged it with the weed-whip—I get a discount on the rent—and paused every now and then to cool off with a glass of lemonade and talk with Mrs. Hammer, who was weeding her garden under a wide-brimmed straw hat. When there was nothing else to do in the yard, I still had the afternoon to get through. I decided to put it to some good use.

I looked up David Paul Douglas in the staff directory, thinking I could talk to him and his wife, Fiona McClure, but they weren't listed. Next I tried Scott Hall, the composer, who'd apparently been the closest thing to a friend Turner had had in the Music School—at least until Turner showed him some music he'd composed and asked for his opinion.

His address was in a little town full of antique stores and fudge shops on the St. Croix River, about forty minutes southeast of Minneapolis. I decided to drive out there without calling first, since it's too easy to say no over the phone. And besides, it's a pleasant drive.

I'd attended a concert of Scott Hall's music about six months earlier, a retrospective celebrating forty years of composing. According to the program, he'd begun his career writing the kind of atonal, experimental music that was popular in so-called classical music circles back then, but midway through his career, about twenty years ago, he'd changed and begun writing much more lyric and melodic music—almost romantic. The program I'd heard had included music from all periods of his career. I'd liked some of the earlier stuff—at least, I'd found it interesting in small doses—but I preferred the later, more melodic stuff. I'm old-fashioned enough to think music is supposed to be emotional, not cerebral.

The Halls lived in a tall house of glass and weathered cedar on a bluff overlooking the river. The woman who answered the door was dressed all in gray, and her hair was the color of old snow. Only her eyes, large and bright under arched, dark brows, gave away the life in her, while the bone structure of her face indicated that she'd once been very beautiful.

I told her my name and that I was a campus cop investigating the death of Evan Turner. I asked her if I could speak with her husband.

"Evan?" she repeated with a frown. "His death was an accident, wasn't it?"

"His grandmother isn't satisfied that it was," I said. "The University has asked me to look into it."

She laughed softly. "I don't imagine Mrs. Farr had any trouble persuading the University to do that! The wonder is that they assigned a mere campus policewoman to the task instead of one of the big detective agencies. You must be a very good detective. Are you?"

"I think so," I said.

"You're certainly brash enough, barging in on us on a Sunday afternoon without phoning first." She smiled. "Well, I've always believed brashness should be rewarded—especially in a woman. Come in. Scott's up in his loft—I'll ask him if he'll see you. We liked Evan and were sorry he died, especially in such an awful way. We'd been

for living. Mrs. Hall cr[...] end table, picked it up, presse[...] for a few minutes.

When she returned, she nodded to[...] to a gallery running halfway around the[...] up,'' she said. ''His study's the last door on the[...] bring coffee up in a minute. Do you take cream or s[...] We like ours black.''

''I do too,'' I said. ''But please don't go to any trouble.''

''Oh, I'm not,'' she assured me with a smile. ''I was making coffee for us when you arrived.''

''Is that a real Picasso?'' I asked her, pointing to a small painting on the stairs.

She smiled. ''It's a real Picasso *signature,* but it's probably not a real Picasso painting. He sometimes signed work done by younger artists who needed money, if he thought they were promising.''

''Nice of him,'' I said, ''but it must drive collectors nuts.''

''Not if they know what they're doing,'' she replied as she went to get the coffee.

I climbed to the gallery, went down to Hall's study, knocked, and went in. The room looked out on the river, the back wall a huge window that offered a spectacular view. The other three walls were lined with built-in bookcases jammed with books and piles of paper with musical notations on them. A bronze bust of Beethoven at his most passionate stood on the top shelf of one bookcase, his hair looking as though it were being whipped by a high wind, while on the opposite bookcase, Haydn in wig and white marble seemed to be watching him with a serene, slightly patronizing smile. I've never cared much for white marble—or Haydn either, the patron saint of classical music

... on a podium...
...ted until he looked up at me

"... hair," he said. "Is that color real?"
"...ar."
"... se it is! Of course it is! You can't get color like
...t of a bottle, can you? Come in and sit down." He
...sed the book, an expensive-looking history of rock 'n'
roll, and gestured to a sofa against the wall next to the
piano. "Did I look depressed when you came in?"

"More pensive than depressed, I thought," I said.

"Well, I should be depressed! I just read in this book
that I have the same birthday—same date, same year—as
Ringo Starr. Do you know who he is?"

I told him I did.

"The funny-looking Beatle," he went on, as though I
hadn't spoken. "My sister was madly in love with the man.
So were a lot of other women. Why?"

"I guess some women are just attracted to funny-looking
men," I answered.

"I've never been attracted to funny-looking women."

"No, it only seems to work the other way."

I noticed a treadmill in a corner of the room and, on an
exercise mat next to it, plastic-coated barbells in various
sizes. He saw what I was looking at and said, "Aside from
the fact that everybody should exercise more than they do,
I have to keep in shape for my conducting. It's a lot more
work than most people realize. Try waving your hands in
the air while conducting, say, Beethoven's Ninth, and see
how exhausting it is. It's not at all unlike boxing. I did
some of that too, in my youth."

He put the book aside and said, "So, Alex tells me
you're out on the Sabbath trying to make poor Evan

Turner's death a murder. Apparently, a member of Dulcie Farr's family can't simply fall off a cliff like an ordinary human being, can he—or jump?''

"It's unlikely," I said, "if the family member in question suffers from vertigo."

He raised his eyebrows. "You're saying Evan was afraid of heights?" When I nodded, he frowned, said, "Well, I suppose he might not have been paying attention to where he was walking. I mean, he did climb around on the hill above the lake with that camera of his—I met him up there one morning when I was out hiking, looking for things to take photographs of. He was quite the avid photographer, you know."

"Was he near the cliffs?"

He pursed his lips. "Well, no. No, he was on the path in the woods, before it reached the cliffs—focusing his camera on, I believe, a mushroom or a fern. He didn't want to be disturbed."

I asked him if he'd seen much of Turner that week.

"Not much, no," he said with an apologetic smile.

"I'm surprised," I said. "I've been told that you and he were old friends."

"Friends?" he repeated, seeming to savor the word for possible unexpected nuances. "*Friends* is perhaps too strong a word. After Evan was hired, Alex and I took him and his wife under our wings. We got together fairly regularly—for dinner and cards, things like that. But after their daughter was born, we drifted apart." He smiled regretfully. "Childless couples have nothing to bring to a marriage with children, and vice versa—especially vice versa."

"How about the Friday he died?" I asked. "Did you see him then?"

"Probably, but I have no recollection of it. I taught my class and then left immediately, drove back down here."

"Oh, you didn't spend the weekend up there?"

"No. A German choral group was in town that night. They were going to be performing a set of my songs. I decided I wanted to hear them, so I drove down. The natural vanity of an old man, I suppose," he added with a smile.

His wife, coming in with a coffee thermos and three cups on a tray, said, "Oh, Scott!" As she was pouring the coffee, I started to get up to help her, but she waved me back to the sofa, brought me my cup, and then took her husband his. Then she went over and sat down in a rocking chair in a corner and picked up a basket of knitting.

A genre painting, I thought. *The composer and his wife, at home.* I felt like an intruder. There was, of course, a good reason for that.

"I've heard some of your songs," I said, "at the concert in your honor last year. They were quite beautiful."

"Thank you," he said, pleased. "I must say, it's nice being grilled—if that's what you're doing here—by a cop who knows something about music. I suppose I'm a snob, but I'm very pessimistic about the musical knowledge of my fellow citizens."

"It's probably no lower than it's ever been," I said. "I don't suppose a lot of people flocked to hear Mozart play on days when there was a good public execution."

"That's a depressing thought!" he said. "But you're probably right."

"One thing puzzles me a little," I said, returning to business. "Turner got his Ph.D. here and then you hired him right away. I was under the impression that universities didn't hire their own graduates."

"You're right, of course, as a rule they don't," he said. "It leads to too much inbreeding. Under normal circumstances, we would only hire one of our own if he—or she, I suppose—were an exceptional candidate, and Evan wasn't that."

"Then how'd he get hired?" I asked, although I suspected the answer.

He gazed at me—through me—for a few moments before answering. "You know who his grandmother is, of course?"

I nodded.

"Well, to celebrate Evan's getting his Ph.D., Mrs. Farr threw a party—a big party. She invited the entire Music School faculty—plus the president of the University and a lot of other wealthy local movers and shakers. You should

have seen it!'' He shook his head, remembering. ''A garden party in that sculpture garden she has for a backyard, with Chinese lanterns and waitresses in matching uniforms. She even imported a pretty decent string quartet to play background music! Our director at that time, Alrikson, was a snob and a drunk, and in those days the director could hire whomever he damn well pleased—and after that party, it damn well pleased him to hire Evan. I don't know what the University got out of it, but I do know the Music School got a new concert hall soon afterward, funded largely by Mrs. Farr.'' He grinned. ''So it wasn't a bad trade-off.''

'' 'Who pays the piper . . .' '' I said.

Scott Hall laughed. ''Most appropriate!'' he exclaimed. ''Most appropriate!''

''Later, though, he got tenure and promoted,'' I said. ''Was that also thanks to Mrs. Farr?''

''Well, the family connection certainly didn't hurt. But Evan had published some fairly good articles on popular American musicians of the nineteenth and early twentieth centuries in some respectable journals by then. They weren't anything I was particularly interested in, and they weren't going to set the world on fire with their originality, but they were soundly researched and well written. Those, plus Mrs. Farr, did the trick for him.''

''And later,'' I pointed out, ''he also made full professor.''

''Yes, yes, he did. On the basis of a book he wrote, a social history of the guitar in the U.S. from its origins up to when it became the instrument of choice for pimply-faced kids in the fifties. It wasn't very interesting or valuable, in my opinion, but it got a few positive reviews and so Alrikson—by that time virtually senile—got him promoted to full professor. None too soon either, since Alrikson had a stroke that even the dean of the college couldn't fail to notice, and he was forced to retire soon afterward.''

''Turner succeeded him as director of the school,'' I said. ''How'd that happen?''

Hall chuckled. ''None of the rest of us—the other full professors, I mean—wanted the job! Why would we? Why would anybody? It's just trying to balance the budget, sit-

ting on committees all over campus with other pompous fools just like yourself, and kissing the dean's derriere to try to get a share of the increasingly limited funds available to the humanities. The job pays a little extra, of course, but not enough to be worth the bother. So we persuaded Evan to take the job and he jumped at the chance.''

"I imagine that the other faculty also thought Turner's connection to Mrs. Farr would continue to be useful,'' I said.

"Oh, that might have occurred to some of us,'' he said with a little smirk.

All Dulcie had been, I thought, was the whorehouse pianist. What was the Music School faculty?

"But Evan wanted the job too,'' Hall continued. "In my opinion, he was no longer interested in doing research and publishing, so he thought he'd give administration a fling.'' He sniffed disdainfully, waved a hand—he had great-looking hands and knew it, which was why he didn't use a baton when he conducted. "After all,'' he went on, "what is an administrator except a failed scholar, or one who has been seduced from his true calling by the temptations of power?''

I said, "It sounds to me as though just about everything Evan Turner had was on account of his grandmother. He must have known that. And he must have known that all of you—the other faculty members—knew it too.''

Scott Hall shrugged, said nothing.

"Something like that could be very demoralizing,'' I said.

"I suppose so,'' Hall said indifferently. "But nevertheless, he was still upset when we didn't elect him to another term as director. He wanted a second term—perhaps because director was the only identity he had left and now he was going to have to try to find something else to justify his existence.''

"How'd Professor Asher manage to win?'' I asked.

"The younger faculty,'' he said sourly. "They don't agree on much, but they agreed on her, and they had the votes.'' His face clouded over. "Geraldine is going to be

a very different sort of director from Evan, I'm afraid. She's going to want to change things.''

He sipped his coffee, waited for me to ask another question. For a few moments, the only sound in the room was the soft clicking of his wife's knitting needles.

"Tell me about the big fuss in the school a few years ago," I said, "when Professor Asher and some of the younger faculty—''

He raised a hand as though to quiet an orchestra. "I know what you're going to say," he said, his voice resigned. "Everybody knows about how she and some of the young turks she's allied herself with tried to ram a crazed feminist down our throats.''

I told him I'd like to hear about it.

He shook his head as though in disbelief. "This woman—this Marilyn Schaeffer—had written a ghastly book on Beethoven—something about how his music's a form of violence against women—'' He broke off, shot me a narrow glance. "Do you like Beethoven's music?''

"Yes," I said. "I like it a lot. Just about all of it.''

He nodded. "Good! Well, anyway, she was working on another book equally ghastly, this one on what she called 'phallocentric music'—music by human beings born with penises, in case you aren't up on academic jargon. It would have been a disaster for the school if we'd been forced to hire her—a disaster!'' He smiled suddenly. "We managed to nip that one in the bud!''

"How?''

"God," he went on, rolling his eyes to the ceiling, "or whoever it is who looks out for the integrity of higher education, intervened in the form of the dean of the college, who declared a college-wide budgetary emergency and retrenched the vacant position. The woman was forced to go elsewhere.''

"And that was it?'' I said. "A budgetary crisis saved you from this monstrous woman?''

"Yes!''

"How convenient.''

"Yes," he replied, looking like a cat trying to hide canary feathers, "it was.''

The University had had its share of budgetary crises over the years, during which some vacant positions were taken away from departments and schools to save money. I wondered if that was all this had been.

I got the photograph of Elli out of my shoulder bag and took it over to him.

"What's this?" He studied it a long time without saying anything. "Who is she?" he asked finally as he handed it back.

"I wish I knew," I replied.

Out of politeness, I handed it to his wife. She looked down at it, then looked up quickly—but not at me, at her husband, something glittering in her dark eyes. He returned her gaze steadily. When she handed the photograph back to me, her hand was trembling slightly. I hadn't noticed that it trembled when she'd poured my coffee.

I could have hung the photograph on the tension that was suddenly in the room with us.

"Well?" Hall demanded.

"Turner probably took the picture," I said, my eyes moving between them. "He called her Helen, but she told him she wanted him to call her Elli."

Alex Hall cleared her throat. "And how do you believe she's connected with Evan's death?"

"All I know is that she was involved in the break-in in the Music School," I answered.

"Really!" Hall exclaimed. "And how do you know that?"

I told them. I described my encounter with one of the burglars in Turner's apartment too.

"I find it hard to believe that Evan could have been in—in cahoots with the burglars," Hall said. "Let me see that photograph again."

He examined it a moment, tilting his head this way and that as though considering buying it for his collection. "She's rather ordinary-looking, isn't she?" he said. "But she's young, and that's all that counts with some men. It looks to me as though she's about to remove her clothing, perhaps as a prelude to making love. Chances are, she had a key to Evan's apartment—his 'love nest'—and she let

one of her accomplices use it after Evan's death."

He shook his head sadly as he handed me the photograph.

His wife's head was bowed over her knitting, but the needles were still. "Do you know this woman?" I asked her.

She looked up, startled.

Before she could reply, her husband said, "Of course we don't!"

He pulled himself quickly out of his chair and, towering over me, said, "Mourning for Evan Turner wasn't how I and my wife wanted to spend this beautiful summer afternoon on the river. You've darkened the day for us, Officer. I'll show you out."

His wife started to get up too, but he waved her back down with one of his beautiful hands.

Fifteen

I got to the Music School the next morning at a little after nine and walked down to the main office, hoping Professor Douglas would be in sometime that day, or at least that I could get his home phone number.

The receptionist, a young woman in her late teens or early twenties, glanced up from contemplating her long, elaborately decorated fingernails and asked me if she could help me. I asked her if Professor Douglas would be in that day.

"I don't know," she said, her eyes filled of wonder, as though I'd asked her one of life's heavy questions. "You want me to check?"

"Would you?"

"No problem!" As if to prove it, she flipped through a sheaf of papers clipped together on her desk and reported: "All the professors are coming in today on account of there's a big faculty meeting at ten."

"Thanks," I said, and turned quickly, hoping to leave before she could say "No problem!" again. I didn't make it.

I met Douglas coming in the front door. It seemed to take him a moment to recognize me. "Ah, the party crasher," he said sourly, smiling down at me, "out bright and early on this beautiful Monday morning. Are you ready to make an arrest yet?"

"Not exactly *ready*," I said. I asked him if I could talk to him about Turner.

"Not this morning, I'm afraid. We're meeting at ten to discuss the future of the school, and I have to prepare my-

self mentally and spiritually for it. It should drag on until noon, I imagine.''

''How about after lunch, then?''

''You are persistent, aren't you?'' He shook his head in mock disbelief, said, ''Sure, I'll be around this afternoon.''

''Can I come back at one-thirty?'' I pressed, showing yet more persistence.

He sighed. ''Why not?'' He waved graciously and disappeared into the building's gloom.

Lieutenant Bixler hadn't come in yet when I got to the station, but he'd said he wanted paperwork, lots of paperwork, so I found a vacant office and used the word processor to type up a three-page report that was replete with complex sentences studded with words of more than one syllable, knowing he'd tire his lips out before reaching the end.

I called the Lake Superior highway patrol and asked to talk to the officer who'd been in charge of the Turner investigation. I explained who I was and asked him if he could tell me if they'd found keys on Turner's body or in his cabin.

He put me on hold, during which time Ginny came in carrying a mug of coffee and one of the low-fat muffins that, no matter what it's called, tastes like cooked prune. I told her what I was waiting for.

''Nope,'' the cop said when he returned, ''no keys. Not surprising, though, when you think of what that body went through. The only thing still on it besides clothes you wouldn't even give your brother-in-law for Christmas was a watch and a handkerchief. No prints on either,'' he added with a chuckle, ''and unlike in detective stories, the watch couldn't even tell us what time he died. Damn thing was still keeping perfect time!''

I thanked him for his help and hung up.

Ginny said, ''No keys on the corpse, huh? Didn't Agatha Christie write that?''

I asked her if she'd heard anything from her contacts at the University hospital about Ben Anderson, Marcy Turner's friend with the Microbus, but they hadn't gotten back to her yet. She'd call them again after lunch, she said.

*   *   *

I had lunch with a couple of midwatch cops, then biked back to the Music School and went down to Douglas's office. His door was open and he was at his desk, his head bent over a piece of music. I knocked softly and waited for him to notice me. He continued studying the music for a few minutes longer, his sharp face focused in concentration, then shoved it reluctantly aside and looked up, nodded, and told me to come in.

"Scott Hall," he said, "mentioned at the meeting this morning that you found one of the Music School burglars camped out in Evan Turner's apartment. And Evan had been taking nude photographs of one of them too. Is that true?"

When I told him it was, he shook his head, scratched his thin mustache, and said, "Very odd—very odd! What do you make of it?"

"Nothing, yet." I brought out the photograph of Elli and handed it to him across his desk. He looked at it, looked back up at me.

"This is the woman?"

When I nodded, he looked down at her again. "You think she may have killed him—or one of her burglar friends? She looks capable of it! But then, so many kids her age look capable of murder, don't they? I guess it's just the style. It doesn't mean anything—not yet, anyway. Most murderers probably look like income tax accountants now," he added with a chuckle, "just to set themselves apart from the crowd."

"You knew Turner a long time, didn't you?" I said. "Going all the way back to his days as a street musician. Would you mind telling me what he was like then?"

"I honestly can't tell you much," he said, propping his chin on his clasped hands, "since we were never really friends. But we both taught at the Riverside Music Academy—a private music school run by old hippies. It's gone now—the University got the land condemned so they could build a parking lot for the new School of Business there. Symbolic," he added with a sigh.

"Evan taught guitar and I taught piano. I was an assistant

professor here at the time, but the pay was lousy so I moon-lighted at night at the academy. Turner also performed in the bars and coffeehouses around there, but I didn't, of course. I was building my reputation as an accompanist, and it wouldn't have helped much if word got around that I played for tips in coffeehouses. I only recall Turner as being a very purposeful young man—maybe too serious for his own good—lean and full of energy and a pretty good musician, if you like that kind of music. It surprised me when he gave it up and returned to school. I have no idea why he did.''

He twisted his long thin lips into a smile. "As Fiona made sure you knew the other night at Marcy's, she and Turner were lovers back then. I knew who she was, of course, and like every other heterosexual male who'd spent any time with her, I lusted after her, but I don't think she was even aware of my existence. My turn didn't come until later—after her last divorce.''

I asked him if he could think of anybody who might have hated Turner enough to want him dead.

He gave me an exasperated look, the kind he probably gave students who hadn't practiced their scales. "Damn it, Officer, you didn't know the man! If you had, you'd know that nobody could hate Evan Turner that much. As I told you at Marcy's Friday night, he *jumped* off that cliff.''

"Why do you think so?''

"Any number of reasons, I suppose. I think he'd been depressed lately. He probably realized he'd made a mistake in leaving his wife and daughter. I suspect he was the do-mestic type—he needed somebody to come home to at night, be there for him—even though he might have re-sented being dependent in that way. I don't know, I'm not a shrink,'' he added with a modest shrug.

"Another thing,'' he went on, "his career was at a stand-still. He hadn't published anything other than an occasional book review in several years and he'd just lost the chance for a second term as director.''

He glanced back down at the photograph of Elli. "Maybe he thought she'd be the answer. A lot of men do, you know. Instead of changing jobs, they change wives.''

He laughed, flicked his eyes up at me. "Can you imagine what it would be like for a man such as Evan Turner—a plump middle-aged man who'd spent the last twenty-some years of his life as a domestic animal—waking up one morning and finding himself in bed with *this* woman?" He shuddered, but without conviction.

That could have happened, I supposed: Turner could have awakened one morning and realized that Elli wasn't the symbol of youth and promise he'd thought she was— the youth and promise he may have felt he'd betrayed in himself. That might explain why he'd gone back to his wife and asked for a reconciliation. And when she'd turned him down, he might have killed himself.

I said, "I've heard that a few years ago there was a big fuss in the school when the younger faculty wanted to hire a feminist musicologist, but some of the older faculty feared she'd infect the school with her subversive ideas."

"Oh, you've heard about that, have you?" Douglas said. "Yes, it's true. In my opinion, getting rid of that woman was Turner's only worthwhile act as director—although Fiona doesn't agree with me, do you?" he asked, smiling up at his wife, who'd just stepped into the doorway.

"No," she replied, coming into the room. To me she said, "Do you mind if I join you?"

Without waiting for an answer, she crossed the room to an old sofa in a corner and made herself comfortable on it. She was wearing sandals, a white, ankle-length summer dress held up by thin straps, and her long silvery hair was piled in a messy knot on top of her head.

"David told me you'd be coming to talk to him about Evan this afternoon," she said, "so I thought I could hurry your investigation along by joining you. I assumed you'd want to talk to me too, since Evan and I were lovers once." She gave me a smile, the one that, twenty years ago, must have blown away a lot of the men. I imagined it was still pretty effective. "Such meaningless connections are grist for the detective's slow-grinding mill, aren't they?" she added.

"They are if the man in question died unexpectedly," I said.

"A man who falls off a cliff," she retorted, "can't really be said to have died unexpectedly."

"In case you're wondering," Douglas stuck in gruffly, perhaps feeling neglected, "it didn't bother me at all that Fiona and Marcy were friends, any more than it bothered me that a colleague of mine had once been my wife's lover. I only wish she'd had better taste in men."

"So do I," she said, staring at him. He flushed, lowered his eyes.

"We were just talking about the feminist scholar who apparently didn't get hired here," I said, before the little poisoned darts turned into bombs.

"She was a phony," Douglas said, "and her book only got published because she was a woman. I'll bet even she's embarrassed by some of what she wrote, now that she's a few years older."

"Maybe some of her ideas were too extreme," Fiona said. "But that wasn't why the old boys lost their heads. It was because *her* ridiculous assumptions threatened the ridiculous assumptions their ideas rest on. They couldn't stand for that. They had to drive her away. If they could, they'd have burned her at the stake!"

Douglas gave me an apologetic smile. "Fiona and I have argued about this before," he said mildly. "I feel confident that our decision not to hire the woman was based on solid academic grounds."

"Oh, absolutely!" she said with a sneer.

"You said getting rid of her was Turner's only worth-while act as director of the school," I jumped in. "How'd he do it? I thought you couldn't hire her because of a budgetary crisis in the college."

Fiona burst out laughing. "There are people who think the crisis came on when your Dulcie Farr called up President Hightower and expressed her dismay over the hiring of some kind of crazy feminist dyke—"

"Fiona!" exclaimed her husband, appalled.

"What?" she demanded. "Don't you like the sound of the truth, David?"

"There's no evidence that Evan or his grandmother talked to the dean," he said. "That was just a rumor."

"But everybody knows it's true," she replied. "Marilyn Schaeffer—that's the woman we're talking about—had the votes and she would have been hired—except for the 'budgetary crisis.' And a few months later, the college got a couple of big traveling grants for faculty—from the Dulcie Farr Foundation."

"That was in the works long before the flap over Schaeffer," he said.

"How do you know?"

He didn't reply, just batted the question away with a hand.

I wondered if Turner had ever gone to his grandmother and asked her to intervene in a University matter. I had no doubt she could if she wanted to. The way I was spending my days lately was proof of that.

Fiona looked at me and laughed. "It gets kind of ugly around this place sometimes," she said. "Kind of like the Roman empire, crumbling from within and with the Huns at the gate—and all the guys going around pretending it's just business as usual."

I asked them both to tell me how they recalled Evan Turner at the conference center.

"I didn't pay any particular attention to him," Fiona said.

Douglas thought a moment, pursing his lips. "I thought he seemed a bit depressed, myself. He taught his courses, met his students for office hours, then disappeared into the woods with his camera. We didn't exchange many words, just an occasional hello."

"According to somebody who knew him," I said, "he had vertigo."

"Vertigo!" Douglas exclaimed. "Evan?"

Fiona shrugged dismissively. "I'm not surprised," she said. "It must have been his punishment for having sold out twenty years ago and become a teacher. He fell off his Pegasus."

"Except, as a friend of Evan's once told him to his face, his Pegasus wasn't a horse, it was a donkey," Douglas said.

I glanced at Fiona. "Isn't that what you once told Marcy?"

Douglas laughed. "You told Marcy that, Fiona? Quoting lines from an old lover without attribution? That's called plagiarism."

"Try not to be stupid, David," she snapped.

"Chris was the name of the old lover who told Turner that?" I asked.

"Yes," Douglas replied, before Fiona could say anything. "He wasn't a very nice guy, but Evan thought he was a genius and worshiped him—right up to the moment he stole Fiona out from under him, so to speak."

"He didn't have to steal me, David," she said levelly. "I threw myself at him. Just so you know."

"Oh, I know that! I'm just trying to make you look better in the cop's eyes, that's all. What was it you once said, dear—'Chris Stavrakis took possession of my soul'?"

She flushed angrily. "You could never have that effect on anybody, David," she snapped, her voice rising. "He could play the guitar better than Evan and the piano better than you."

"And do booze and drugs better than anybody! And live off other people—including his women!"

"Chris Stavrakis," I repeated. I can only take so much domestic bill-and-coo before I break out in a rash.

"Right," Douglas replied, making it sound like a curse. "But he couldn't have had anything to do with Turner's death—unless you believe in ghosts. He died twenty years ago. He choked to death on a carrot." Seeing the look on his wife's face, he didn't say that sarcastically.

I asked him if he had been there when it happened.

"No, but Fiona was. There was a lot of weeping and wailing over on Riverside when he died—especially among the women."

I turned to her, gave her a questioning look.

Suddenly close to tears, she demanded, "What do you want from me? The death certificate? I don't have it."

"What about Turner? Was he there?"

"Why would he be? He thought Chris had stolen me from under him, as David so nicely put it. Evan hated the man—Evan hated me too."

"You say Turner worshiped Chris Stavrakis," I said,

"but it doesn't sound as though Stavrakis thought much of him."

"It wasn't anything personal," Douglas said. "Chris was incapable of liking anybody or anything. It was part of his charm. Women—and men too—wanted to break through his coldness, warm him up, make him human."

"He didn't like mediocrities," Fiona snapped. "He predicted that David would spend his life playing 'secundo' to other people's 'primo.' It's almost as though he had second sight."

"Everybody was a mediocrity to Chris Stavrakis," Douglas retorted, "except women. Women weren't even that! Women were just—"

"Shut up!" she screamed, lunging up from the sofa.

He averted his eyes quickly from her mad face.

"What was his connection with all of you?" I asked.

Fiona stared at me a moment, as though only just remembering I was there. She sank back onto the sofa. "He taught at the Riverside Music Academy," she said, her voice suddenly calm, but still breathing heavily, "along with Evan and David. He also performed in the bars and coffeehouses around there."

"He teamed up with Turner sometimes," Douglas couldn't resist putting in, "which was how he met Fiona and swept her off her feet."

Her eyes flicked to him and away. "He was a wonderful musician," she said. "He was a great lover too."

"God knows, he'd had enough practice," Douglas shot back wearily, as though tired of the fight. She didn't look as though she had any more energy for it either.

"He'd also been a student here, twenty-five, thirty years ago," he went on. "If you're interested in the man, talk to Scott Hall. Hall was his adviser. Stavrakis even lived with him for a while, until Hall threw him out. And we've got a box of his music in the music library too—or we did ten years ago, which was the last time I saw it. Gathering dust."

Fiona's eyes suddenly filled with tears and she stood up. "I'm tired of this. Chris choked to death in a stupid accident. Who cares how Evan died?" She started to the door

but stopped when she saw the photograph of Elli on her husband's desk. "What's this?"

"A clue, my dear," he told her in a mocking voice. "Something the sleuth here has found in Evan's dirty underwear."

She looked at him uncomprehendingly, then used a finger to turn the picture so she could see it.

It was a strange thing to see: a woman turning to stone.

The silence stretched out for half a minute or longer, until she must have noticed it herself and glanced up quickly. "Who—" She had to clear her throat to finish the simple sentence. "Who is she?"

"I'm hoping you'll tell me," I said.

She darted a quick look at me and then her eyes went back down to the photograph. She shook her head, then tried a laugh that came out sickly. "You mean *this* is why Evan left Marcy?" she asked, trying to make it sound funny. Her lips were still bloodless.

I didn't say anything, just went on staring at her.

"She was one of the Music School burglars," her husband said.

"Was she?" Her eyes strayed back to the photograph in spite of herself and then she jerked them away. "Was she?" she said again with a quick, confused smile. "So little Evan had a—a woman on the side! I wouldn't have thought it of him. A young woman maybe—but not one who looks like this!"

She made a show of looking at her watch. "I have to go now." She gave me a quick nod and left the room—almost fled. Her husband stared after her a moment, a frown on his face, then took another long look at the photograph on his desk, picked it up, and handed it to me.

"Do you recognize her too?" I asked him.

He tried to look puzzled, as though he didn't understand what I meant. "I've never seen her before," he said. "Now, I've give you enough of my time—more than enough. What else do you want to know?"

"A few minutes ago, you told me Chris Stavrakis lived with Scott Hall, but Hall threw him out. Why?"

"The rumor around here was that he made a pass at

Hall's wife—or was it the other way around? I don't remember—it was just a rumor and there are lots of those going around, as I'm sure you've learned by now. I do remember that after Stavrakis left school, Hall sometimes went into the places where he was playing. He'd sit way in back. I saw him there once."

He gave a nasty laugh. "So it wasn't only women Chris Stavrakis cast his spell over. He had that effect on men too—some men, anyway. But not me. I was immune to his charms. Now good-bye, Officer."

Sixteen

Scott Hall's door was closed. I knocked, but there wasn't any answer, so I went down to the main office and, with a smile and a wave at the receptionist I'd dealt with earlier, went back to the executive secretary's office and asked if Hall was still in the building.

"Yes," she said, "but he doesn't want to be disturbed this afternoon. He's in one of the rehearsal rooms, working."

"Do you think he'll be available tomorrow?"

"I couldn't say. None of the faculty have regular office hours in the summer, you know."

Geraldine Asher came out of her office then, gave me a distant nod, and turned and handed the papers she was carrying to the secretary. She started back toward her office.

I asked her if I could have a moment of her time. She gave me the look she might give a conductor whose orchestra was drowning her violin, then nodded and led the way back into her office, glancing at her watch as she went—why, I can't imagine, since that hadn't done any good the last time we'd talked.

She sat down behind her desk, placed her hands flat in front of her, and waited, her mouth a thin line of distaste. I put the photograph of Elli on her desk and told her what I knew of it.

She pulled glasses from a blouse pocket, studied it a moment, then looked up at me. "Well?"

"Turner took it," I said. "He probably took the one on the wall behind her too—it's also of her."

She peered at it again, more closely. "How can you tell?"

I pointed to the bracelet in the two photographs, said, "The design is called the 'Greek key.' "

"Ah, yes," she said. "How very observant of you. Who is she?"

It was easy not to let her effusive praise go to my head, all the more so since it wasn't deserved. "Turner called her Helen, she told him she wanted to be called Elli. She was one of the Music School burglars."

"And some kind of friend of Turner's too," she said with a wry smile. "A close enough friend to pose nude for him, apparently. Well, well."

"I take it you don't recognize her."

"I certainly don't—not as the classical Helen on the wall or as the contemporary Elli with the sneer. Of course, we get hundreds of students in our big undergraduate survey courses, so I suppose she could have been one of those. You might want to show these photos to Turner's teaching assistant last quarter, see if by any chance she recognizes her."

She leaned back in her chair, sighed heavily. "The last time you were in here, Officer, I described how Evan once told me he was trying to find himself. Don't you think it's likely that his efforts to find himself ended in something sordid, like the young woman in that photograph? Isn't that usually how middle-aged men go about 'finding themselves'? And when it ended badly, when he'd thrown away his marriage, he took the easy way out and jumped from that cliff?"

Everybody I'd talked to seemed to want to dismiss Turner's death as a midlife crisis that had turned fatal. "His vertigo would seem to rule out suicide," I reminded her.

She threw out her hands. "Does it? I can see avoiding cliffs if you want to live, but they might be just the place I'd seek if I wanted to die."

I wasn't sure an expert on vertigo would consider that very sound psychology, but it interested me that Professor Asher was so generous with her time and her ideas now, and so enthusiastic in sharing them with me.

I asked her if the name Chris Stavrakis meant anything to her.

She thought a moment, then shook her head. "No. Where does she come in—or is Chris a he?"

"A he," I said, "and I don't know yet. Maybe just more of the wild goose chase I seem to be on."

I got up to leave, got as far as the door, and then turned and said, "There's a rumor going around the school that Turner used his grandmother to prevent the hiring of Marilyn Schaeffer."

"There are always rumors going around the school, Officer," she said. "Frankly, I'd rather that a child of mine, if I had one, learned the facts of life in the gutter than here. She'd be more apt to get them right."

"So you don't think it's true?"

"How could I know if it's true or not?" she snapped. "Behind-the-scenes transactions aren't put in writing, are they? But it's not inconceivable that your friend Dulcie Farr invited President Hightower to dinner at the mansion one evening, dropped a word here about the terrible feminist—possibly even lesbian—scholar threatening her grandson's precious Music School, and a word there about the University's financial needs. The main reason Hightower is president is because he's quick to pick up on the meaning behind two apparently unrelated comments, when they're made by a wealthy donor. If something of that sort happened, all he'd have to do would be call the dean of the college and suggest the college has too much money, if it's spending what it has on frivolous things like crazed feminist musicologists. It's really very simple, Officer," she said. "I'm surprised you need to ask."

"I know that's how the University works," I said, "but I don't think that's how Mrs. Farr works. She has gay friends of both sexes, and she likes outrageous people and ideas. Is it possible that Turner, as director, could have gone to the dean and lied about his grandmother's interest?"

She narrowed her eyes. "I suppose it's possible. The dean wouldn't call Mrs. Farr to check. He's no friend of feminism himself."

She picked up a pen and poised it over a legal-sized

notebook, waited for me to catch her drift and go. I did and went.

Out in the main office, I asked the secretary for the name of Turner's TA in the spring quarter. "Kathleen Baker," she said, "but she's not on campus this summer. I can give you her home phone number, if you want it."

She wrote it down on a piece of paper and handed it to me. When I asked her how long she'd been the school's executive secretary, she gave me a thin smile and said, "Ten years. I wondered if you'd think to ask me about Professor Turner."

She glanced around to make sure nobody was within earshot, then went on, "All through the faculty meeting this morning, Professor Douglas whined about how Mrs. Farr has hired a campus cop to try to prove her grandson's death was murder rather than suicide or an accident, and how you crashed Turner's widow's birthday party Friday night. Professor Hall said you'd come out to his home—his home, mind you!—Sunday afternoon. It must be nice to have Dulcie Farr behind you."

"Sometimes," I said ambiguously, and asked her what her opinion was of Turner's death.

"Oh, I think it was an accident," she answered. "The faculty thinks it might've been suicide. I guess that would be my second choice."

I asked her what she'd thought of Turner. "Of course I'm sorry he died," she said. "He was a pain in the ass to work for—he dumped most of the day-to-day business of the school on me—but that doesn't mean he should have to fall or jump off a cliff, or that I might push him if I had the chance. There'd be a lot of worried administrators on this campus if that were the case. But it annoyed me that he took the director's salary without earning it."

"Did you notice any change in him the last few months of his life?"

"Personally," she said, "I thought he was having an affair. What else would account for his being away from the office so much of the time?"

I showed her the photograph of Elli and asked if she'd

ever seen her before. She studied it a minute, then shook her head. "She could be any one of a hundred undergraduates taking courses in the school. God, how I hate that facial jewelry, which I suppose is the point. I just hope the fad goes away before my daughters reach the age where they can get holes punched in their bodies without my consent."

"There's sure to be something worse then," I said.

"What could be worse?"

"Don't ask."

To be on the safe side, I showed the photograph to the receptionist in the outer office. "Cool," she said, but added that she'd never seen this particular Elli before, although she'd known one in high school. She glanced behind her to make sure the executive secretary wasn't within earshot and added that Professor Hall was back in his office now. "But he still doesn't want to be disturbed," she said, giving me a wink.

"Thanks," I said, giving it back.

"No problem!" she assured me, probably just to see me wince.

I walked down to Hall's office and knocked, waited until I heard a muffled "Come in," and did. His head was bent over a musical score. Distracted, he looked up, didn't seem to recognize me for a moment. Then he said, "Oh, it's you again! I told the secretaries I didn't want to be disturbed this afternoon."

"I'm sorry," I lied. "I guess I should have checked with them first before knocking on your door."

"But that's not your way, is it, Officer?" He slapped his pencil down on his desk impatiently. "Well, what is it today?"

"There's an old student of yours who interests me," I said. "Chris Stavrakis. Do you remember him?"

"Chris—! How the hell is he involved in this investigation of yours?"

"His name keeps coming up."

"Not in the company I keep!"

"He was a friend of Evan Turner's," I said, "until he stole Fiona McClure from him. And he was your student.

Somebody told me he lived with you—until you threw him out.''

''And did 'somebody' also tell you Stavrakis died some twenty years ago—under anything but suspicious circumstances?'' he asked acidly.

''Yes, but I'm still interested in him. I'm especially interested in trying to find out why a man who died so long ago is still so alive in so many people's minds.''

He gave me a sharp glance, perhaps to see if I included him in that number, then said softly, ''He was not an easy man to forget.''

He got up suddenly and walked over to the window. ''Chris Stavrakis was a very talented guy,'' he went on after a few moments, still with his back turned. ''Maybe even as talented as he thought he was, but he wasted his talent. He threw it away as though it were nothing, as though—by throwing it away—he could demonstrate how meaningless and absurd the struggles of the rest of us are to create something.'' He shook his head. ''I couldn't understand that. I still can't.''

When Hall didn't say anything more for a minute, just continued to stare out the window at the New Campus across the river, glittering in all its sterile glory, I asked him how Stavrakis had come to live in his home.

He turned to face me. ''He didn't live in the house, he lived in the room over the garage. And there was nothing between him and my wife. Nothing! Just in case that's part of the story you've heard.''

''I'd like to hear your version of the story,'' I said.

He sighed, stomped back to his desk, and slumped down in his chair. ''When I came here some thirty years ago, Stavrakis was already here. He was a grad student in composition. A few weeks after the fall semester began, he had some kind of disagreement with his adviser, Lassen, who went to the chairman and demanded that Stavrakis be assigned to somebody else. The chairman assigned him to me.

''I knew Stavrakis had gone through several other advisers before alienating Lassen, but being arrogant and rather naive, I assumed the problem was that Lassen was

over the hill and that Stavrakis, like me, was young and impatient with everything old.''

He gave a short laugh. "Well, we were not a good match, Stavrakis and I, to put it mildly. For one thing, I was only a few years older than he—I'd been a bit of a prodigy and the youngest person ever hired as a full professor. And for another, at that time I wrote very avantgarde music, very cerebral, you know, and Stavrakis hated that kind of music. He loved melody.''

"As you do now," I said.

He smiled faintly. "Yes, that's right. I forgot that you know a little about my music, don't you? Yes, I love melody now too. But I had to work through the kind of music that was popular in academic circles back then, and what I compose today is not a retreat or a rejection of that music, it's a synthesis. All meaningful advance is a synthesis of the old and the new.''

I nodded encouragingly, as students do.

"Anyway," he went on, "Stavrakis became my advisee, and things went well for a time. Then, one day, he came to me and said he'd been evicted from his apartment—the landlord, he claimed, planned to turn the building into an office complex or something. I discovered later that that was a lie—he'd been evicted for not paying his rent. I offered to let him stay with my wife and me until he found a new place to live. You see, the U had lured me away from Berkeley with the offer of a good salary, and I'd just got a fat commission to write a symphony, my second. So Alex and I had splurged and bought a big old Victorian house—quite different from the one you invaded yesterday—with a large yard and a garage on the alley in back. We offered the room over the garage to Stavrakis at a reasonable monthly rent, and he moved in. I might add that we rarely saw that reasonable monthly rent," he added with a grimace.

"Friction developed very quickly between us. He wasn't interested in listening to advice from me. Indeed, he wanted to give *me* advice on how to write music! He made no attempt to hide his contempt for the kind of music I was writing. He said it came from books, not the heart. During

one heated exchange, for example, I told him that all his contemporaries had died with Rachmaninoff. He retorted that Rachmaninoff might be dead, but his music was still alive—meaning that the opposite was true for me.''

Hall laughed at the memory. ''I didn't mind—I still thought of him as a wayward genius, somebody I was going to do my best to save. Besides, I got in the last word. I asked him why he didn't go out to Hollywood and write for the movies.''

The smile faded from his face. ''The end came one night after I'd conducted a concert at the University auditorium. I arrived home late and found Alex waiting for me, with Stavrakis passed out in a pool of his own vomit on my living room floor. She told me he'd come up to the house and she'd let him in, not realizing he was drunk or high. She tried to make him leave, but he ignored her.

''I woke him up, led him out of the house and over to his room. The next day, I told him he had to move out. He didn't apologize for his behavior, he just left, and I didn't see him again until the party the director of the school, Alrikson, always had to celebrate the end of school year.

''There was a lot to drink—there always was at Alrikson's parties—and Stavrakis drank more than his share of it. Then, about halfway through the evening, he went over and sat down at the piano and started to play. Whatever it was—probably something of his own that he made up on the spot—attracted people's attention and they gathered around to listen, as people always did when Chris played. When he'd got everybody's attention, he segued into one of my best-known pieces and began, ever so subtly, to parody it. He turned it into a kind of silly march.''

Hall shook his head, smiled at me, but his eyes were sad. ''I have to admit, it was quite brilliantly done, but oh, it was savage! Of course, the people who were listening were terribly embarrassed. They moved away from the piano quickly and began talking loudly, but that just made it all the worse, of course. And Stavrakis played on.

''The crowning moment came when Alrikson, drunk, went over to Stavrakis and said, 'I like it—what is it?' He was probably the only person in the room who didn't rec-

ognize it as mine. Stavrakis, still playing, looked up and said, 'The Academic Whore's Overture.' Then he brought the piece to a grand climax, got up, and walked out.''

Scott Hall had started the story calmly. When he finished, his voice was trembling with emotion. ''And that was the last we saw of him in the Music School. He didn't even bother to withdraw formally. We learned later that he'd become some kind of a hippie—this was the late sixties, you understand—who earned a living of sorts playing for tips in bars and coffeehouses and teaching at that so-called 'music academy' over on Riverside. And that's my version of the story you've heard,'' he concluded. ''Take it or leave it.''

''And you never saw him again?''

''No,'' he said, his eyes meeting mine without blinking, ''I never saw him again.''

''Someone mentioned to me,'' I said, ''that there's a box of Stavrakis's music in the library. How'd that get there?''

He shrugged. ''His father brought it in, right after Stavrakis's death. He told the secretary he'd found it when he was cleaning out his son's apartment. He left it with her and went away. She looked up Stavrakis in the files, saw that I'd been his adviser, and brought the box to me. I gave it to the music librarian and she filed it with all the other material that's donated to us. For all I know, it's still there somewhere, gathering dust.''

''Did you look at it?''

''Of course I did!'' he snapped impatiently. ''But it was just scraps—uncompleted work that was hard to decipher in places and, when I could decipher it, turned out not to have been worth the effort.''

''So you don't think he left any real music behind?''

''If he did, I never saw any of it.''

As I got up to go, I said, ''Evan Turner's wife told me that he'd recently tried his hand at composing music too, before taking up photography. Apparently he showed some of it to you.''

Hall raised his head and looked at me, perhaps puzzled by the change of subject, or the fact that I was still there. ''Yes—so what?''

"What was it like?"

"Treacle. Pretty noises with no structure, rather like what they call 'New Age' music. Pretentious, effusive, empty."

"Did you tell him that?"

He twisted his lips in a smile of sorts. "I wasn't kind to him, I confess. I have no patience with people who abuse their talent, or with people who have none."

Seventeen

I got my bike and headed back to the station, dodging students who darted into the street without looking first, deep in thought or conversations with others either walking beside them or on their cell phones, sometimes both. Because I usually take the dog watch, I don't often see the campus in broad daylight and full swing.

At the south end of the Mall, in front of the union, students were dancing to the music of a rock group called, according to the words on the bass drum, No Plans 4 the Future, that was performing as part of a summer program called "Rockin' the Mall." To my ears, No Plans 4 the Future didn't sound as though it had any plans for the present either, but the dancers didn't look as though they cared. They seemed to be trying to exorcise something—what they'd learned in class that day, perhaps.

I stopped to listen for a few minutes, wondering if I would have loved this music as much as I loved the rock music that outraged people who were my age now when I was a kid. I also wondered where the kind of music No Plans 4 the Future was playing would fit into the history of music, and if Evan Turner, had he lived, would someday have had to find a way to include it in his survey course in music history, along with Dylan, the Stones, and the Beatles, now considered safe enough for elevators and television commercials, right up there with Mozart, Beethoven, Gershwin, and Fats Waller.

Off to one side stood a cluster of fundamentalist Christians sweltering in dark clothes under the afternoon sun and brandishing Bibles as their leader, Pastor Floyd, harangued

the dancers and passing students. The rock music drowned him out from where I was standing, but I'd heard him before, and knew the air around him was blue with lurid descriptions of the consequences of premarital sex, atheism, homosexuality, feminism, vegetarianism, witchcraft, crossdressing, bisexuality, rock and roll, and other perverted practices and persuasions. I'd never seen anybody—in public, anyway—quite so sexually aroused as Pastor Floyd became with his own rhetoric.

I waved to a campus cop I knew who was keeping an eye on things—students without a sense of humor sometimes take Pastor Floyd's insults personally and try to beat him up—and continued on up the Mall on the pedestrian path, walking my bike. Card tables lined the path on both sides, their owners hawking many of the -isms Pastor Floyd was railing against, while people who looked as though they'd been caught in a time warp and just come from a hard night in the Age of Aquarius displayed hand-made jewelry, candles, incense, jams, jellies, and perfumed oils.

I'd almost cleared the pedestrian crowd and was about to mount my bike when I spotted Fiona McClure sitting in the shade of a big oak tree on the grass in front of the auditorium. She was playing her Celtic harp and singing quietly, but I could easily hear her clear voice, as light as honey, above the din of the rock band at the other end of the Mall. Although she seemed to be playing just for herself, a small crowd had gathered and was sitting in the grass around her, listening. She'd let her hair down too, and a breeze was blowing it gently around her face.

I leaned my bike against a tree and strolled over, sat cross-legged on the grass, and thought about her reaction when she'd seen the photograph of Elli. She'd recognized her, I was sure of that—but how? And why did she always speak with such bitterness about Evan Turner? She was the one, after all, who'd broken off their relationship, dumped him for Chris Stavrakis.

What link was there between Elli and Turner and Fiona McClure? There didn't have to be a link, of course. And Turner could have fallen or jumped from the cliff above Lake Superior.

Alex Hall had reacted strongly to the photograph—and maybe her husband had too. What had they, and Fiona Mc-Clure, seen in it that I couldn't?

Thinking of Alex Hall made me wonder whose version of why Hall had kicked Chris Stavrakis out of his house was the true one: that he'd made a mess on the Halls' living room rug or a pass at Hall's wife—or she'd made a pass at him. It wasn't hard to see that she had been beautiful thirty years ago—and her eyes were still full of passion, even as she sat knitting in her husband's study.

Chris Stavrakis must have been a charismatic guy, I thought, considering that Fiona McClure had never got over him. He'd "taken possession of her soul," according to her husband. I laughed to myself at that, tried to recall if I'd ever known a Greek male except in classical art and literature.

Greek. A bell rang somewhere in my head at the word: Elli wore a bracelet with the Greek key design on it.

I reached into my shoulder bag and pulled out the photograph of Elli—and Helen. I continued staring at it a long time, trying to make sense of it. Helen, of course, was a Greek name. It meant "light."

A shadow fell over the photograph and I looked up. I hadn't noticed that Fiona McClure had stopped playing. Now she was standing over me, looking down, cradling her harp in her arms, the sun shining through her long hair. For a brief moment, I wondered if I'd died and there really was an afterlife complete with angels.

"You must find her very attractive," she said dryly.

"She's Chris Stavrakis's daughter, isn't she?" I said.

"I don't know."

"But you think so."

"I didn't know he had a daughter! I *don't* know that he had a daughter!"

"Yet you recognized him in this woman's face."

"So what? It could just be a coincidence. She could be some relative of his. If he had a kid, he never mentioned her to me. Besides, what difference does it make who she is?"

"She might have had something to do with Turner's death."

"You mean she might've pushed him off that cliff? So what if she did? The world's a better place without him! Marcy'll get the insurance money and his retirement income, and Annette will be no worse off for the loss of her father. Everybody lives happily ever after," she added bitterly.

"Except you."

She made an impatient gesture, started to turn away.

I asked her how long she and Stavrakis had been together.

She hesitated, turned and glared down at me, said nothing.

"I want to know about him," I insisted, meeting her eyes without blinking. "I'm going to find out all about him."

"Why? He died a long time ago. He choked to death— on a carrot, for God's sake!"

"I need to talk to this woman," I said, tapping the photograph. "She's connected to Turner in some way, and obviously related to Stavrakis."

Fiona stared off over the Mall a moment, then made a face and sat down in front of me, spreading her skirt around her, her harp in her lap. She reached out and took the photograph, studied it a long time, then handed it back without saying anything.

"Once," she said, "I could have told you to the day, but now I can only remember the months we were together—there were eleven of them. That was a long time for Chris to stay with one woman! I thought it meant—" She laughed, but her eyes were shining with tears. "I thought it meant we were soul mates, that we were meant for each other."

And I once believed in Santa Claus. "If this is his daughter," I said, "she may have been from a relationship before you and he got together."

She shrugged, looked away.

"He must have been quite a guy," I went on. "Tell me about him. I just know from Scott Hall that he was a gifted but self-destructive musician. Was that true?"

"Scott Hall!" she spat. "Well, he was right about that, anyway."

"What was his problem?"

"His mother died when he was a teenager," she said. "Some kind of cancer. Chris never got over it. He never wanted to talk about it, but once, after a party, he did. He was fifteen years old when the cancer was diagnosed, he told me. He watched her gradually waste away—it took a year to kill her—and all the while he prayed to God to spare her."

She stared out over the Mall, and for a moment there was just the rock music in the distance and an occasional shouted phrase from Pastor Floyd.

"Chris promised God he'd devote his life to writing music in His honor if He'd spare her," she went on. "He even wrote songs to entertain her. He was playing them for her when she died. He told me, after that, he didn't believe in anything but sex and death, sex and death."

She glanced over at the photograph of Elli in my lap, then gave a quiet, bitter laugh. "Maybe I should have paid more attention when he told me that. But he was terrified of death, which is why he became a health nut. Even though he drank a lot and did a lot of drugs, he was a vegetarian. And that's what killed him—he choked on a carrot! Some kind of Nemesis at work there, wouldn't you think? Very appropriate for a Greek."

She was silent for a moment, just plucked the strings of her harp idly with the nimble fingers of one hand, a snatch of something sad. Then she looked up at me quickly and said, life coming into her voice, light into her eyes: "But at the time he died, he was starting to compose music again—writing down the songs he'd composed for his mother, reworking them. He said he planned to turn them into a song cycle based on women characters in Greek plays. I was his inspiration for taking them up again, he said—and I believed him. I thought I was special. I thought I was his muse!" The light died in her eyes and her mouth twisted in a bitter smile.

"Did you ever see them or hear him play them?"

She shook her head. "I asked him to play some of them

for me, but he said nobody was going to hear any of them until the whole cycle was finished—he said they had to be heard as part of a whole.''

"Do you think the songs actually existed?''

"I always thought they did, but now''—she glanced down at the photograph of Elli—''I'm not so sure. He didn't like me looking over his shoulder while he worked, so I never actually saw them. But he was working on something, anyway. He told me he'd lost the originals, the ones he'd written for his mother. He left them home when he moved down here, and thought his father had probably thrown them out. His father hated the fact that Chris wanted to be a composer.''

"Scott Hall told me that Stavrakis's father brought a box of his son's music to the Music School right after he died,'' I said. "It's still in the music library. He said it was just scraps of music—nothing worth trying to preserve.''

She made a face, nodded. "Yes, David told me about the music a couple of years ago, not long after we got married. I went down to the music library and looked through it. I didn't see anything worth saving there either.''

"Is his father still alive?''

"I doubt it. He was old back then.''

"How about brothers and sisters?''

She shook her head. "Chris was an only child. I don't know about aunts and uncles. He didn't talk much about his family.''

"Did you go to his funeral?''

She smiled wryly. "No. You see, I was the one who called his father to tell him Chris was in the hospital, where they'd taken him from the Boardinghouse. He drove down and found me in Chris's room and I made the mistake of telling him what our relationship had been. I forgot that Chris had told me he was a deeply religious man. We were standing by Chris, the old man on one side of his bed, as old and wrinkled as a Greek olive, and me on the other. Chris looked exactly as I'd seen him many times before when he was sleeping, except this time he wasn't sleeping. He was brain-dead, kept alive by machines.

"His father called me a whore and told me to get out—

and Chris just lay there with his eyes closed and a half-smile on his face, the meaningless smile of some ancient stone god. And that was the last I saw of him.''

She scrambled to her feet suddenly. As I started to get up too, she reached down and gave me a hand. "So, under the circumstances," she said, "I thought I'd skip the funeral. Chris would've skipped it too, if he'd had any say in the matter.''

She picked up her harp. "So now you've heard my tragic love story," she said. "Why don't you tell me one of yours in return? Do you have one, Peggy O'Neill?''

I said no, I didn't.

"That's too bad! You mean you've never met anybody who possessed you completely, who you were convinced you couldn't live without?''

"No," I replied, "and I hope I never do!''

"How rational you are, Peggy O'Neill!" she said, her eyes bleak. "Well, at least you'll never have to worry about falling very far, will you?''

"I don't believe love includes having to worry about falling," I said as we walked over to my bike.

I thanked her for her time and started to ride off. She called after me: "If you do find that woman, Peggy, that Elli or Helen, I'd like to know her story. Will you tell me?''

"If I can," I called back.

Eighteen

I biked back to the police station and slipped into Ginny's office. "It must be really sweltering out there," she greeted me. "You're looking unusually hot and bothered."

"Not me," I snapped. "I've got ice water in my veins. I'm a vampire who feeds off the pathetic life stories of people whose hearts are where their brains oughtta be."

"A vampire with ice water in her veins, huh? What do you suck, ice cubes? Sounds like heat stroke to me. Let's see, where do we keep the salt pills?"

I asked her if she'd found out anything about Ben Anderson, from her spies in the hospital.

"Not a lot," she said, bringing out a bag of chocolate-flavored rice cakes and offering me one, which I declined. "Only that he and Marcy Turner have been an item at the hospital for some time."

"How long?"

"It first made the nurses' hot line three, four months ago. A great deal of flirting, going off on their breaks together, that sort of thing."

"That must have been around the time when Marcy Turner threw her husband out," I said. "She told me she'd worked to save the marriage right up to the end."

"Well, either she worked fast to fill the void or she lied to you. You don't think people lie to cops, do you?"

I asked her what he did at the hospital.

"He's an intensive care nurse. Divorced and fortyish. No kids. Tall, nice-looking in a rugged sort of way, and heavily into outdoor stuff like sailing and skiing."

"How'd you find all this out?"

"You can't keep secrets from people who work in hospitals. It's been the gossip du jour for months. In June, Anderson went out of town to some kind of IC nurse's convention—and Marcy took some vacation time then too."

"What else?" I asked.

"Anderson has a cabin on a lake about an hour's drive northwest of the conference center. Pelican Lake. Didn't you tell me that Marcy and her daughter were up there somewhere the weekend Turner died? I thought so. Well, of course she and her kid might've been staying with somebody else entirely, since the area is littered with lakes and half the metropolitan population owns property on them."

"I'll keep an open mind," I said. "Anything else?"

"Just one more thing, possibly not relevant at all. As you know if you read the papers, the U hospital's going to merge with the Highland Medical Center before the end of the year. If that happens, a lot of nurses at both places will be looking for new jobs, depending on how much seniority they have. Anderson's job isn't in danger because he's got plenty of seniority, but what about Marcy Turner's?"

"She returned to nursing a year and a half ago," I said.

"That might not be long enough to save her, the way hospitals have been closing around here lately. Laid-off nurses with seniority get hired first, the others work as secretaries if their PC skills are strong enough. And Anderson, as you could tell from his vehicle, isn't exactly raking in the bucks either. How much insurance and retirement money are we talking about here?"

"A lot," I answered, "if Turner died before changing his will. And very little or nothing in the way of child support if he'd been serious about resigning from the U."

Ginny sat back, dug out another rice cake, held it up. "Okay, so what we have here is a woman—a single mother with an uncertain employment future—who was going to lose a lot of money in a divorce, in love with a big strapping outdoorsy nurse with a cabin within an easy drive of where her husband fell off a cliff. It doesn't take a genius to figure out that, at the very least, she wouldn't be unduly distraught to hear about his tragic fall. Maybe she lured

him to an isolated place, then she or Anderson killed him and tossed him over that cliff.''

That was obviously what Annette Turner feared had happened. After all, she was at Anderson's cabin that weekend too. Could she have overheard something or seen something?

"Looks open-and-shut to me," Ginny said, biting off a piece of rice cake and munching contentedly.

I told her about my suspicion that the mysterious Elli, or Helen, was related to Chris Stavrakis—probably his daughter—and brought her up to date on who Stavrakis was and how he figured in the lives of Evan Turner, Fiona McClure, and Scott Hall and his wife.

"Kind of interesting," Ginny said, "in a lurid and somewhat overwrought way. And probably completely unrelated to Turner's death."

I asked her how long it would take her to find out who Chris Stavrakis's survivors were, assuming there were any.

"Me?" she asked, raising an eyebrow and brushing rice cake off her shirt front.

"Yeah, can't you do those wonderful things computer nerds with thick glasses and no lives always do for the sleuth in detective novels?"

"No, but I can use my hacker skills to conjure up a map that shows the location of the University library, if you want. I'll even print it out for you. You might also try the phone book." She tossed it across her desk to me.

I hate sarcasm, unless it's mine. I found two listings under Stavrakis and called them. A man with a heavy Greek accent answered the first number and said with a hearty laugh that every other Greek he knew was named Helena or Christos, depending on their sex, but he didn't know any who matched my descriptions. The woman who answered the second number said much the same thing. She had a sister named Helen, she said, but she was in a rest home in Michigan, and her niece's son Christopher was alive and well, thank you very much.

Then I called Kathleen Baker, who'd been Turner's teaching assistant, and got a recorded message telling me

to leave my name and phone number and she'd get back to me.

A cop stuck his head in Ginny's door and said, "Bixler wants to see you, Peggy. Chop-chop."

"Chop-chop?" I repeated.

He threw up his hands and backed away. "His words, not mine. Don't kill the messenger!"

"Why not?"

When I got to his office, Bixler had the report I'd written earlier in front of him. "You need to take a refresher course in unarmed combat," he said, placing a plump finger on the place where I'd described my encounter with Muscle Boy in Turner's apartment on Saturday.

"I think so too," I said, but wondered if any cop I knew, male or female, could have subdued Muscle Boy unarmed.

"What'd he do, take you by surprise?"

"Yes."

His little pig's eyes glittered with pleasure. "Good cops aren't taken by surprise," he said.

"Then maybe it's time I came inside and got a desk job," I replied, the words *like you* trembling unspoken in the air between us.

The papers in his hand shook as he bit back a response to that. Bixler and I live on the uneasy border between "hostile environment" and "insubordination."

"What's this photograph business?" he asked, ducking back down into my report.

I told him I didn't know yet.

"A real 'mystery woman,' " he sneered, "just like in the movies. You think she could've pushed Turner off that cliff—or her boyfriend who jumped you?"

I replied that that was one of the things I wanted to ask her.

He shook his head, tossed the report aside. "What a waste of taxpayer money!" He gave me a look that indicated he thought it was all my fault. "Turner jumped." He made a diving motion with one of his fat hands. "Probably on account of this gal Elli or Helen dumped him. First his wife, then his girlfriend. The old lady just don't want to believe it. She called, by the way," he added.

"Who? Mrs. Farr?"

"Yeah, 'Dulcie.' " He still hadn't forgiven me that slip. "Her butler did, I mean. Sounds batty. Wants you to call him back."

"Okay," I said briskly, "I guess I'd better get right on it. Do you want me to pass on to her your theory about what happened to her grandson—that he jumped?"

He glared me out of his office.

I went back to Ginny's office and called Dulcie. Butler answered. "Ah, Miss O'Neill," he suppurated, "thank you for returning my call so promptly. Dulcie is anxious to hear what progress you've made. Can you join us for tea this afternoon?"

"I don't have my car," I told him, "and I don't intend to bike to Dulcie's in this heat, since it's all uphill."

"Oh, that won't be necessary," he said with a chuckle. "I'll pick you up at your police station in the car, if you'll give me directions."

With a sigh, I did.

It was an ancient Rolls-Royce and as I climbed in, I felt like a thirties movie actress—perhaps playing in Ginny's *No Keys on the Corpse.* I flung an imaginary boa around my neck, settled back in the cushions, and said, "Dulcie won't be happy if I tell her everything I've found out, Butler."

He glanced at me in the rearview mirror. "Don't underestimate her, Miss O'Neill," he replied, the veneer of butlerhood gone suddenly, reminding me that he'd once been an actor. "She's thought a lot about her grandson since you last spoke with her. She's a tough old bird. She can handle anything you can dish out."

We drove the rest of the way in silence. I passed the time counting the number of people in cars we passed who did a double-take at the sight of us.

She was sitting under an umbrella at a white wrought-iron table in her sculpture garden, dwarfed by a huge abstract iron sculpture behind her that, according to the artist's

intent, years of rust and bird droppings would complete. I liked it.

As I pulled up the chair opposite her, I said, without wasting any time, "Have you ever intervened in Music School politics?"

She gave me a startled look. "Of course not! I don't meddle in University business."

"We both know better than that, Dulcie," I said. "I wouldn't be here now if you didn't meddle in University business."

"That's different. That's—"

"You also forced your grandson down the Music School's throat, and you undoubtedly used your influence later to get him promoted."

She looked a little taken aback that her tame cop could speak to her like that, but recovered quickly. "So what if I did? They got a wonderful concert hall out of it, and some scholarships too. And Evan turned out well for them!" Her eyes narrowed. "Why did you ask that question?"

Butler appeared with a tray of tea things and cookies, his mask back in place.

"There's a rumor in the Music School," I said, "that you used your influence to block the appointment of a feminist musicologist a few years ago."

She gave me a blank look, shook her head. "That's not true! I don't believe I've ever heard of a 'feminist musicologist.' It's one thing, Peggy, to use my influence to get them to hire Evan, it's another thing to meddle . . ." She stopped, a cookie halfway to her lips, as something seemed to occur to her. "You don't think Evan would have used my name to keep this woman from being hired, do you?"

"I think he was capable of it," I said.

"You do?"

"Yes."

She shrank back in her chair and brooded a few minutes, then nodded and said, "Yes, I suppose he was. Of course, it doesn't really matter if he did or didn't do it, if his colleagues believe he did. Which might well give someone a motive for hating him enough to kill him, I suppose, if they

felt strongly enough about this—this musicologist. Is there such a one?''

"I don't know if she hated him enough to kill him," I said, "but she's not sorry he's dead."

"That woman who replaced him as director, I suppose you mean," she said. "A marvelous violinist, but I know she and Evan didn't see eye to eye on much. He said he was almost sorry he didn't choose to stay on as director for another term, when she succeeded him in the position."

"He didn't 'choose' not to stay on," I said. "He was voted out."

She sat up straight, as though I'd thrown water in her face. "That's not what he told me," she said. "Why was he voted out?"

"Everyone I've spoken to," I replied, hoping she was as tough an old bird as Butler thought, "from the new director down to the secretary, tells me he wasn't doing his job. He just liked the prestige it gave him, and maybe the extra money."

Dulcie's thin mouth almost disappeared into her wrinkled face and her old hands clutched the arms of her chair like claws. Behind her, Butler's moon face hovered, looking worried.

When she picked up her teacup, her hand was steady. "Is that all you've found out, Peggy O'Neill," she said bleakly, "that my grandson wasn't the man I thought he was?"

Instead of answering that, I asked her if the name Chris Stavrakis meant anything to her.

She repeated it to herself. "Doesn't sound familiar. Butler?"

"That was a name Evan mentioned often, I believe," he said, "back when he was playing guitar. He was a musician too, if I recall correctly, and Evan seemed to be somewhat in awe of him. However, I don't recall Evan mentioning him after he abandoned music for the groves of Academe."

"Did we ever meet him?"

"I don't believe so, Dulcie."

She asked me why I was interested in him.

I got out the photograph of Elli and slid it across the table to her, told her how I'd got it.

Dulcie studied the photograph a minute. "Who is she?"

"I don't know. All I know is that she looks a lot like Chris Stavrakis and was involved in the Music School burglary, along with a man whom I found living in your grandson's apartment."

She stared at me in disbelief as I described my encounter with Muscle Boy in Turner's apartment. "Surely you don't think Evan was mixed up in some kind of criminal activity with these people, do you?" she asked when I finished.

I said I didn't know that either.

"It's more likely Evan was having a fling with this girl," she said, "and got in deeper than he expected to. Do you think she could be why Marcy divorced him?"

"Marcy claims she doesn't know anything about her," I answered. "She claims she divorced him because he'd been neglecting her and their daughter for years. She finally got tired of it."

She nodded grimly. "I understand you've spoken with Annette," she said.

"Yes."

"I like Annette," she went on.

"No, *I* like Annette," I corrected her. "You love her."

She glared at me a moment. "We won't quibble over words," she said softly.

"I like her mother too," I added. "What little I've seen of her."

She started to get angry again, then gave it up with a sigh. "So do I. How'd she take those years of neglect—alleged neglect?"

"I don't know," I said, and put my teacup between my face and her eyes.

Dulcie laughed suddenly. "I'll bet you don't, Peggy! I wouldn't blame her if she took a lover. In her shoes, if what you say is correct, I'd do the same thing."

Butler hove back into view bearing a watering can with an elegantly curved spout. She watched him pour water on a hanging plant, a little smile playing around her lips, a

blush coloring her lined old face, of shame, of remembered passion, perhaps of both.

"But I didn't kill Three," she went on, meaning her husband. "I stuck it out. Women did, back then—in our way. Modern women don't handle these matters as discreetly as we did. Do you think Marcy could have killed Evan? Or was it this woman—this Elli?"

"I don't know," I said, my refrain.

We sat a few more minutes in a silence broken only by a fly checking out the lemonade and Butler puttering, plus the occasional bird working on the sculpture. Finally Dulcie said, "Maybe, if I had some assurance she hadn't murdered Evan, I might consider some kind of . . . what's the word I want, Butler?"

"Rapprochement," he supplied, somehow always within earshot.

"Yes. Rapprochement. She reminds me a little of myself at that age." Then she looked up at me with an anguished look on her face. "You have to relieve Annette's mind about her mother, Peggy!"

"I'll do my best," I said.

"It would be terrible for Annette if her mother turned out to be a murderer! It would scar her for life."

"Yes," I agreed.

She gave me a stern look. "I would be very unhappy if she turned out to be Evan's killer, Peggy."

· Nineteen

It was almost six when Butler dropped me off back at the U, where I got my bike and rode home. I checked my answering machine for messages—nothing. I thought about the skinny man at the bar who I was sure was the leader of the burglars. Had he or Lanny shown the note to Elli?

I dumped a salad into a bowl, poured the dressing that came with the package over it, and took it out onto the deck along with the photograph of Elli, which I propped up on a vase of flowers, an uneasy mix of bleeding hearts and jack-in-the-pulpits that Mrs. Hammer had put on the table from her garden. Elli, standing on one leg, caught in the act of pulling off a boot, stared back at me, a mixture of amusement and scorn on her face under the curly dark hair. Her eyes seeming to dare me to figure her out.

Was she taking off her clothes because they were about to make love or because she was going to pose for him nude, as she'd done for the photograph on the wall behind her?

She wasn't beautiful in any conventional sense—her face was too full of character and intelligence for that—but she was young, and for some middle-aged men, as Scott Hall had said, that's enough. Was that all it was—a midlife crisis that had nothing to do with Turner's death? A lot of people who die unexpectedly leave puzzling loose ends behind them. If they didn't, there wouldn't be anything for conspiracy theorists to do; they'd have to get lives of their own.

Elli may have had nothing to do with Turner's death, but I had to be sure. Trying to locate her through the people involved in the burglary had been a dead end. All I had

left to try was her connection to Chris Stavrakis.

I'd first heard of Stavrakis through Stilwell at the Boardinghouse. I wondered if he might know if Stavrakis had left behind a daughter, or knew how I could get in touch with his family. The difficulty would be in getting Stilwell to talk to me about anything, so, recalling how he'd become positively garrulous for Pia Austin Friday night, I called her, hoping to enlist her help.

"What are you doing tonight?" I asked when she picked up the phone.

"Andy's coming over and we're going to watch a movie. You want to join us?"

"No, I want you to seduce somebody for me."

"Tonight? Sure! Who? Somebody rich, I hope."

"Stilwell."

"Stilwell? Stilwell is short, dark, and loathsome," she reminded me, not that I needed it.

"But he may be rich," I pointed out. "After all, he's a bachelor, he obviously puts no money into the Boardinghouse, he has no known vices—so he's gotta have a lot of money stashed away somewhere. Right?"

"Peggy, what's this all about?"

"I want to find out what he knows about somebody who used to hang out in Riverside twenty years ago."

"Who?"

"It's a long story. I'll tell you about it when you get here. Will you do it?"

"I suppose so. When?"

"How about ten? I've never seen Stilwell in the place much earlier than that, and I've got something I want to do first."

"Okay, but I'm bringing Andy, unless you think he'll interfere with my femme fatale act."

"He'll probably be a help," I said. "Stilwell only lusts after women he can't have."

It was eight-thirty when I got to the Turner home. I parked and got out, did a double-take when I saw Ben Anderson's old VW bus in the driveway. I went up to the

front door and rang the bell and, a minute later, Marcy
Turner opened the door.

"You do like to drop in unexpectedly, don't you?" she
said dryly, "and at inconvenient times. Is this something
we can't talk about over the phone?"

"You told me you wanted to see the photograph of Elli,"
I said, "and I happened to be in the neighborhood."

"Right!" she said sarcastically. "Let's see it," she said,
holding out her hand, still blocking the door.

"I'd also like to talk to the owner of the old bus out
there, Ben Anderson," I said.

A startled expression washed over her face, quickly followed by an exasperated laugh. "You're very good at what
you do, aren't you? All right, come on in. Annette's at a
friend's, but she'll be home soon. I'd rather you weren't
here then. She's still extremely upset over her father's death
and you'd be hard to explain to her. I wouldn't care to have
her know Dulcie thinks I shoved him off that cliff," she
added dryly.

Anderson was sitting on the couch in the living room, a
can of beer in his hand. He was just as Ginny had described
him: tall, with a full head of brown hair starting to turn
gray in places, a large nose, slightly crooked, that saved
him from being too good-looking.

"Ben Anderson, Peggy O'Neill—the campus cop Evan's
grandmother sicced on me. Peggy's caught on to us somehow. How? Have you been shadowing me or something?"

"You made it easy," I said, and told them about passing
the bus the night of her birthday party and seeing it again
the next day when he'd stopped to talk to Marcy. I didn't
tell her about the gossip Ginny'd picked up from the other
nurses.

She gave Anderson a glare. "I told you I didn't want to
get into the bus with you that night!"

"You were worrying about the neighbors," he said
mildly, "not a campus cop."

She turned back to me. "I'd offer you a beer, but I'm
sure a professional like you doesn't drink while on duty."

"I'm fine," I said, and without waiting to be asked went
over and sat down in an easy chair that matched the couch,

and Marcy went over and sat on the couch with Anderson, but at the opposite end. She looked at the photograph for a long minute. "Elli, huh? Well, if Evan left me for her, he's probably better off dead, because she doesn't look as though she's into nurturing, does she?" She glanced up at me. "You think she was his latest hobby?"

"I think she's the daughter of Chris Stavrakis."

"Chris . . . ?" She looked bewildered a moment, then recognition dawned.

"Who's Chris Stavrakis?" Anderson asked, taking the opportunity to slide closer to Marcy on the couch.

She explained briefly, then turned to me. "I don't get it."

"Neither do I," I said. "Do you know if he had a daughter?"

She shook her head. "All I know is what Fiona told me about him—that Evan worshiped him until Fiona dumped Evan for him. Evan never talked about him. Does Fiona know about this woman?"

I nodded. "She claims she doesn't know anything about her either."

She shook her head, then looked at the photograph again. "It's funny, in a way, isn't it? We were married almost nineteen years. I had his child—and yet I didn't really know him at all." She looked at me. "What more can I do for you? Annette's going to be home any moment now."

"You told me the other day that you were spending the weekend your husband died with friends on a lake up north," I said. "Friends, or a friend?"

She laughed, turned to Anderson, and said, "We don't seem to have any secrets from her, do we?"

"We also don't have anything to hide, Marcy," he replied.

"You obviously know Annette and I were staying with Ben that weekend," she said to me. "But we weren't anywhere near the conference center until we drove back here and Annette wanted to stop in and say hello to her dad."

"Did your ex know you were up there that weekend with Ben?"

"Yes. I didn't see any reason to keep it a secret from

him. I even offered to let him have Annette for a night or two, if he wanted her. He said no.''

I asked both of them how Annette felt about Anderson. Anderson replied. ''I think she likes me,'' he said. ''At least she did until her dad died. Now I'm not sure what she's think—''

A car pulled up in front of the house and a door slammed.

''Damn it! Here she comes,'' Marcy Turner said. ''Who shall I tell her you are?''

Before I could reply, the screen door opened and the subject under discussion slouched into the room. She was wearing yellow headphones with an aerial on them, giving her the vaguely Martian look so many kids affect these days. Without pausing, she started across the room to the hall, then took a second look at me and stopped.

I gave her a smile and a nod. She shoved an earphone off one ear and stared at me.

''This is Peggy O'Neill, honey,'' Marcy said brightly. ''You remember, she was at my—''

''Yeah, Mom, I know,'' she said dully. ''She was at your birthday party. She's a friend of Grandma Dulcie's.'' She continued to stare, then turned and started toward the hall again, pulling the earphone back down over her ear. Her mother didn't try to stop her.

''Hold on a sec,'' I called after her, loud enough to be heard over whatever she was listening to. She paused and half turned.

''I don't think—'' Marcy said.

''Dulcie learned about your husband's vertigo from Annette,'' I told her.

''From *Annette*?'' She turned to her daughter. ''Why didn't you tell— Oh, my God!'' She jumped up and ran over to her. ''You don't think I had anything to do with your father's death, do you?''

Rigid and red in the face, Annette shouted, ''He didn't fall off that cliff by accident! He couldn't have!''

''How do you know?''

Annette told her what she'd told me about her father and

the Ferris wheel, and what he'd said about not going near cliffs while he was up at Lake Superior.

"But then it's all the more likely that it was an accident, Annette," Anderson said. "He got too close to the cliff without realizing it. He got dizzy and fell."

"Is that how it happens, *Doctor* Anderson?" Annette asked him with a sneer that was ruined by trembling lips.

"Annette!" her mother said. "Why do you think I—or Ben—pushed him over a cliff?"

"Because the night before he went up north, Dad came over and tried to make up with you and you told him no, it was too late. So then he got mad and I heard him tell you he was gonna quit the U, and he asked you how you were going to keep your nice house then!"

"Oh, God! How'd you hear all that?"

She managed to give her mother a look of complete exasperation through tears. "Mother, I can hear everything you say through the heat register over there, okay? You and Dad weren't exactly whispering, you know."

"Oh, darling—I'm sorry!"

"I also heard you and Fiona talking about it too, later, on the phone after Dad left." She glared at Anderson. "I'll bet you told Ben too," she added, turning her eyes on him accusingly.

"You mean you didn't overhear that too?" he asked with a weak smile. Marcy Turner darted a glance at me, perhaps hoping I had the common decency not to listen to this little domestic squabble.

"Who else had a good reason to kill my dad?" Annette demanded, turning to me.

"I haven't found any *good* reasons," I said, feeling helpless. "He might have killed himself. I've talked to a lot of people—"

"Don't you listen?" she shouted, near hysteria, her face red, her eyes wild. "My dad was afraid of heights! Besides, he would've left a note!"

"Mine didn't," I said quietly.

She started to say something more and then what I'd said penetrated. She blinked. "Didn't what?"

"He didn't leave a note."

"Your dad committed suicide?" When I nodded, she said, "How do you know he wasn't murdered, if he didn't leave a note?"

"Because he killed himself in his study." As I spoke, I began to feel the tears welling up in my eyes too, as it always does when I talk about it, as though the words have the power to bring back the moment—which they do. "His study was next to my bedroom. The blast woke me up and I rushed in there and found him. There was nobody else there but him."

She looked at me as though I were the horror I was describing. It has that effect on people sometimes, which is why I save it for special occasions. "Why'd your dad do it?" she asked, wiping her nose with the back of her hand.

"He was drunk. He was a failure in his business, he was unhappy in his marriage, he was a rotten father, and he knew all of the above."

"Oh," Annette breathed.

She thought about that a long time before saying anything. Then, "My dad wanted to get back together with Mom, but she said no. She said she'd rather flip burgers at a McDonald's for pennies than stay married to him. Maybe he killed himself on account of that."

"People don't usually kill themselves on account of just one thing," I said. "From what I've been told by the people who knew him, he was a pretty unhappy man."

She turned and looked at Anderson. "But you knew about the insurance, didn't you?"

He nodded. "But I'm a nurse, Annette," he said. "I think people have a right to live. I wouldn't kill anybody— maybe not even in self-defense."

"You wouldn't?"

"I hope I never have to find out."

She looked at him a long time before saying anything. He met her gaze without flinching. Then she started to turn away.

"Wait a minute," I said.

She turned back. "What?"

"I'd like to ask your mom and Ben some questions, with

you listening—listening where we can see you, I mean.
Would you mind?''

"Now just a minute!" Marcy flared. "You—"

I think she was about to tell me to get out of the house,
but before she could, Anderson put a hand on her arm. "I
don't think we have much choice, Marcy, she's pretty well
got us trapped. Besides, Annette seems to know a lot anyway, which is probably the cop's point. Annette might as
well hear the rest in the room with us, instead of in the
hall."

Annette came back into the room, stood with her back
pressed against the door, her big eyes in her tear-streaked
face moving from one to the other of us like spotlights.

I said, "You were at Ben's cabin the weekend Evan died,
but you say you didn't go anywhere near the conference
center, is that right?"

"Yes," they both said, and then looked at Annette.

Anderson sighed. "We didn't go near the center," he
said, "but I'm sure Annette's thinking about where I was
Friday night. I told her I was going to visit my mother,
who's in a nursing home up there. She has Alzheimer's."

"I asked you if I could come with you," Annette said
accusingly.

He nodded. "I know you did, Annette. But Mother's
often irrational and says things she doesn't mean. It would
have been very unpleasant, and I didn't want you to experience that."

"Thank you very much," she said, "for sparing me an
unpleasant experience."

He flushed, looked miserable, and I grinned in spite of
myself. Annette caught the grin, tried not to grin back. We
both wiped our eyes at the same time.

"You can check with the nursing home," Anderson said,
turning to me. "With any luck they'll remember I was
there." He gave me the name and the town it was in. "It's
on the main street. You can't miss it, since it's also the
only street."

"When did you get back to the cabin?"

"I don't remember, exactly. It's a long drive." He
glanced at Annette, perhaps to see if she was still there.

She was, so he sighed and said, "It was after Annette was in bed."

"Asleep?" I asked her, since we'd all learned that for her, being in bed was not a precise synonym for being asleep.

"I didn't hear him come back," she said.

Which meant the nursing home was no alibi at all, whether he'd been there or not. After all, nobody knew the exact time Turner had been killed.

"Thanks, Annette," I said, "you've been a big help."

She nodded and started to leave the room, then stopped and turned back. "I've thought about it a lot," she said to me. "I've been thinking that if Mom was planning on murdering my dad, she would've agreed to take him back. Then she would've waited until things died down and everybody thought they were all lovey-dovey again. And *then* she would've killed him—or *he* would've," she added, her eyes darting to Anderson. "So since she told him no and got in a big fight with him right before he died, she probably didn't kill him. Isn't that what you think?"

I started to agree with her, then saw something glittering in her eyes that made me change my mind. "That's how it often is in books and on television," I said, "but real life isn't usually like that, so I have to keep an open mind."

She'd been holding her breath. She let it out noisily, said, "What did you do, after your dad killed himself?"

"I threw up," I said.

"No—I mean afterward. After it was all over."

"I grew up."

She laughed, but waited for me to go on.

"I had help with that," I said. "A therapist. I was lucky to find one who didn't want me to go on believing I had a terminal illness, just because an adult out of my control had done something terrible. Maybe that's something you ought to consider doing."

She shrugged. "I'll think about it," she said.

"If you do, just be sure it's somebody who doesn't want to spend a lot of time with you," I told her. "You've got

better things to do with your life than pick at sores to keep them from healing.''

She managed a laugh at that, then nodded and started to turn away. She saw the photograph of Elli on the coffee table, went over and looked at it. ''Who's this?''

''I think it's the daughter of an old friend of your dad's,'' I told her. ''I don't know for sure yet.''

She studied the picture a moment, frowned suddenly. ''This is Dad's apartment, isn't it? Did he take this picture?''

''I think so.''

''Huh,'' she said, considering. ''What's her name?''

''Elli,'' I said. ''Your dad called her Helen.''

''Was she his girlfriend or something?'' she asked, trying to sound indifferent.

''He was probably just using her as a model,'' her mother answered, too quickly.

Annette looked at her mother as though she were something the cat had brought in, much the worse for wear. ''Who was Dad's old friend?''

''Annette . . .''

Annette turned to me. ''A man named Chris,'' I told her.

''The one with the Greek last name? The one Fiona dumped Dad for?''

''How do you know about that?'' her mother asked, appalled.

''Fiona told me when she came over and stayed with me while you and Ben went off for the weekend last month.''

''Fiona told you! Why?''

Annette rolled her eyes. '' 'Cause I asked her about him, Mom! Once, back when you and Fiona were just starting to be good friends, you and Dad got in a big fight about it, on account of Dad didn't want you being friends with her.''

''But that was a long time ago!'' her mother exclaimed. ''You were just a—''

Annette shook her head, gave me a *What can you do?* look. ''I wanted to know what he had that my dad didn't,'' she explained to me, one adult to another, ''and when she told me, I wanted to know why she didn't marry him. She said it was because he died.''

She took one more look at the photograph and started to leave the room. She hesitated, turned back, and announced, "I loved my dad, just in case anybody wants to know. And I don't think he killed himself."

She stood there striving for the look of an avenging angel, the effect marred only slightly by the trembling chin and the earphones with the antenna. Then she turned and stomped out of the room.

Marcy Turner put her head in her hands, and Anderson began massaging her neck.

"That was a dirty trick," she said after a moment, looking up at me.

"But it worked out for the best," Anderson said.

"But she didn't give a damn about that," she snapped.

"I knew Annette could handle it," I said.

"How could you know that?"

I just smiled, picked up the photograph of Elli, and left.

Twenty

I wasn't troubled in the least by having forced some things out into the open that Annette had suspected and was worried about. I only wish every suspect I interviewed had a thirteen-year-old child present. At that age they're pillars of morality for about one more year.

I drove over to Riverside and found a place to park on the side street next to the Boardinghouse. Pia and Andy were waiting for me by the door.

I filled them in on what I wanted and why I wanted it, and then we went in. On the little stage, a poet was reciting something slowly, obviously thrilled with each turn of phrase that slipped from her lips, since she grinned proudly after each one, like a mother showing pictures of her new baby, while at tables nearby a few people listened, their noses buried thoughtfully in their espressos.

We ordered lattés from Stilwell and I thought I saw something resembling pleasure flit across his pasty face at the sight of Pia, but I couldn't be sure. To put as much distance between us and the riotous cultural event taking place on the stage, we took our drinks to the distant corner where, three nights before, I'd sat with Pia and Andy, Sam and Christian.

"Denise doesn't know Derrida from Dairy Queen," an intense woman with more than a hint of a mustache was assuring her companion at one table as we passed, while at another two sallow men who looked like Mafia goons were dissecting a French film by a director who'd died of ennui around the time I was born, and the chess players sat frozen over their board under the Picasso. Someday, I thought, I'd

go over and pinch one of them, to see if he was real.

After we'd been there awhile, Stilwell drifted over to us, trailing a rag across the tops of tables as he passed. I watched him approach out of the corner of my eye, while pretending to be deeply engrossed in conversation with Pia and Andy. When he got within earshot, Pia looked over at him and said, "Help us out here, Stilwell, will you? Tell us what you know of Chris Stavrakis."

"Stavrakis?" he said, darting her a glance. "Who wants to know?"

"She does," she said, aiming a thumb at me. "She enlisted me to get you to tell her what you know about him. A simple but, we think, effective stratagem."

"Why?" he asked, directing the question at her while busily scrubbing a puddle of dried coffee off the neighboring table.

"Because you're hopelessly in love with me on account of I look like an abandoned waif, and that brings out the dirty old man in you, whereas you wouldn't give a mature woman like Peggy O'Neill here the time of day."

"I mean," he said, taking no offense, "why's she so interested in Stavrakis? The other night she wanted to know about Evan Turner."

"She's not convinced Turner just fell off that cliff by himself. She thinks somebody might've assisted him. She's interested in anything that has to do with the man. This Chris Stavrakis seems to have been an important figure in his life."

Stilwell shook his head in disgust. "Stavrakis didn't push Turner off that cliff, if that's what she thinks. I told you the other night, he died twenty years ago. He choked to death on a carrot, about where that poetess is standing now."

"The past can reach its bony hand into the present in a variety of ways," Pia said. "If it didn't, there'd be fewer detective stories and no psychoanalysis. Now pull up a chair, Stilwell, and tell us all about him. Next to me," she added, scooting over. "You're unlikely ever to get this close again." Andy hid his face behind his coffee cup, perhaps in embarrassment.

With a helpless look around the room, as though in search of a hole into which to escape, Stilwell pulled up a chair—as far from Pia as he could get without getting close to me.

"So what does she want to know?" he asked reluctantly.

"Everything," Pia replied, "for starters."

"Stavrakis was a con man," he began. "Maybe he was a genius too. He thought so, anyway."

"But you didn't," Pia prompted.

"What I thought was, he was a genius at conning people." Stilwell squeezed out a short, tormented laugh. When he'd recovered from his fit of levity, he said, "He even conned me, and that's not easy to do, so you can see how good he was at conning people."

"Conned you how?"

"Borrowed money and didn't pay it back. He owed everybody money. He seemed to get a kick out of borrowing money from people he'd burned before. Once I heard somebody ask him why he never paid back the money he owed 'em, and he answered—I can still hear him—'Why should I have to pay for the pleasure you get from loaning me money?' "

"What kind of power did he *have* over you?" Andy broke in, appalled. Andy's so tight he squeaks.

"He didn't have any power over me!" Stilwell said, offended. "The one time I loaned him money and he didn't pay it back, that was it, as far as I was concerned! But he conned a lot of other people over and over again, I don't know how. Some kind of whammy he put on 'em, maybe. They thought he was a genius who was gonna make it big someday and then they could talk about how they'd known him when."

"Why?" Pia asked. "If he never actually *did* anything, why did people think he was a genius?"

Stilwell shook his head angrily, as though being pestered by mosquitoes. " 'Cause he had everything going for him— looks and personality and talent." He snickered, a horrid noise. "The gals hung around him like flies on shit. They'd come up to the piano and put their hands on his while he was playing—just lay their hands on his and let 'em ride

along. And Stavrakis would laugh and play on, pretending to try to shake 'em off—but making music! He got lots of gals that way, and every one of 'em thought he was in love with her. But actually, he didn't love them at all. He faked that too.''

"So he was just an attractive phony," Pia said.

Stilwell shook his head, looked as though he'd like to tear his hair out in frustration. "He wasn't a phony! I mean, he wasn't *only* a phony. He could make up beautiful songs, really beautiful songs, right off the top of his head.''

"How do you know they were his songs?" Pia demanded. "You said he was a con man. Maybe they were melodies he'd stolen from somebody else.''

"He wouldn't've bothered," Stilwell said. "Besides, when he conned you, he always let you know, so he could laugh at you afterward.''

He looked around the room, as though Stavrakis might be lurking somewhere in the shadows. "But nothing he had and nothing he did meant anything to him," he went on in a low voice.

"I remember once somebody asked him why he didn't try to record his music. He said, 'Why should I? In a couple million years, everything's gonna be just dust anyway, floating in space. Beethoven's music, Mozart's. Just dust floating in space.' ''

"That's no reason not to create!" I blurted in spite of myself.

Stilwell looked at me as though trying to place me.

"So what was his connection with Evan Turner?" Pia asked.

"They was both trying to earn a living making music and they both taught at that so-called music academy they had here back then. So they knew each other and sometimes they played together, Turner on guitar, Stavrakis on piano. If Stavrakis was playing, you could be sure a lot of people would show up.''

Stilwell scratched his terminal three-days' growth of beard. "It was funny," he went on. "Turner loved Stavrakis. I don't mean he was gay—nothing like that—I mean he was Stavrakis's biggest fan. He thought he was a

genius and he was always tryin' to get him to write his stuff down. But Stavrakis just laughed, told him he didn't want to add nothin' to the cosmic dust. He told Turner he should give up playing the guitar, which he said he wasn't any good at anyway, and become his Bosworth.''

''His what?'' Andy asked.

''Some guy who wrote down every word some other guy said.''

''Boswell,'' Pia said.

Stilwell gave her an uncomprehending but adoring look. ''Stavrakis could tell you to your face that you were ugly and talentless, and you'd come back for more,'' he added, a kind of grudging admiration in his voice. ''I guess that's the definition of *charisma*, huh?''

''Or being able to pick your friends carefully,'' Andy said in disgust.

Stilwell glared at him, as though he'd made a slurring reference to the Holy Ghost. I've known a few self-styled geniuses of the kind he was describing. Their major creations are wrecked lives.

''And then Fiona McClure dumped Turner for Stavrakis,'' I said.

His eyes flicked to me, back to Pia. ''Anybody could see it coming a mile away,'' he told her. He got that moonstruck look in his beady eyes again. ''Fiona was this gorgeous gal with long golden-blond hair and eyes the color of . . . of . . .''

''Windex?'' Pia suggested.

''Yeah, Windex. And she was famous too. She'd just been busted for doing a topless gig in Riverside Park. I didn't see it,'' he added, his voice heavy with regret, ''but I heard about it. It got in all the papers and made her famous, and she spent a night in jail until Turner went and bailed her out. She got community service and a fine. I heard Turner was embarrassed by it and made it clear he didn't like what she'd done, but Stavrakis thought it was great. The upshot was, she dumped Turner for him.''

''How'd Turner take that?'' Andy asked.

''Hard, real hard. 'Cause Turner thought they was

friends. He should've known Stavrakis didn't care about anybody but himself.''

"And then Stavrakis died," Pia said. "How soon after this harpist fatale dumped Turner?"

Stilwell thought about it. "A year maybe. Somethin' like that. Fiona was still with him. That was a long time for Stavrakis to stay with one woman."

I asked him to tell us about the night Stavrakis died.

"I wasn't there when it happened, of course," he told Pia. "I hadn't come in yet. But I heard about it, naturally, from some of the people who were. Fiona was playin' that night to a crowd of folk music lovers—her crowd, right?— and all of a sudden Stavrakis walks in and jumps up on the stage and starts playing along on the piano, accompanying her. She liked that 'cause she was really in love with the guy and he could do no wrong, but the crowd didn't. They weren't his people, they were into serious folk music and had come to hear her, not him. But that just made him crazier—that they were pissed at him.

"About halfway through the program," Stilwell went on, "Stavrakis sits back on the piano bench and lets Fiona play a solo number. She's playing away and singing when, all of a sudden, he whips a carrot out of his jacket—he was a health food nut too, did I mention that?—and he holds it up, turns to the audience, and says, 'What's up, Doc?' You know, like Bugs Bunny does in the cartoons. Then he takes a big bite of carrot, laughs—and sucks it right into his windpipe. And that's the end of Chris Stavrakis. Braindead. He died in the hospital the next day."

Stilwell sat there a moment without saying anything, his head resting on his palm, staring at nothing, or at something that had happened in the Boardinghouse twenty years ago. A smattering of applause from the little cluster of people by the stage broke the silence.

"Didn't anybody know the Heimlich maneuver?" Pia asked.

"I guess not," he said. "I know what it is now, of course, but I'd never heard of it back then. Nobody else must've either, since they all just stood around wringing their hands—except Fiona, who was kneeling next to him,

crying and begging for somebody to do something.''

"Was Turner there?" I asked.

He looked at me as though I weren't too bright. "How should I know? But I never heard that he was. But he wouldn't've come to hear Fiona after what she did to him, would he? Anyway, he was with some other woman by then. I heard later that he married her."

"Marcy?" I said.

"Yeah, something like that. A French name, anyway."

I sat back with a long sigh, thinking. "And so Stavrakis died and Evan Turner gave up trying to be a performer and went back to school."

Stilwell nodded. "Yeah. It's a funny thing, I remember Stavrakis told Turner once that he'd end up as a professor. He said something like, 'Turner, a man with your lack of talent should be a waiter or a professor.' Stavrakis knew about Turner's grandma, see, and he wouldn't let Turner forget it. Like he knew that when the going got rough, Turner would go crawling back to the old lady and she'd bail him out. Plus, Stavrakis just loved to make fun of people who were trying to make something out of themselves. He thought people with dreams and ambitions were stupid. He was just as nasty to Dave Douglas—that's what Douglas called himself before the U hired him and made him a professor, Dave. He calls himself David Paul Douglas now."

Stilwell snickered again. "Now Fiona's married to Douglas—at least she was, last I heard. What is he, her third husband or something?" He sighed. "Anyway, after Stavrakis died, she never set foot in my place again."

I asked him if Scott Hall had ever come in here back then.

He frowned a moment, perhaps in thought, then his face lit up and he laughed. "The composer, right? Yeah, he did. I wouldn't've known him from Adam, except once he came in when Stavrakis was playing, and Stavrakis spotted him. He told the crowd that they were honored to have a great composer in their midst, and asked Hall to stand up. Hall made a beeline for the door, with Stavrakis laughing fit to die. Never saw him in here again."

"My feelings for Stavrakis are getting warmer by the minute," Pia muttered under her breath.

I got the photograph of Elli out of my shoulder bag and slid it across the table to Stilwell.

Without much curiosity, he picked it up and looked at it. After a couple of moments, his eyes grew very big.

"Jesus!" he said, still staring. "It's like a ghost! He had these same big eyes that were always laughing at you, and the big mouth—see the start of a sneer there at the corner? That's how he looked at just about everybody. I saw it a lot, I wouldn't forget it. Who is she?"

"As far as you know," I asked, "he didn't have any children?"

"Stavrakis? You gotta be kidding! Leastways, he never said nothing about a kid that I ever heard. Or a wife either. I suppose she could be a niece or something," he added doubtfully.

"You said he was involved with a lot of women. Can you think of one of them who might've had a child by him?"

He shook his head. "Uh-uh. Fiona was the only one he was ever with for very long that I knew of." His eyes flew up as a horrible thought struck him. "She ain't Fiona's kid, is she?"

I said I was sure she wasn't, asked him if he remembered when Stavrakis had died. He stared out into the room a moment, eyes narrowed, lips moving. "It'll be twenty-one years come January, or maybe February. It was cold, anyway, and snowing."

He held the photograph up and stared at it some more, then put it down on the table. Pia thanked him for his help, asked him to get us all refills on our lattés. He went off, shaking his head.

"Too bad Stavrakis wasn't murdered," Andy said, " 'cause then it might've been the harpist who did it. You know, if she'd discovered he was cheating on her with some other woman."

"It's hard to get somebody to choke to death on a carrot in front of a crowd," Pia pointed out.

"Maybe," Andy went on, "she knew the Heimlich ma-

nuever but didn't use it on him, just knelt there carrying on for effect, and watched him die. It would be the perfect crime, wouldn't it, because legally it wouldn't be murder at all. I mean, nobody *has* to save another person's life. You can just stand there and watch him die without lifting a finger and the law can't do anything about it.''

"But it would be murder anyway," Pia said grimly.

We sat and drank coffee for another hour or so and then they left. I stayed on awhile longer, staring into the dregs of my latté, as if the pattern of foam and espresso could tell me where to find Elli. I considered driving over to the Dungeon and throwing myself on Lanny's mercy again, but decided the chances of success were no better now than the last time I'd tried that.

My mind drifted, playing with pieces of the puzzle, or puzzles, I'd picked up so far. It seemed to be a puzzle about obsessions: Evan Turner obsessed with finding himself, Geraldine Asher obsessed with restoring the Music School to whatever greatness it might once have had, a woman scholar obsessed with showing that Beethoven was a rapist. And just about everybody obsessed with a dead man named Chris Stavrakis.

As I got up and walked out into the night, I wondered what was wrong with me. I had no obsessions, unless trying to avoid becoming obsessed counted as one. It probably did.

I checked my answering machine when I got home. There were two messages. One was from Kathleen Baker, Turner's teaching assistant, telling me she was sorry she'd missed my call and to feel free to call again. The other was Gary.

"*I'm glad you're not home,*" he said, "*because it's easier for me to tell this to your voice mail. I've thought a lot about what I want in my life since we last talked, Peggy. I love you, but I'm old-fashioned enough to want a marriage—a real marriage, not a commuter one. And I want kids—two, if possible.*"

There was a long pause. Then, "*Although I think Loon Lake would be a great place to raise a family, I'd be happy*

to live in Minneapolis if you'd agree to marry me, and if you'd be willing to have kids—at least one. I don't need to live up here. I could live down there, in the city, as long as we could spend our vacations at places like this."

There was another long pause, just the dull sound of the tape. "*That's all,*" he continued. "*I'd like to hear from you in the next day or two—I have to decide about buying the paper soon. If you want to talk about it, call me anytime. Or I'll come down there.*" Another long pause. Then he laughed softly and said, as though talking to himself, "*Oh, hell! I wish I could erase this and start over.*" And then he hung up.

It was late, but I called him anyway.

He answered on the second ring.

Twenty-one

I didn't sleep well and called Kathleen Baker at a little before nine in the morning.

"Jeez," she mumbled into the phone, sounding half asleep, "this had better be good."

I apologized for calling so early and told her who I was and that I wanted to talk to her about Evan Turner.

"Professor Turner? What about him?"

I told her I'd been asked by the University to look into his death.

"Oh, yeah? You mind telling me what there is to look into?"

"I'd like to discuss it with you in person." I also wanted to try to find out why she sounded so hostile, now that she seemed fully awake. "Can you give me half an hour of your time today sometime?"

She thought it over a minute. "I'm going over to the music library this afternoon to study for my prelims," she said finally. "I'll be there from one until about four. You know where it is?"

"You couldn't make it earlier, could you?"

"Not for Evan Turner," she said, and she hung up. I'd met another of Turner's fans.

It was raining when I left the house, just a fine mist, and the weather report said it was going to rain all day, so I took my car. I arrived at the police station around eleven, used Ginny's office to write up a brief report for Bixler, and managed to slip it into his mailbox without him seeing me, since his door was closed. He was probably busy with his hunting or girlie magazines.

I had lunch with Ginny and a couple of other cops and then, at a little before one, walked over to the Music School, the hood of my raincoat up against the drizzle. As I entered, I thought of the last time I'd gone in there when it was raining, but this time the lights were on and I could hear the discordant, muffled sounds of musical instruments being played somewhere behind closed doors.

As I got to the stairs that led down to the basement, where the music library was, Scott Hall and David Douglas were coming out of the main office. Neither of them seemed to find the sight of me enough to brighten the gloomy day. I smiled and said hello and continued on down the stairs.

There was only one person in the library, sitting at a table littered with books and papers, a small blond woman in her twenties, with glasses, a sharp nose, and an equally sharp, determined-looking chin.

I told her who I was and sat down opposite her at the table.

"I saw Professor Hall in the office a little while ago," she said, "and mentioned you were coming to talk to me about Turner. So his grandmother's behind this, huh? What makes her think he was murdered?"

"She just thinks the police up north were a little hasty in calling it an accident."

"And she's got the money to reopen the case!"

"Something like that," I said as I sat down. She shoved her papers aside and watched me expectantly. I asked her when she'd last seen Turner.

"A few days before he left here to go up to the conference center," she said. "In his office. A student was unhappy about the grade he'd received in Turner's spring survey course and wanted to discuss it, so, since I'd been the grader for the class, Turner called me and asked me to deal with it. After I'd gone over the student's blue book, I agreed with him that the grade was too low, so I filled out a change-of-grade report and took it in to Turner to sign. He signed it without bothering to ask why. He never had much time for students. That was the last I saw of him."

"How'd he seem?"

"You mean his mood? About the same as usual, as far as I could see. Preoccupied, the way he usually was, with his own business."

"Do you have any idea what business that was?"

"None," she answered, making it clear she had no interest in knowing either.

"He was an avid photographer," I said. "Did you ever see any of his work?"

"He showed me some of it. Why?"

"What was it of?"

She shrugged. "The river, a lake somewhere, trees—stuff like that. He seemed to like nature."

"Did he ever show you pictures he'd taken of people?"

"I saw a few of his daughter. They were okay. Good photo album pictures."

I slid the photograph of Elli across the table to her. She glanced at it, asked me if Turner had taken it. I told her he had.

"Figures," she said with a sniff.

"You know who she is?"

"No, but she came to Turner's office sometime in May when I was in there. She knocked on the door and poked her head in without waiting for him to tell her to come in. I could tell he wasn't exactly thrilled to see her. She had a stud in her nose, rings in her ears and on her eyebrows, like she does in this photograph."

She laughed. "He didn't introduce us, but he called her Helen. She said she was just passing by and thought she'd come in and tell him the band was playing on the Mall at noon, in case he wanted to go hear it."

"The band?"

"Yeah. As though Turner would know which band it was. They have a regular program on the Mall in the summer that features local bands."

"Did you ask him about it?"

She grinned. "Yeah, just to embarrass him a little more. He said she was a friend of his daughter's. I didn't believe him. With my dirty mind, I figured she might be the reason his marriage broke up, or else she was somebody he'd found to console himself with afterward." She tossed a

thumb at the photograph, said, "Helen's such a nice old-fashioned name, isn't it? She didn't look much like a Helen to me."

"He played guitar himself," I said, "before he went back to school to become a teacher."

"So I've been told," she said indifferently.

"You don't act as though you cared much for him," I said.

"I didn't, but that doesn't mean I'm exulting over his death."

"Why didn't you like him?"

She made a face. "Oh, just little things—like, he killed my adviser. My ex-adviser, I mean." Her eyes were angry behind the glasses as she waited for me to deal with that.

I asked her who her ex-adviser was.

"Drew Channing. I assume by now you've heard about the Marilyn Schaeffer scandal, right? The feminist scholar the younger members of the faculty wanted to hire?"

I nodded.

"Well, when Marilyn Schaeffer wasn't offered a tenured position, Professor Channing left in protest and managed to get a job at the University of Chicago. About a month ago, she was hit by a car and killed while crossing a street."

"And you think Turner did it?"

"I *know* he did it," she replied, raising her voice. "Indirectly. Drew—Professor Channing, but she wanted her students to call her by her first name—wouldn't have left here if Schaeffer hadn't been screwed by Turner with the help of his grandmother. And if she hadn't left here, she wouldn't've been in Chicago to get hit by a car, would she? She was a wonderful scholar, and she really cared about her students—unlike Turner."

Her eyes glittered with tears. "Damn it! Now I think about it, I'm sorry Turner's dead, because I'd like to kill him myself! I'd leave here too if I wasn't about ready to take my Ph.D. exams. Well, at least now I won't have the son of a bitch on my examining committee." She dabbed at her eyes with a Kleenex, said, "Sorry. You want me to confess?"

"What makes you think his grandmother had anything

to do with Marilyn Schaeffer not getting hired?''

''That's what everybody thinks,'' she replied. Hearing how weak that sounded, she said, ''Besides, it makes sense. Turner was totally opposed to Schaeffer, but Schaeffer had the votes, and all of a sudden the dean retrenches the position, claiming the college didn't have the money. Wasn't that convenient! I don't agree with everything Marilyn Schaeffer writes, but at least she's creative and forces people to think about music in new ways—something the old men around here haven't had any reason to do in three hundred years! Isn't that what scholarship's supposed to be all about?''

''You don't have to convince me,'' I said. ''But for what it's worth, I don't believe Mrs. Farr intervened in the Schaeffer business.''

''Why not? Look around you! How many buildings on this campus were built with money from the Dulcie Farr Foundation? What's the name on our new concert hall? You think she couldn't block the hiring of one faculty member, if her precious grandson told her he wanted her to?''

I waited until she'd run down, then said, ''I asked Mrs. Farr about it and she told me she didn't know anything about Marilyn Schaeffer. I believe her. I also believe that she'd have as much sympathy for Marilyn Schaeffer's crazy ideas as you do. And I think Evan Turner would have known he couldn't talk his grandmother into using her influence in that way.''

She didn't say anything to that for a minute. Then she wiped her eyes again and went on, ''Well, anyway, Drew was probably happy to leave here. She probably would've left anyway.''

''Why?''

''It was an open secret that she and Gerri Asher had something going—Drew lived with Gerri for a while—but they broke up. The last year Drew was here, things were a little frosty between them.''

''Are you sure this isn't just more Music School gossip?''

She shrugged, didn't say anything to that.

I looked around the library, at the rows of bookshelves and the book-lined walls. I told Kathleen Baker I'd like to see a box of music that was supposed to be down there somewhere, and asked her if she could help me locate it.

She led the way over to the card catalogue on the other side of the room. I gave her Stavrakis's name and, after a moment of thumbing through cards, she said, "It's over in the area with the unclassified stuff. We get boxes and boxes of junk from people who've died and left behind stuff their families don't know what to do with, so they dump it on us. Some of it might be valuable—to social historians, for example—but we don't have the money to catalogue most of it, so it just collects dust over here."

She got up on a stool and looked at the labels on boxes on the top shelf, shifted a couple of them around to look behind them. She sneezed, wrinkled her nose. "Nope, it's not here," she said after a minute. She got up on tiptoe, peered down at the shelf, used a finger to check for dust. "It was until recently, though," she added. "Something was, anyway."

I thanked her for her time and started for the door.

She said, "You're not much of a sleuth, you know."

"I'm not?" I asked, turning back.

"You never asked me if I'd ever seen her again—your Helen."

"Did you?"

She laughed at my eagerness. "I left Turner's office a few minutes after she did and saw her standing outside on the street corner. About a minute later a van pulled up and she got in—an old zebra-striped van. Probably carrying the band's equipment for the concert on the Mall."

Upstairs, I headed down to Scott Hall's office, knocked, and waited until I heard a gruff "Come in" before I entered.

"Yes," he said, staring at me.

"I was just down in the music library talking to Kathleen Baker," I said, unaffected by the acid in his voice, since I've encountered worse. "We weren't able to find the box of Chris Stavrakis's music you said was there."

"Really?" he said, raising an eyebrow. "And what do you conclude from that?"

"I'd just like to know where it is," I said evenly.

"And I'll bet your shrewd detective's mind is playing with the possibility that I took it away," he went on, "perhaps because it contains evidence that points to me as Evan Turner's killer."

"It would have to be some box, to do that," I said with a smile.

"Indeed it would!" He aimed a finger at one of his bookshelves. "It's that box over there, on the bottom shelf. After we talked yesterday, I brought it up here and looked through it to see if there was anything in it I would now consider worth trying to save. Don't ask me why."

"Was there?"

"No."

I went over and looked at the box, an old cardboard one, the kind you get from the grocery store when you're moving. I opened the lid and peered in. It was half full of spiral notebooks and loose sheets of music paper with musical notations all over it, some of it scribbled out or erased. It meant nothing to me, of course. I closed the lid and put the box back, turned to Hall.

"The last time I was here," I said, "you told me you never saw Chris Stavrakis after the end-of-semester party at Alrikson's home, but I've heard that later you attended his performances sometimes—and he even laughed you out of the Boardinghouse once."

"My God!" he said, his eyes widening in amazement. "Who could still remember something like that from so long ago?"

"Things like that tend to stick in the mind," I replied, "if you're well enough known."

He nodded, his eyes moving around the room, finally coming back to me. "Yes," he said finally, "I went to hear him perform—more than once, to be honest with you, but he only spotted me that one time, the last time—and a long time before he died. I wasn't there for that."

"Why'd you go hear him?"

"I don't know." He laughed softly. "Morbid curiosity,

I suppose. I knew what a great talent he had, and I wanted to see how he was wasting it. That's all. You know so much, you probably know I couldn't have been responsible for his death.''

"The photograph I showed to you and your wife on Sunday," I said. "You recognized Chris Stavrakis in it, didn't you? Your wife certainly did."

He looked at me steadily. "You have an overheated imagination, Officer. We did no such thing." He continued to stare at me, daring me to call him a liar. I didn't see what I could gain from doing that, so I thanked him for his time and got out of there.

Twenty-two

It was almost three by the time I left the Music School and ran back to the station to get my car. The drizzle had now turned into a steady, all-day kind of rain. I drove to Lanny Nelson's place and into the unpaved parking lot behind the building. Lanny's zebra-striped van was parked next to the Dumpster by the alley. I ran to the back door, hopping over puddles.

I climbed the back stairs to the third floor, walked down to Lanny's apartment, and knocked. No answer. No sounds of anybody inside either, just the muffled noise of a guitar coming from the apartment behind me. I knocked some more, waited, then crossed the hall and knocked on that door.

The music stopped and, after a moment, the door opened and a man, naked to the waist and barefoot, stood in the doorway. He was holding his guitar loosely at his side by its neck, like a dead goose. He could have been anywhere from twenty-five to forty, with a lined, unshaven face, dark glasses, and a blond crewcut.

"Yeah, what?" he greeted me effusively, looking me up and down and not finding anything of even passing interest anywhere.

I told him I was looking for Lanny Nelson.

Without saying anything, he gestured across the hall with his index finger, started to close the door.

"I know," I said quickly, "but he's not home, although his van's in the lot. You haven't seen him today, have you?" I tried to peer around him at a woman who'd just come into the room.

He scratched his head and gave me a puzzled, overdone squint. "Do I look like Lanny's social secretary?"

Having no answer to that, I put a frustrated look on my face and said, "Damn! I'm a writer—freelance—doing a piece on the local rock scene. Lanny said he could help me meet some musicians." I attended Catholic schools throughout my childhood, so trying to pass off lies as truth comes as naturally to me as breathing, and was once just as necessary.

A spark of something not entirely unlike interest appeared in the man's eyes, but you had to be looking for it. "Yeah? How do you know Lanny?" He stepped back and let me into the apartment.

"From the Dungeon," I said. "We got to talking one night."

"Oh." He gave a scornful laugh. "And Lanny sold you a line of bullshit, said he's an expert on the local rock scene, huh?"

"He's not?" I suppressed the urge to gasp.

He rolled his eyes.

The woman looked me over curiously. She was wearing a thin terry-cloth bathrobe and drying her hair with a huge towel. She had the required rings and studs all over her face, including a fat nose ring like those worn by prize winning bulls at the State Fair, still almost a month away. The fact that I didn't find it hard not to stare probably meant the fad was almost over.

"I'm Leah," she said. "He's Skate. Who're you?"

"Peggy." I didn't know anything about the local rock scene, so, recalling the name of the band I'd heard playing on the Mall the other day, I said, "I wanted to talk to No Plans 4 the Future, but Lanny said they weren't available."

"How would he know that?" she wondered aloud.

"They suck," Skate contributed.

"Right, but they just got a record contract," Leah retorted, with a lot of emphasis on "they."

The apartment was minimally furnished, the most prominent feature a king-size waterbed on the floor.

Leah said, "You only want to write about groups that've made it?" She finished with the towel and tossed it over

her shoulder, where it landed on the radiator under a window. Her hair, sticking out in all directions, was crayon yellow, which gave her the appearance of a punk sunflower.

"No, not at all," I said quickly. "I want to talk to groups that are still struggling too—the whole spectrum. Are you in bands?"

"I'm trying to put something together," Skate said vaguely.

"I work nights in a used CD store," Leah said. "Which is why we eat," she added with a sour glance at Skate.

I decided to risk it. "The person Lanny said he was going to arrange for me to talk to is a woman named Elli. Do you know her?"

"I know *an* Elli," she said. "You mean Lanny's ex-girlfriend?"

"Yes," I said. "He told me she'd be able to give me a lot of personal insights into what it's like to be a woman trying to make it in rock music today." When a lie's going well, it feels as though you're tap-dancing on quicksand.

"Lanny's right, for once," Leah said, "she'd be a good person for you to talk to. She's authentic—*so* angry."

"Yeah, but what's she angry about?" Skate wondered aloud with an aggravated laugh.

"About how shitty women are treated in the music industry, for one thing, Skate."

He threw up his hands, guitar included, in mock surrender, and flopped down onto the waterbed and began playing chords, his back to the wall.

"Elli what?" I asked.

"Just Elli. She used to be Lanny's girlfriend, but she's not anymore. They're still friends, though. Lanny's her business manager." She laughed. "Not for long, though. Elli's ambitious. She sings and plays guitar and keyboards, and Lanny ain't gonna be able to take her where she wants to go. She's got a lot of talent."

Must run in the family, I thought.

She broke off suddenly and gave me a big-eyed look. "Now, that would be something for you to write about! Stone Pucker! Elli plays with 'em sometimes."

"*Played* with 'em, you mean," Skate said, practicing

riffs now. "Past tense. Stone Pucker's no more."

Leah cocked her head at me. "You know about Stone Pucker?"

"Just that they played the Dungeon Saturday night," I said, remembering the name from the Dungeon's marquee.

"You heard 'em play Saturday?" she asked, her eyes wide.

"No," I said, wondering what the fuss was about, "I was just in the Dungeon that night—sometime after midnight. Stone Pucker was gone by then. Some other band was playing. Gacy's Diner."

"Too bad you weren't there earlier," she said, looking disappointed. "You could've seen their last performance. It's historic."

She made it sound like I'd missed the Beatles' final concert or something. I gave her a puzzled look.

"You don't know, do you?" she said.

"Know what?"

"Josh Wills got offed," Skate said from the floor. "Pucker was his band. Don't you read the paper or watch television? What kind of a music writer are you, anyway?"

Leah threw him an exasperated look. He'd ruined the climax she'd been building to. I suppose if I'd been a real freelance writer interested in rock and roll, I'd have paid attention to something like that. "Offed?" I asked. "How? When?"

"Saturday night or Sunday morning," she said. "After Pucker'd played the Dungeon. The cops think Carl did it, but they haven't caught him yet. Carl's Pucker's drummer."

"And Elli played with them?"

"Sometimes. Lanny was their business manager too. You could do a real story on that, couldn't you? I mean, it's got everything—sex, murder, rock and roll."

"Why sex?" I asked.

"Because after Elli dumped Lanny, she and Josh got together. Carl was jealous—that's what they say, anyway. He's a mean drunk, Carl. He does hard stuff too, like crack."

"Is he a big guy?" I asked, the hair rising on my neck. "Maybe a weight lifter?"

She nodded eagerly, eyes bright. "Yeah, that's Carl. He works out regularly with weights, which makes him a dangerous guy to be around sometimes. He destroys things."

She didn't have to tell me that.

"And Josh?" I asked. "A tall, skinny guy with long hair?"

"Yeah. Josh was the band's creative intelligence. Carl's nothing but trouble, but Josh was a major talent. Who knows how far he might've gone?"

"Creative intelligence!" Skate repeated with a laugh, and began strumming the first ominous chords of Chopin's "Funeral March," which was pretty much where I'd come in.

Leah didn't have much more to tell me about the murder, just what she'd heard from customers coming into the store where she worked. As soon as she'd closed the door, I stepped back across to Lanny's apartment and knocked again, still without getting an answer.

I walked outside, stood contemplating Lanny's van, annoyed, as the rain splashed down around me. Was he home and just didn't feel like answering his door? Well, it didn't matter, since I'd got more from Leah and Skate than I'd expected, and probably more than I could have got from him. I slid behind the wheel of my car and used my cell phone to call my friend Buck Hansen, a homicide inspector with the city police. I know his number by heart.

"The murder of that rock musician on Monday," I said by way of greeting. "Is it your case?"

"Josh Wills," he said. "Yes. Why?"

"Does the body have a nasty-looking gash running the length of its right forearm on the inside?"

Buck didn't have to check. "The medical examiner says it's about a week old."

"Would you like me to come in and tell you about it?" I asked.

"Would you?"

Twenty-three

Buck and I have been friends a long time and we get together regularly for dinner. He's a gourmet cook and likes to try out new and elaborate recipes on me, in the hope of improving my taste. When it's my turn, we either go out or else I order from one of those gourmet delivery services.

I nosed my car down into the police garage under city hall, showed the attendant my shield, parked, and took the elevator up to Buck's floor. The sign on his door says his name is Mansell Hansen, but nobody calls him "Mansell" twice. I think he doesn't change the name on the sign because he likes to interview suspects in his cluttered, homey office and "Mansell" on the door is more apt to relax a suspect than "Buck." He's a little under six feet, but looks taller because he's thin and keeps himself in such good shape, with silver-blond hair and blue eyes with laugh wrinkles around them that offset their chilliness, at least when he's talking to people who aren't murder suspects.

He poured me a cup of freshly brewed coffee—he knows some of my vices well—and waited while I settled myself comfortably in an old leather armchair I'd sat in often before.

I told him how I'd been spending my time lately and how Josh Wills had got the gash on his arm and I'd got mine on my neck. When I finished, he slid some eight-by-ten photographs out of a folder and reached them across his desk to me.

They were the crime scene photographs. The man I'd encountered at the burglary and the Dungeon was lying on the floor, barefoot and wearing jeans and a white T-shirt.

His arms were thrown out at his sides, the T-shirt was dark with blood. The gash from the fence showed clearly on the inside of his right arm. I thought of the first time I'd seen him, in the noise and chaos of the thunderstorm, frightened and angry, trying to shake his foot free of my grip.

In death, he didn't look frightened or angry at all. It was strange to think that, only a few hours before this photograph was taken, he'd been on a stage playing guitar and singing, a mob of people dancing at his feet. He was very still now. It was a quiet photograph.

"It happened Sunday morning," Buck said. "One of the other tenants of Wills's apartment building saw them come in around two—Wills and Carl Lorenzen, the band's drummer. They were arguing and Wills was trying to calm Lorenzen down. Their band, with the evocative name Stone Pucker, had been playing a gig at the Dungeon. We got a call at a little after three that somebody was out of control in Wills's apartment—hollering, breaking things.

"Before the cops arrived, a man witnesses have identified as Lorenzen came running out of the building looking like all the demons of hell were on his tail. The apartment looked like a cyclone had hit it. We haven't been able to locate Lorenzen at any of his usual haunts. People who knew him say he never lived any one place very long."

"What was his motive for killing Wills?"

"According to people who knew them, Wills was supposed to be a pretty talented guy and Stone Pucker showed promise of going places—there was even talk of a record contract for a while. But Lorenzen's drug use was getting worse and bars were increasingly reluctant to engage the band.

"That's when your mystery woman enters the picture. She'd been playing in bands since high school herself and she's supposed to be a good all-around musician. She played and sang with Stone Pucker off and on. She sang with them Saturday night, in fact, so you must've just missed her. You may be lucky you did," he added with a bleak smile.

"Wills wanted her to join the band full-time," he went

on, "but she said she wouldn't as long as Lorenzen was in it. Wills was reluctant to let Lorenzen go—they'd been playing together a long time, since high school—but after their gig Saturday night, when Lorenzen, under the influence, played badly and Elli told Wills she'd never play with them again, Josh had finally had enough and fired him. Lorenzen doesn't take rejection well."

I said, "It sounds like Elli was lucky not to be at Wills's place when Lorenzen arrived. Did you talk to her?"

"Oh, yes." He flipped a page in his notebook. "She was born Helen Hadley," he began.

"Hadley!" I repeated. It seemed so ordinary—no wonder she used just her first name. To make sure we were talking about the same person, I showed him my photograph of her.

He glanced at it. "Yep, that's her. She acts tough and I don't think it's all an act either, but I also got the feeling there's something genuine behind the facade. I liked her. Of course, I didn't know she was a burglar when I talked to her. That might've made me like her less."

"How old is she?"

He consulted his notes. "Twenty, she says. Why?"

I felt a pang of disappointment. "Everything was pointing to her being Chris Stavrakis's daughter, but he'll have been dead twenty-one years in February, according to somebody who should know. Doesn't give him much time to be her father."

"It takes time to be a father," Buck retorted, his eyes suddenly bleak. "It only takes a moment to be a sperm donor." He has a daughter in her early twenties whom he doesn't see very often. I've never been able to get him to talk about her, although I've tried.

I shrugged. "Well, however it happened, it seems she inherited his face and his musical talent. Could I have her address?"

He wrote it down on a piece of paper. "She doesn't have a phone," he said, "and probably won't be there now anyway. She works at the Farmington Mall in one of those boutiques that sells the jewelry kids hang all over their bodies."

We talked for a few more minutes and then I finished my coffee and stood up to leave.

"Thanks for the tip about Lanny Nelson," Buck said. "His name hadn't come up in the investigation yet. He may know something useful about where Carl Lorenzen could be holed up."

"If you can get him to talk," I said.

"We'll also check Evan Turner's apartment," he went on, "just in case Lorenzen figured it would be safe to go back. He doesn't sound like Ph.D. material."

I headed for the door, then paused, remembering that Nelson hadn't answered his door when I'd been there, but his van was still in the lot. There were any number of innocent explanations for that, but I mentioned it to Buck anyway.

"We'll check it out," he said, as he reached for his phone.

Twenty-four

It was four-thirty by the time I got back to my car. I thought of driving to the address he'd given me for Elli and waiting for her to come home from work, but I didn't know how long it would take her to do that or even if she'd come directly home, so I decided to drive to the mall and see if I could catch her there before she left. I'd lived all but three days of my life without knowing of her existence, but now that I did, I didn't want to waste any more time before meeting her and hearing her story.

Farmington Mall is the oldest mall in the state, its name a mocking reminder of what used to be done there before the land had been turned into a large middle-class suburb where they raise, instead of wheat and corn, consumer kids who want their bodies pierced and painted.

I parked as close to one of the entrances as I could get, ran inside through the rain and looked for the nearest directory. My heart sank—there were eleven jewelry stores, nine if I eliminated the upscale ones. I started with the nearest and worked my way around the mall. No Elli worked for Gretchen's Ear Boutique, Ears for Tears, BeDecked, or Cheri's Salon.

It was almost five when I reached A Piercing Scream, tucked in an out-of-the-way corner of the mall. The saleswoman, idly spinning a rack of costume jewelry and dreaming of God knows what, asked me how she could help me.

I told her I was looking for Elli.

"You just missed her."

The story of my life, I thought bitterly.

"She doesn't hang around much after five," she added,

"on account of she has a bus to catch at a quarter after."

"Where?"

"The bus shelter's on the west side of the mall," she replied, chewing gum, spinning the jewelry rack, and giving my face a professional once-over, as though looking for holes or wanting to add some.

I thanked her and went quickly back to my car, since it was quicker to drive around to the west side of the mall than walk.

The rain was starting to come down seriously now. I turned on my headlights and wipers and got in the line of cars leaving the mall, their drivers on their way home for dinner. I was about a hundred yards from the bus shelter when I saw Lanny's van pull away from it and bully its way between two cars, heading for the exit. I changed lanes quickly and followed, eight or nine cars behind it. The van, luckily, stood out in a crowd.

It turned north out of the mall and headed back toward downtown, weaving in and out of the rush-hour traffic. I managed to keep it in sight until I got out of the mall too, then gradually worked my way up until I was only two cars behind. I had no way of knowing if Elli was actually in the van, but it would have been a great coincidence if Lanny had just happened to be passing the bus stop where Elli was waiting for her bus.

We came to the Dungeon a couple of miles north of downtown, and I thought that's where they were going, but instead of stopping, the van continued on another mile or so, then turned east on the street that, according to the address Buck had given me, Elli lived on. It was nice of Lanny, I thought, to give his ex-girlfriend a ride home in the rain—although maybe he was only protecting his investment, since he was also her business manager.

A minute later, the van's taillights glowed red as it slowed and then turned into an alley between two-story buildings that housed small businesses on the ground floors, apartments above. With the exception of a Chinese take-out place in the middle of one of the buildings, the businesses were closed, their windows dark.

I pulled over to the curb and parked, waiting to see if

the van would come back out. I was eager to talk to Elli, but not with Lanny around. I waited about five minutes, then decided I was going to have to try again later that night when, I hoped, Lanny would be gone. Buck had said she didn't have a phone.

I put my car in gear and was moving off when my cell phone rang. I dug it out of my shoulder bag, pressed send, and said hello. "It's Buck, Peggy. I'm calling from Lanny's apartment. He's dead—his throat's been cut."

As I jumped out of the car, I told him where I was and what I'd been following.

"Stay where you are," he said. "We'll have cops there in a couple of minutes."

"No, I'm going in there," I said, running down through the rain to the alley. "I'll try to stall him or distract him."

"Peggy, no!"

"I'll keep the line open," I said, "but don't say anything more now."

"Wait, Peggy! You don't know what he's going to do!—" he hollered, but I'd already dropped the cell phone back into my shoulder bag and so Buck sounded tiny and ridiculous.

The van was parked under an old wooden balcony that ran the length of one of the buildings on the second floor. I glanced inside, saw that it was empty. The smell of Chinese cooking mixed with the odor of gasoline and rain. An Asian man in an apron and a cook's hat came through the screen door behind the restaurant with a bag of garbage. He gave me an incurious glance as I ran up the rickety flight of stairs to the balcony. There were three apartments. I went to the first, pulled on the screen door. It was hooked from the inside. No light escaped from the curtain covering the window of the inner door. I ran along the balcony to the second apartment, yanked at the screen, which flew open in my hand. I turned the knob on the door and pulled. It was locked. A gap in the curtain covering the window let me see into a small, dark kitchen. I hesitated, frustrated, about to go to the next apartment, when something caught my eye on the linoleum floor inside—a leaf. A leaf caught in a wet footprint.

I pulled out my cell phone. "It's the middle apartment," I said.

In the distance, faintly, I could heard sirens, and then a muffled scream from inside the apartment. "He's hurting her!" I said into the phone, and twisted the doorknob and hit the door with my shoulder. Nothing.

I used the phone to break the window. A tiny hysterical voice asked me what I was doing. "Breaking and entering," I answered.

I reached in over the jagged pieces of glass, slid the bolt open, and unhooked the chain, then opened the door and went in.

Another scream, louder this time. I ran through the kitchen and into the living room, holding the cell phone in my right hand now and telling Buck what I was doing, my car keys clenched in my left hand with the ignition key protruding between my index and middle fingers. The living room was empty, but I heard another scream coming from the room beyond it.

The sirens were growing louder as I ran across the living room. I heard a man shouting and the crash of something falling. The woman screamed again as I ran into the bedroom. The sirens were so loud now that they filled the room, the police cars' emergency lights casting a garish, bloody glow over the two figures struggling at the foot of the bed across the room, Carl holding Elli by one muscled arm around her neck, a knife at her throat, pieces of a shattered vase on the floor around them.

"How'd they find us?" he hollered. "How the fuck did they find us?" Blood was pouring into his eyes from a gash on his forehead. "Well, so what?" he said. "What've I gotta lose now? What've I gotta lose? It's all your fault, bitch!"

She twisted away, kneeing him in the groin, but he slammed her back against the window like a rag doll and then lunged toward her, the knife in front of him. I had a moment to see her terrified face and then I screamed, "Carl!" and ran across the room.

He twisted his head around. His eyes widened in his bloody face as he recognized me. "You!" He forgot Elli

and started for me, the knife in front of him.

I could hear Buck's small metallic voice holler, "Peggy! Peggy!" I waited until Carl was about a foot away from me and then tossed the phone into his face and jumped aside—and tripped on a small rug and fell down on one knee.

He was over me before I could duck away. He grabbed my hair with his left hand and pulled me up to the knife. I grunted and punched at one of his eyes with the key in my fist, but he turned his head aside and I only struck his cheek. I tried to twist away—and then suddenly he was crashing to the floor with Elli on top of him, hacking at his eyes with a piece of pottery. He screamed, dropped the knife, tried to cover his eyes with his hands, and then the room was full of cops and everything calmed down quickly.

"Who are you?" Elli asked me, breathing hard. She was bathed in the garish glow of the squad car lights—red, white, yellow, blue—and naked to the waist. One eye was swollen shut and she was covered with blood—Carl's blood. Light flickered on the jewelry on her face, and the bracelet that had led me to her glittered dully on her wrist.

"My name's Peggy O'Neill," I said, "and I've been looking for you. Thanks for saving my life."

"Yeah, you too," she answered. "What do you want?"

Twenty-five

She refused to go to the emergency room, finding instead what she needed in her bathroom. She took her time, and when she came out to talk to Buck, she was barefoot and wearing a clean shirt and a clean pair of jeans. She had a bowl of ice and a washcloth that she used on her swollen eye.

Lanny's van had been waiting at the bus stop when she got there, she told us. He'd picked her up a few times before in bad weather, back when they were going together. She couldn't see anybody in it but, figuring Lanny had gone into the mall to find her, she ran over to it and climbed in, to wait for him to come back. People were jammed into the bus shelters, out of the rain, waiting for their buses and paying no attention to her. Then Carl had jumped into the van next to her, put the point of his knife in her side, and told her to slide under the wheel and drive. She'd tried to calm him down, told him that his killing of Josh hadn't been in cold blood, he'd been under the influence of drugs, the courts would take that into account.

He'd just laughed. She'd recognized the laugh, knew he was high on drugs now, too. Once in the apartment, he took her upstairs, told her he'd killed Lanny and now he was going to rape and kill her—or vice versa, if she'd prefer, he wasn't particular. It was all her fault, he insisted, over and over, because she'd made Josh kick him off the band. They'd struggled and then I'd arrived.

"The cavalry," she added, as though not terribly impressed, but giving me a smile too. "I guess we're even now."

"More than even," I said, remembering Carl and the tree branch.

Then Buck and the other cops had gone away and left us there in Elli's apartment.

She asked me if I wanted a beer or something.

"A Coke, if you have one."

I looked around while she was out in the kitchen. There wasn't much in the way of furniture: a fat sofa in a faded floral pattern squatted against a wall, with a battered old footlocker in front of it for a coffee table and a couple of canvas chairs around it. Stereo speakers bracketed a CD player in one corner and an electronic keyboard took up part of another wall. She'd stuck posters of female rock stars on the walls with tacks and tape. The bedroom, in addition to the bed, had a small desk with a computer on it. I could see, through the shattered pottery on the floor and Carl's blood, that she kept the place very neat.

I sat in a somewhat shaky canvas chair. She came into the room with a can of beer and a Coke and put them down on the footlocker between us, then sprawled back on the sofa and we sized each other up.

She looked pretty much the way the caretaker at Turner's building had described her: about five-six, with short, light brown hair that curled over her high forehead, dark eyes under heavy dark brows, and a wide mouth. Her ears were outlined with colored glass, three thin gold rings hung from one eyebrow, and there was a ruby-red stud in one of her nostrils.

"So how'd you find me?" she asked. She had a pleasant, slightly hoarse voice. Except for the black eye, she didn't look any the worse for her ordeal.

"Through a photograph of you that Turner left at a shop to be framed." I got it out of my bag for the last time and passed it across the footlocker.

She glanced at it and smiled sadly. "The only picture Evan took of me that I liked enough to want a copy of. He told me he was gonna have it framed for me as a present. I forgot all about it." She tossed it onto the footlocker and sat back on the couch. "So what do you want?"

I told her I'd been investigating Turner's death and

wanted to talk to her about it, learn what the connection was between her and Turner.

She looked at me as though I were nuts. "You think maybe I pushed him off that cliff? Or Carl did? Not me, anyway! I've never even been up to Lake Superior, and why would I want to kill Evan? Carl didn't have any reason to either—not that Carl needs much of a reason to kill people, I guess," she added, dabbing at her eye with the washcloth and taking a swallow of beer.

"But you did rob his apartment and the Music School."

She cocked her head and looked at me. "You going to arrest me for that?"

"Not me. I'm only interested in your relationship with Evan Turner."

She thought about that a moment, then shrugged. "Okay, so we robbed his apartment—Josh and Carl and me—but we didn't need to kill him to do it, on account of I had a key."

"Why?"

"It wasn't what you're thinking. I wasn't living with him or anything like that. Evan was old enough to be my dad. But he gave me a key the day before he went up north. See, he once promised me I could have his keyboard—that one over there," she added, pointing with her beer can. "He didn't want it anymore and he knew I did. At the time I didn't have a place to put it—I was crashing with friends before I got this place—so I couldn't take it then. But then I got this place and, the day before he went to Lake Superior, I reminded him about the keyboard and asked him if I could still have it. He said sure. But I couldn't get Lanny's van that day, so Evan said I could pick up the keyboard while he was away, and he gave me a spare key."

"It sounds like he trusted you," I remarked.

She glanced quickly up at me. "You can't steal from the dead," she said matter-of-factly. "Anyway, I hadn't got around to getting the keyboard yet when I heard about Evan dying. Oh, shit! I thought. There goes the keyboard."

A real overflow of powerful feeling.

As though reading my mind, she shrugged and went on. "I needed it and he didn't—and besides, he'd promised it

to me. I figured my only chance to get it was if I took it right then, so I got Lanny's truck and we went over, Josh and Carl and me.''

I looked over at the keyboard. That many people weren't needed to carry it.

She followed my glance. ''It was just gonna be me and Josh, but Carl wanted to come along too. Saying no to Carl wasn't a good thing.''

''And then you saw all the other stuff Turner had in his apartment and decided to take it too.''

She nodded. ''That's about it. He was divorced, so nothing he had really belonged to anybody anymore. Besides, his ex had dumped him for another guy, he told me, and she had a good job and would probably get his insurance too. So it wasn't like it was hers, or she needed it or anything.''

She took another swallow of beer. ''So we took his computer—I took it, I mean. Josh wasn't interested in it 'cause he said you couldn't sell it for much. But Evan had a program in it that lets you compose music if you hook it up to the keyboard and I thought I could use it. Josh took his guitar—it's a good one. He thought he might want to keep it, in case he got interested in doing something acoustic sometime. Carl took Evan's stereo.''

''Tell me about the Music School,'' I said, trying to get the image of carrion birds alighting on a corpse out of my head.

''That was Josh's idea. He found the keys just lying on Evan's desk and he knew what they were. So after we unloaded the other stuff, we were sitting around his place and he said he thought it would be fun to go over and look around in there. He'd been a music major for a couple of years, so he knew how much good stuff they had. I don't know that I would've gone along if I hadn't been a little high, but I was, so I did. That was lucky for you, wasn't it?''

She laughed suddenly. ''It was like a big music store in there! If you hadn't come along, we could've had everything we'd need to start our own recording studio. That's why Carl was so pissed at you—you spoiled it for us. He

wanted to run that tree branch right through your head. That's another reason he was pissed at me—I made him miss.''

I asked her how she'd happened to meet Turner.

"He was a friend of my dad's a long time ago.'' She looked down at the gold bracelet on her arm, began fiddling with it. "I know it's stupid," she went on, "but four, five months ago I got the idea I'd like to know something about him—my dad, I mean. You know, get a different opinion about him than the one old Christos and Ma had given me.''

" 'Christos and Ma?' ''

"My grampa and my mom, except I never called him 'Grampa' or anything like that, I called him Christos. He was an old Greek guy. He'd been a religious nut when he was younger, according to Mom, and he was still pretty weird about religion when I knew him. He died last year, ninety-some years old—sort of like the clock in that old song, you know? 'Ninety years without slumbering, tick-tock, tick-tock,' '' she sang, moving her head from side to side like a pendulum as she dabbed at her eye with the washcloth.

"That was pretty much old Christos's life,'' she continued. "He owned a little greasy spoon in Wausau, a town right smack in the middle of Wisconsin, almost to the day he died—'his life seconds numbering, tick-tock, tick-tock.' ''

She laughed quietly. "I miss the old bastard. He could be kind of nasty, but I liked him and I think he liked me too—at least, he liked me listening to him talk. He mostly talked about Greece. He loved Greece almost as much as he loved God. More, probably.''

"Is your mother still alive?''

"Oh, sure—she still lives in Wausau. She's married and all, and they have two kids. A real *Leave it to Beaver* kinda life now.'' She smiled, added, "She's happy.''

"How did your mom and dad get together?''

"Mom was Dad's girlfriend in high school, before he moved down here to go to college. They kept in touch, though. Mom got a job as a waitress in old Christos's café

and she lived in a little apartment upstairs. She thought that, sooner or later, she and Dad would get married—at least, that's what she hoped would happen. He'd tell her stuff like he needed to get his degree and get a job before he could marry her.''

She shook her head in disbelief. "He must've been a real con artist, my dad, on account of Mom's not stupid. But she really believed what he told her. According to old Christos, the only time he'd come home was when he needed money, and even though Christos knew that, he'd give it to him anyway.''

She stared at me a moment, through me. "Dad came home about two weeks before he died. He visited Mom in her little apartment over Christos's café the way he always did—except this time she got pregnant. And before she even knew it, Dad was dead. A real old-time American romance, wouldn't you say?''

I nodded, couldn't think of anything to say.

"Anyway, I got the idea I wanted to know more about him—maybe get a different opinion about him than old Christos and Mom had given me.''

"Why?" I asked, because I'd occasionally had similar feelings about my own father, but it would mean trying to talk to my mother about something meaningful, and I wasn't sure either of us was up to it.

"Why? Beats me! I knew enough to realize he must've been a pretty selfish guy, but he had to be more than that too. See, I was starting to mess around with his music, trying to make it into songs and putting words to it.''

"You can read music?" Before she could say what her face told me she was about to say, I added quickly, "I mean, I've read that some of the best rock composers don't—Paul McCartney, for example. He's managed to write an oratorio and a symphony, plus all those songs, without knowing how to read music.''

That mollified her. "Yeah," she said condescendingly, "I can read music. The guy Mom married had an old up-right piano, and I could sit down and make stuff up, just like my dad could, even before I took lessons, so Mom let me have piano lessons. When Christos heard about it, he

didn't want her to, on account of he said music was what ruined my dad, but Mom thought it was a shame not to let me develop my talent.''

"Christos accepted you as his granddaughter?''

She laughed. ''Not at first he didn't! He even fired Mom from the café when she told him she was pregnant. And he was furious when she told him his son was the father! But a few years later, about the time I started school, he came to the door one evening and asked to see me. I guess somebody'd tipped him off that I looked a lot like my dad. There was a big scene with lots of noise and tears—I remember it—and after that he treated me like a granddaughter, which I was, of course. One year, he gave me this bracelet for my birthday. It belonged to his wife—my grandmother. I never knew her.''

Smiling, she let the bracelet slide up and down her arm, this woman who looked so much like her father. I watched it for a moment, fascinated, thinking of the woman who'd owned it, and of her son who'd made up music for her as she died—and how all that had led me here to this place, now.

"You want another Coke?'' Elli asked me, breaking the spell.

"I'm fine, thanks.''

She jumped up and went out to the kitchen and got herself another beer. When she came back, she said, ''Later, I found an old guitar in Christos's attic that he said was my dad's. I taught myself to play it, with the help of a friend. When I learned to read music, I had a lot of fun playing with the stuff Dad had written, and after a while I got to thinking maybe he was speaking through me, you know? Or maybe we were talking to each other through the music.''

She gave me a dazzling smile. ''Probably stupid, right? I guess he was selfish and fucked up, but at least he left me something—his talent and his music. And I liked what I got to know of him through the music. Does that make sense?''

I nodded. It made sense to me.

"I started playing in bands in high school and then, after

I graduated, me and a couple of other girls started our own band and went around playing all over the place, wherever we could get a gig. But after doing that awhile, I decided I needed to settle down in one place, so I decided to come here. It's a good music town—there's a lot of musicians and bands and places to play you know?''

"And it was where your dad had lived," I said.

"Yeah, sure." She pressed the cold cloth against her eye, held it there a minute. "I had an old address book in a box of stuff Christos had taken from Dad's apartment after he died. I looked up some of the names in the phone book, but after twenty years, I only managed to get hold of Evan and one of his old girlfriends. She made it pretty clear she didn't want to relive old times."

"Fiona McClure?"

She shook her head. "No, it wasn't her. Evan told me about her. She was one of Dad's lovers, but she wasn't in the book."

She laughed suddenly. "When I got Evan on the phone and told him who I was, it was like I'd told him I was Death or something—Nemesis?—coming to get him. He sounded like he was having a heart attack! I don't think he believed me, but he said he wanted to meet me, so we got together for coffee someplace. One look at me and he was convinced. He told me what he remembered of Dad—how they used to play together in bars and coffeehouses around the U and stuff like that."

"And he told you about Fiona McClure."

"Yeah." She smiled. "She's a harpist. I thought about looking her up once, but Evan said he didn't think I should."

"When did you first meet Turner?"

"In April, I guess. After he'd told me everything he could remember about my dad, I figured that was the end of it—I mean, Evan and I didn't exactly have anything in common. But then he got interested in *me* and wanted to know all about my life—you know, a woman trying to make it as a musician. Then he asked me if I'd pose for him. He said he was tired of being a professor—all that *talking* about creativity instead of being creative—and he

was trying photography. He offered me money, twenty bucks an hour for a couple of hours a week, so I said yes. That's a lot of money for doing nothing.''

"How long did this go on?"

"Off and on until a couple of weeks before he went up north. At first we'd go down to the river and he'd take pictures of me in the trees and bushes or sitting on the shore—stuff like that. Plus he did a lot of close-ups. He was fascinated by my face—on account of how much I look like my dad, probably. Evan was really hung up on my dad.''

She laughed. "Finally he screwed up the courage to ask me if I'd pose naked for him. I'd seen it coming a mile away. I said sure, why not? Being naked's no big deal. But I made it clear to him that he wasn't going to touch me—I was up front with him about that. No monkey business.''

"When I searched his apartment," I said, "I couldn't find any photographs or negatives of you.''

"That's right, you couldn't!" She laughed. "When we went in to get the keyboard and stuff, I took them all with me. Pictures like that could come back to haunt me someday. I burned 'em.''

"And so that's all there was to your relationship with Turner.''

"You sound disappointed," she said with a grin. "What were you expecting, that we'd been lovers or something, and I killed him because I caught him with another woman?''

"No, you're just a loose end in the life of a man who died violently and unexpectedly.''

She drank beer a moment. "When I heard about him dying," she added, "I wondered if maybe he'd jumped.''

"Why'd you think of that?"

"Well, see, me, Tracy, and Lisa had just started Furies—that's our band—and we were starting to get busy, writing music together, rehearsing, and running around trying to line up gigs and stuff, so I told Evan I didn't have time to pose for him anymore. To be honest, I was getting bored with it too. He took it pretty well, I guess, but then he said

he'd like to try to take pictures of me and the band. We rehearse in Lisa's parents' basement—Lisa's our bass player. He said maybe he could do a kind of documentary in pictures of a band that's just starting out. He'd written a book on the guitar and he figured this could be a kind of continuation of that or something. I talked it over with Tracy and Lisa and we all agreed to let him try—I figured I owed him that, on account of he'd been my dad's friend. So we let him hang out with us and take pictures, and he did that for a couple of weeks."

She laughed suddenly. "He even suggested we cut an album and call it *Greek Light*, because Helen means "light" in Greek, and that was my dad's mother's name too. My mom named me that, probably hoping to soften up old Christos, and Evan was always calling me that, even though I told him I didn't want him to. Also, the songs we were working on were my dad's."

"Your dad's? You were rehearsing your dad's songs?"

"Sort of. We're turning them into rock music."

"It was the music you found in your grandfather's attic?"

"Yeah, stuff my dad left behind when he came here and went to the U. Old Christos told me he'd composed them for his mom when she was sick, but when she died, he lost interest and left them all behind when he moved down here. Only a couple are finished, the rest are just melodies, with the harmonies sort of sketched in. We're having a lot of fun with them now, trying to turn 'em into rock."

"How did Turner react when you told him it was your dad's music?"

"He was really blown away when he heard some of it. He wanted to see the original stuff my dad had written down. When I showed it to him, he asked if he could make a copy of it. He said he knew a composer at the U who might be able to finish the songs the way my dad intended, some guy who's written some beautiful songs himself.

"I told him no," she went on with a toss of her head. "My dad's music is mine now. He tried to write music the way they teach you to do it at the U and he couldn't, so I wasn't gonna let somebody at the U have it now!"

"And Turner didn't argue about it?"

"Uh-uh. He knew he couldn't change my mind."

"You said you thought he might've committed suicide. Why?"

"On account of I finally had to tell him we didn't want him hanging around anymore. He was starting to get on everybody's nerves. He showed us some of the pictures he'd taken of us and, to be honest, we didn't think they were any good. They weren't rock and roll, if you know what I mean."

Her eyes bored into mine across the footlocker. "We're professionals, you know. We've all been in and around rock music all our lives and it's what we do—it's our lives! Evan was just an amateur, an old guy who didn't have a clue. Frankly, we even wondered if maybe the real reason he was hanging around was so he could kind of live his life through us. Does that make sense?"

From what I'd learned about Evan Turner, it made perfect sense. "I don't suppose he took that very well," I said.

She looked down at the scarred surface of the footlocker. "No, it was like I'd stabbed him in the stomach or something. I felt a little bad about having to do it. He said, 'But can we go on being friends and see each other sometimes?' I told him I didn't think we had enough in common to be friends. He didn't like hearing that either."

"That was the day before he went up to Lake Superior?" She nodded.

That night, I recalled, Turner had gone back to Marcy and asked if they could try to put the marriage back together.

"I thought maybe I should string him along a little longer," Elli went on, "at least until I got the keyboard. But I decided I couldn't do that and still be true to myself."

"But he said you could have the keyboard anyway?"

She nodded. "Yeah. Evan was basically a nice guy. A little fucked up, but nice. He told me dad's death really shook him. It was what made him decide to give up music himself and become a professor. He said he regretted it now."

"Did he tell you how your dad died?"

"Yeah, but I already knew. The doctor told Christos he choked to death on a carrot while he was playing somewhere in front of a crowd of people. A pretty horrible way to die, so I can see how it might've shook old Evan. Plus, of course, he blamed himself."

I glanced up at her. "Who did? Turner? He wasn't there!"

"Yeah, he was. He told me he was, anyway. Uh-huh. He told me Dad was really in a groove that night. He wasn't supposed to play, somebody else was—that Fiona something, his lover. But he came in and joined her on stage and started playing too, and they were really jamming together—if you can imagine a harp and a piano jamming, which I can't. But then my dad took a break. He brought a baggie of vegetables out of his jacket—Dad was a health nut, according to Evan—and just then Evan came into the place. When Dad saw him, he pulled a carrot out of the baggie and waved it at Evan. He called out, 'What's up, Doc?' the way Bugs Bunny does in the cartoons, and took a big bite and laughed—and that was that."

"Why did Evan—Turner—blame himself?"

She shrugged. "I dunno. It didn't make sense to me. But he did. He said if he hadn't come into the place when he did, Dad wouldn't've laughed as he tried to swallow the carrot."

She smiled sadly. "I asked Evan, didn't anybody know the Heimlich? Everybody does today. But he said nobody must've, because nobody tried it on him, they just pounded on his back and made it worse. I knew Evan's wife was a nurse, so I said too bad your wife wasn't there, 'cause she probably knew it, but he said they weren't together then."

But they were, of course.

We talked a little longer and then, suddenly tired, I got up to go. Elli didn't seem tired at all. She thanked me again for coming to her rescue and I thanked her for coming to mine. At the door, I thought of something else and turned. She was still on the sofa, looking at the photograph of herself.

"You said earlier that you'd considered looking Fiona McClure up, but Evan discouraged it. Did he say why?"

"Yeah. When I told him once that I'd sort of like to meet her and hear what she had to say about my dad, he said he hoped I wouldn't—said it would upset her too much, to find out he'd been cheating on her."

She smiled. "Like I said, Evan was a nice guy. So Fiona McWhat's-her-name can keep her illusions about my dad. Besides, I'm not interested anymore, I've got his music. I don't need what some old girlfriend remembers about his life. I don't live in the past."

Twenty-six

When I got home that night, I microwaved something and ate it without knowing what it was, made myself an espresso, and took it into my living room. I let my mind play with what I'd learned about Evan Turner from Elli and all the others I'd talked to, and what they'd told me about themselves while they were telling me about him. And when I'd worked the story out to my satisfaction, I wondered what I could do with it. After a while, I got up and went to the phone and called Fiona McClure.

Douglas answered. When I asked to speak to his wife, he snapped, "It's late—what's this about?"

"I'd like to tell her that myself."

"You can tell her tomorrow," he said, and hung up. I'd heard a woman's voice in the background, asking a question.

I stood there and waited, staring down at the phone until, a few minutes later, it rang. "This is Fiona, Peggy. What do you want?"

"You said you'd like to know Elli's story. I have it, if you're still interested."

A long pause. "You've talked to her?"

"Yes."

"She's Chris's daughter?"

"Yes. Would you like to meet somewhere tonight and talk about it?"

"Will it make me sleep any better?"

"You'll have to answer that question for yourself."

She gave a brittle laugh. "My! You sound like you have something more on your dreary cop's mind than just telling

me a bedtime story! I wonder what it could be."

"I'll be at the Boardinghouse in an hour," I said. "If you're interested, you can meet me there."

"The Boardinghouse!" she exclaimed. "I take it back—there is poetry in you after all, Peggy. I haven't been in—in that place since Chris died."

I didn't say anything to that, just waited.

"I'll think about it," she replied finally. "I'll think about it," she repeated. And hung up.

I got out my cassette recorder and tucked it into my shoulder bag, sat in my living room, and stared out my big picture window at the rainy night until it was time to drive over there.

The place was almost empty, with only the chess players who were always there huddled over their board, lost in contemplation, and a few people sitting alone at tables. I got a latté from Stilwell, who acted as though he'd never seen me before in his life, and took it to a table in the corner up by the rain-splattered front window, where I waited to see if Fiona McClure would come.

A few late-night people, huddled beneath umbrellas or rain hoods, hurried past the window without coming in. A couple of cars sped down the street, their taillights leaving glowing red streaks behind them in the night. An hour passed and Fiona didn't appear. I got another latté from Stilwell, took it back to my table, waited.

I'd almost given up on her when suddenly she walked briskly past the window, a small, determined figure in a dark raincoat, stray wisps of her silver hair blowing around her in the breeze like smoke.

She hesitated a moment at the door, then pushed it open and came in. She stood just inside and looked around the room slowly, her eyes stopping at the empty stage a moment before passing on, and then she walked up to the counter where Stilwell, his back to her, was busy making a new pot of coffee.

He turned after a minute, noticed her standing there, and asked her what he could get her. Then he took a second look and dropped the metal filter full of old grounds he was

holding. It made a loud clang in the quiet of the place as it hit the floor.

"Hello, Stilwell."

He didn't say anything, just stared.

"It's been a while, hasn't it?" she went on with a smile. "You haven't changed much. What's your secret? There's a portrait of you in the basement that's growing old instead of you?" When he didn't answer, she continued, "You are alive, aren't you? You didn't die and the present owners had you stuffed?"

That brought him out of his trance. "Yeah, hi, Fiona," he managed to get out. "You ain't changed much yourself."

"You must be mellowing," she said. "You never used to lie. You serve plain coffee?" When he nodded, she said, "That's what I'd like."

"I'm makin' fresh," he told her. "I'll bring it to your table when it's done. You still take it with milk and sugar?"

"Yes," she said, her voice softening, "I still do." She started to open her purse.

He raised a hand. "It's on the house, Fiona."

"What am I, suffering from a terminal illness?" she asked, then added with a smile, "Thanks, Stilwell." As she turned and came over to me, the smile faded from her face. She slipped out of her raincoat, let it fall over the back of her chair, sat down. She looked smaller than I'd seen her before, and older too.

"Okay, so I'm here," she said nervously. "Sorry I'm late. Nice of you to wait."

"It's okay," I told her. "I like it here."

"You have strange taste. Well, so this Elli is Chris's daughter, huh?"

I nodded.

She brooded on that a moment. I waited for her to ask me to tell her about Elli, but she didn't. She said, "There were a lot of women before me, of course, and even when we were together, there were women hanging around. Elli's mother was one of those?"

I shook my head. "No, she was an old girlfriend from high school, a waitress in his dad's café."

She managed a laugh. "Sure, why not? He used to go home sometimes, to see his dad. I suppose it was to see her too. I would have killed him if I'd found out." She shook one of her long fingers in my face, trying to keep it light. "You don't mess with harpists, you know, at least not young and romantic ones." She lowered her voice to an ominous whisper, leaned over the table. "Maybe I cast a spell on him, got him to swallow a piece of carrot the wrong way." She grinned to indicate she was only joking, but there was no humor in her eyes.

Stilwell arrived then with her coffee, put it down, hovered.

She looked up at him with a smile. "Thanks."

He nodded, gave me a puzzled glance, turned, and went away.

I said, "If somebody who was here that night had known the Heimlich maneuver, Chris Stavrakis might have been on his feet again and back at the piano within a few minutes of choking on the carrot."

She sipped the coffee tentatively. "I suppose so," she said. "But nobody did."

"Marcy must have known it."

"But she wasn't here," she said.

"Was Turner?"

She looked at me. "No, of course not. He hated Chris, so why would he come to hear him play?"

"Because he didn't know Chris was playing that night. He thought you were playing alone, to your fans."

"Evan wasn't here!" she repeated sharply.

"He told Elli he was."

She put her cup down with a clatter. "He lied to her."

I shook my head. "I don't think so. He described the scene to her just the way Stilwell did to me last night, how you were up on the stage playing the harp and singing and Stavrakis came in unexpectedly and joined you on stage. He even mentioned it was a plastic bag of vegetables, not just a carrot, as you and Stilwell told me. But he also added something else Stilwell didn't know, because he wasn't here: he told Elli that Stavrakis spotted him and waved the carrot at him and called out, 'What's up, Doc?' The audi-

ence—*your* audience—wouldn't have noticed that Stavrakis was speaking to Turner, or known what it meant. Why would Turner tell Elli something like that if it wasn't true? He certainly wasn't bragging about inadvertently contributing to her father's death.''

''Why not? Anything to make himself seem important. I'll bet he didn't tell her about me!''

''But he did.''

Her eyes held mine a moment, then darted away. She got up quickly and turned her back on me, staring into the room as though looking for something. All there was to see was Stilwell at the bar, his pale, expressionless face turned to us, and the empty stage with the piano on it. She turned and sank back into her chair.

''Yes, all right, so Evan was here. He came in without realizing Chris was here too. Evan knew I was playing that night, so he must have come in to see me, even though he was engaged to marry Marcy at the time—that's the kind of creep he was. Chris and I had just ended a duet and Chris brought out that goddamned bag of vegetables. He spotted Evan—and you know the rest.''

She shook her head slowly from side to side, as though still not able to believe it. ''His last words were 'What's up, Doc?' Why does everything have to turn out so disgusting?''

''I wonder if Turner knew the Heimlich,'' I said, watching her over my coffee cup. ''After all, he was engaged to a nurse. Marcy could have taught it to him, if he hadn't learned it somewhere else.''

She looked up at me, a sneer on her face, her big eyes glittering. ''Oh, you mean Evan didn't tell Elli he knew the Heimlich and could have saved Chris?''

''No, he didn't tell her that. That's the only thing he didn't tell her.''

Fiona seemed to relax, drank some coffee. ''Had they even invented it back then?''

I didn't bother to answer that. ''I'm thinking about how you and Marcy became such good friends after you married Douglas, and how Turner was so opposed to it. He even made Marcy promise not to talk to you about him.''

"He was a jerk, that's why," Fiona said. She sounded tired now.

"Or was it because he was afraid you'd tell her the story of how Stavrakis died, and she'd realize her husband had stood by and let a man die without doing what he could to save him?"

"How should I know what he was afraid of?"

"A couple of nights after he moved out," I said, "you and Marcy got a little drunk together and she broke her promise not to talk to you about him. According to Marcy, you talked about Stavrakis too."

"But we didn't talk about how he died!"

"You won't mind if I ask Marcy about that, will you?"

"I won't mind at all," she replied, a little smile of triumph on her face.

She drained her coffee cup and stood up, reached for her raincoat. "I can't say this has been pleasant, Peggy, but it's been interesting." She smiled down at me. "Anything else you want to tell me before I go?"

For a moment I thought I must have been wrong, and then the realization hit me. "Annette!"

She paused in the act of turning away, looked back at me. "What about her?"

"You babysat her while her mother and Ben Anderson were off for a weekend together last month. She told me that."

"So?"

"She asked you about Stavrakis—and why you didn't marry him."

"She told you that too?" she whispered, her face the color of chalk.

I nodded. "Would you mind if I asked her if the Heimlich maneuver came up in that conversation?"

Twenty-seven

Fiona stood there unmoving a minute, then sank back down into her chair. As she did, Stilwell hove quietly into view, an apparition from the past, carrying his coffepot like an offering. He caught Fiona's eye and, when she nodded absently, refilled her cup. "Put some in mine too, will you?" I asked him. He pretended he didn't hear me, or else he really didn't hear me, and moved away.

She picked up her cup and held it in both hands, as though to warm them. "I've become a kind of aunt to Annette," she said when he'd gone, "and sometimes we do things together—go to movies, concerts, things like that. Her mother works long hours at the hospital and doesn't always have the time or energy for her. I have both. And she loves listening to me play the harp. She's even planning to take harp lessons from me, starting next month." Fiona smiled, thinking about that.

"A couple of weekends before we went up north, I stayed with her while her mother and Ben were at his cabin, and one night I took her to a pizza place for dinner. As we were waiting for our order, she suddenly asked me why I'd dumped her dad. When I'd recovered from the shock, I asked her how she knew about us. She told me she'd once overheard her parents arguing about me, back at the time Marcy and I became friends, and she'd figured out the reason Evan didn't want her mother to see me was because I'd dumped him for Chris. Imagine—she'd held on to that memory since she was ten or eleven!"

I had no trouble imagining it.

"You've met Annette," she went on, "so you probably

know there's no point in lying to her or holding out on her. I told her it was because I'd fallen in love with somebody else. It didn't seem to bother her that I'd dumped her father for another man, but she wanted to know why I hadn't married him—Chris. I told her he'd died. She wanted to know how. I told her that too. And do you know what she said then?"

I wanted to hear it from her.

" 'Too bad Daddy wasn't there,' she said. I asked her why. 'On account of he knew the Heimlich maneuver,' she replied. I asked her how she knew that, and she said, 'Because when Mom taught it to me and some of my friends, she told us she'd taught it to him on one of their first dates. All the nurses at the hospital had to learn it.' She said teaching it to boys was a great way to hug them without them knowing what you were doing."

Fiona looked out into the room. "There was chaos," she said after a moment, so softly I could barely hear her. "Chris was over there on the floor, gasping for breath, terror in his eyes—the only time I ever saw him scared—but nobody knew what to do. Somebody pounded him on the back, but that didn't do any good. I was kneeling beside him, screaming for somebody to do something. I looked up and saw Evan's head in the crowd. He was staring down at Chris, no expression on his face, no expression on his face at all. Then he looked at me, turned, and vanished. He murdered Chris as surely as if he'd shot him or stabbed him—or thrown him off a cliff."

The silence stretched out for minutes. Then she looked up suddenly, her blue eyes boring into mine. "From the moment Annette spoke those words in that pizza restaurant," she went on slowly, "I knew I was going to kill her father. The only question in my mind was how."

She twitched a smile. "I didn't want it to look like murder, you see. Not because I was afraid I'd be a suspect—how could I be? After all, I had no reason to want Evan dead, as far as anybody knew. But I didn't want suspicion to fall on Marcy or Ben. That's when I decided to accompany David to Lake Superior. I hoped I could find an op-

portunity to kill Evan there and make it look like an accident.

"For most of that week, whenever he'd go into the woods with his camera, there'd always be too many other people around, but I finally saw my chance Friday afternoon, when a lot of people left the conference center for the weekend and David had to drive down here for recitals."

She laughed, too loudly. "You know, Peggy, you did more than just shatter my illusions about Chris with that photograph of Elli. You broke up my marriage."

"How'd I do that?" I asked, since it seemed the polite thing to do.

"Once you began raising questions about Evan's death, I could see that David was starting to wonder why I'd chosen to stay up there that weekend instead of coming back down here with him—much less gone up there in the first place. He knows I don't really care for the North Shore in midsummer—it's too hot and there are too many bugs. When he saw my reaction to the photograph, it all came together in his mind. Last night he told me he wanted a divorce. I suppose he doesn't want to go on living with a murderer. He's such a fastidious man." She shook her head in mock despair, perhaps to cover the real thing.

I asked her how she'd got Turner alone.

"I saw him walk into the woods around five o'clock. Nobody was around, so I simply strolled down the shore until I was out of sight of whoever might have been watching and then climbed into the woods on one of the side paths that go up from the shore.

"It didn't take me long to find him, since he stuck to the trail—Evan always stuck to the trail. He was making his way slowly up in the direction of the cliffs, pausing every now and then to take a picture. He was so preoccupied with his photography that I could have come up on the trail behind him and killed him long before he got to the top, except I didn't have anything to kill him with. Besides, I wanted to get him as close to the cliff as possible—preferably push him off when he was at the edge. And I wanted to talk to him first, before killing him. I wanted

to be sure he'd known the Heimlich and might have been able to save Chris. I wanted him to know why he was going to die!

"I let him see me in a glade of birch about two-thirds of the way up the trail. He almost jumped out of his skin, probably because it was dark in there and he thought he was seeing a ghost. He asked me why I was there and I told him I was just out walking, and I asked him if I could walk along with him. He was confused at first, but then he seemed almost touchingly grateful.

"We walked on and I asked him if he'd take my picture, and he said he'd be happy to. 'But not here,' I told him. 'Higher up, where there's more light.'

"When we got to the top, with only a few yards of bare earth and boulders between us and the cliff, he stopped. I told him I wanted the picture to be of me standing by one of the boulders near the edge. He said yes, but he'd have to take the picture from a distance, since he'd only recently discovered he was afraid of heights. I had to bite my tongue to keep from telling him he'd always been afraid of heights.

" 'Oh, come on, Evan,' I said, and gave him my nicest smile, 'just a little closer.' But he wouldn't go any closer— not even for me. So we sat down on one of the boulders and I took his tripod out of his hands and put it in my lap. I began talking about the last night here twenty years ago. I reminded him of how he'd stood and looked down at Chris, choking to death on the floor over there, and how he'd met my eyes before turning away and leaving. 'You knew the Heimlich, didn't you?' I asked him. The question startled him. 'How'd you know?' he asked me. 'Your daughter told me,' I said. 'Annette!' he whispered.

"He bowed his head and as he sat there, staring down at his hands, I got up and swung the tripod with all my might—I can still feel the shudder run up my arms! I dragged him to the edge of the cliff and shoved him over. I hung over the edge—I'm not afraid of heights!—and watched until he hit the water, and then I threw the tripod after him."

She sat back in her chair, breathing hard. After a moment, she added, "My only regret was that he was unconscious or dead when he fell."

"I don't suppose you thought to ask him if he regretted that he hadn't tried to help Stavrakis, or suffered all these years on account of it," I said.

"If *he'd* suffered! Evan? Why should I?"

"I suppose you're right. Your suffering was so much greater than his could ever have been."

"He never regretted it," she said angrily. "Not for a minute! He was proud of what he'd done!"

"If that's the case," I said, "why didn't he throw Elli in your face, once he'd found out about her? That would have been sweet revenge, wouldn't it? But when Elli mentioned to him once that she'd like to meet you, he asked her not to. He said it would cause you too much pain."

She stared at me wide-eyed for a moment, her mouth open. Across the room, Stilwell stood watching us from behind his counter. Then she shuddered, as though a cold wind had come up suddenly, and she pulled her raincoat more tightly around her.

"Until you showed me the photograph of Elli," she whispered, "I felt that killing Evan was the most beautiful thing I'd done in my life. You've destroyed that for me, Peggy—turned it into a ghastly joke. And now I don't want to talk about either of them anymore."

"But what about Annette," I said, "who will always wonder if her mother—or Ben—killed her father for the insurance?"

"Yes, that's something I hoped I could avoid by the way I killed him," she said, getting up. "But she'll get over it. Sooner or later we all have to learn how hideous life is. And besides, it's better than if she learned the part she played in her father's murder, isn't it? If she hadn't told me Evan knew the Heimlich, he'd still be alive today."

I stood up, reached into my shoulder bag, and dug out my cell phone.

She asked me what I was doing.

"Calling Homicide," I told her. "Asking them to send a squad car to come and take you to jail. I'm arresting you for murder."

"You're kidding, aren't you?"

"No."

"I'll deny I said any of this! It'll be your word against mine. Probably no more than a handful of people knew Evan was there the night Chris died. They won't remember it now, twenty years later, even if you could find them."

I opened my shoulder bag and brought out my cassette tape player and showed it to her.

She stared at it blankly a moment, then gave me an incredulous smile. "You can't do that," she said. "It's against the law—isn't it?"

"No."

"If I'm arrested," she said, her eyes glittering, "Annette'll learn the role she played in her father's death. It'll be your fault."

"Better that than live with the suspicion her mother killed him." I started punching in the numbers.

Fiona reached into her raincoat, brought out a small pistol, and pointed it at me. I hadn't expected that. "Hang up," she said, "or whatever it is you do with those things. And give me the cassette."

She was holding the pistol quite steadily—a beautiful and evil-looking thing. I looked at it a moment, then shrugged and dropped the cassette back in my shoulder bag. "What good would killing me do you?" I asked, meeting her eyes. "Do you think Stilwell would cover for you? Or do you intend to shoot him and the other customers too? If you do, don't bother with the chess players. They're oblivious to their surroundings."

She hesitated a moment, her eyes jumping around the room. The chess players were still bowed over their board. A fat woman and an even fatter man in a low-brimmed hat were squeezed together on a sofa in a corner, their heads together, chuckling at something over their coffee. Stilwell was coming our way with his coffeepot.

"Why not let it be, Peggy?" Fiona pleaded, her voice low and urgent. "Chris and Evan both got what they deserved. A kind of harmony has been restored to the world, don't you see? The only person who'll suffer if the truth comes out now is Annette."

"I'm sorry," I replied, and finished dialing Homicide.

She turned and ran for the door and I started around the table after her, but then Stilwell was in my way with his coffeepot. I dodged left and so did he, dodged right, tried to shove past him but tripped, and we went down together, hot coffee splashing everywhere, as Fiona McClure ran out through the door and a little voice in my hand said, "Homicide, Sergeant Mitchell speaking."

Twenty-eight

I had some explaining to do the next day in Captain Di-Prima's office. His face was bland, unreadable, the report I'd written up the night before in front of him on his desk.

Bixler was standing in a corner, glowering at me. His face is always easy to read, like an open sore. "Not even a rookie would've handled it that dumb," he said. "You should've had a plainclothed cop in there with you for backup."

"But would you have authorized such a waste of taxpayer's money?" I asked earnestly, as though really interested in the question. "After all, until Fiona McClure confessed, I didn't even know we were dealing with murder. Evan Turner jumped, don't you remember?" I made the same diving motion with my hand that he'd made with his in his office on Monday.

His face mottled and his stoat's eyes bulged and I worried about the possibility that he'd have a heart attack right there on the floor. It wouldn't be DiPrima who'd give him CPR.

DiPrima wasn't fooled. "That was a strange time of night to be conducting a routine interview, wasn't it?" he asked, flashing me his patented bright smile under eyes that sparkled like ice. "You must have had some sense that Fiona McClure was a murderer, especially after what you'd just learned from the rock musician."

"Maybe I did," I admitted, feeling myself turn a little pink, "but I couldn't be sure I could get her to confess."

"Yeah, but once she'd told you everything," Bixler growled, "you could've figured she'd try to get away and

done something to stop it. It's not like she was Muscle Boy—who also took you by surprise. You should've been armed."

"Why? I don't shoot people who are running away." It seemed I'd only just had this conversation—at the Music School burglary, where this all began for me.

"Why did you show her the cassette player?" DiPrima asked. "Surely that was just asking for trouble."

"Yes," I said. "That was an error in judgment."

He didn't say anything to that, just locked eyes with me. I blinked first. I gave him that.

Bixler aimed a fat finger at me. "If she kills anybody else before she's caught, O'Neill, the blood'll be on your hands."

DiPrima glanced down at the report a moment, then back up at me. "This Stilwell character. Do you think he tripped you deliberately?"

"I don't see how he could have," I answered.

DiPrima considered that a long moment, his eyes boring into mine. Then he shrugged and relaxed back into his chair.

"Well," he said with a sigh, "I suppose it's easy for us to rewrite the script, once we know how it's going to end. But you didn't have that privilege last night, did you? And we mustn't forget something else: you *were* able to get a woman who'd committed the perfect crime to confess. That's an impressive feat, wouldn't you say, Mel?" he added, turning to Bixler, whose first name is Mel. Mel sputtered something incomprehensible.

"You also did what you were assigned to do," DiPrima went on, "which was answer Mrs. Farr's questions concerning her grandson's death. I understand she's very pleased."

I managed to keep any expression off my face. Before coming to the station that morning, I'd called Dulcie and given her a brief report. I suspected that she'd already spoken to the University president, which was why I was going to escape DiPrima's wrath for letting Fiona McClure get away. Well, Dulcie had intervened on behalf of lesser mortals than I in her time.

DiPrima got up, went to his window and looked out at the little strip mall across the street from the station, his hands clasped behind his back. For a moment there was only the noise of Bixler's heavy breathing. Then he turned back to me.

"You've been a patrol officer a long time, haven't you, for the most part working the dog watch, where your talents are obviously underutilized."

"They're utilized just fine," I replied quickly, trying not to show the panic I was feeling.

"Have you considered taking the sergeant's exam?"

"I've considered it," I said, "but I don't think I'm ready yet. I don't have the people skills required of the rank." By that I meant I don't get along well with idiots and deadbeats, and some of the cops who'd be under me if I were a sergeant would be one or the other. I also like to pick and choose when I see people and when I don't. Being in charge of others doesn't give you that kind of freedom.

DiPrima smiled thinly. "How modest of you, Officer. Well, we can at least bring you out into the light of day, where we can see more of you. How'd you like to be a detective?" He went back to his desk and sat down, waited for my answer.

I felt myself starting to sweat, forced myself not to look at Bixler.

"I like working the dog watch," I said.

DiPrima gave me a startled smile. "Oh? Why?"

I couldn't tell him—especially not with Bixler standing there—how I like being able to walk around in the night alone. It's a privilege not many women have—or men either, anymore. And how I love being able to take my breaks down on the riverbank in warm weather, under an old willow tree that somehow manages to survive the summer flooding and winter ice. Or how I love watching the new day rise from the night and then going home to bed just as other people are starting work.

"It's hard to explain," I said, "especially since people who work days—most people—think those of us who take the dog watch by choice are crazy. But I fell in love with it the first time I got assigned to it. It suits the way I like

to live my life better than anything else I could be doing at this time.''

'' 'At this time,' '' DiPrima repeated with a smile. ''So there is some hope that someday you'll see the light, as it were.'' He turned and looked at Bixler. ''Well, Mel. What do you think?''

I watched Bixler's poached-looking eyes dart around the room as he wrestled with the possibilities. He was clearly torn. Since he knew how much I loved the dog watch, his natural tendency would be to pull me off it. But if he did, and I became a detective, I'd be spending a lot of time with him in the police station during the day, instead of outside, patrolling the campus at night. Bixler didn't like the night, and avoided it when he could.

Ultimately, his eyes encountered mine, which are green and, I'm told, can be chilly when the occasion calls for chilly eyes.

He turned to DiPrima. ''If she wants to stay on the dog watch,'' he said finally, ''let her.''

A few days later, two fishermen on Lake Superior noticed the vultures, and since they weren't having much luck themselves, they went to see what kind of luck the birds were having. They found Fiona McClure's body washed up on shore, not far from where Evan Turner's had been found. She'd driven straight from the Boardinghouse to the conference center, deserted now that the summer programs were over, climbed to the place where she'd thrown Evan Turner's body off the cliff, and jumped. ''*I'm* not afraid of heights!'' she'd told me.

And that was the end of that story.

I received a card from Gary, a day or two after that, and a couple of photographs, the ones he'd taken of us on the cliffs above Lake Superior. In the timed photograph, I was giving the camera a bright, inane smile, and Gary was looking at me. It was hard to make out the expression on his face.

I dated them both on the back and put them in a box with the other things I'm going to put in albums someday,

when I'm old and gray and have nothing better to do with my time, and then I went off to swim with a friend at Lake Eleanor. The winters are long here, so we have to take advantage of every summer day.

Epilogue

The phone rang while I was sitting on my deck with a book and a tall iced tea. I let it ring a few times before getting up and going inside to answer it. It was Butler, calling to invite me to Dulcie's for dessert that evening.

"Why, Butler?" I asked warily.

"It's Annette," he said. "She wants to talk to you about her father's death, if you have the time. She wanted me to tell you that I will be making chocolate eclairs for the occasion."

"I'd probably come anyway," I told him.

Dulcie applauded as I walked into her living room. It could have been worse, I suppose; she could have been at her piano and struck up a march. The others present—Marcy, Annette, and Ben—had the decency to look embarrassed.

Butler served an array of his own pastries, including the eclairs, with coffee for the adults and milk for Annette. Annette asked me to tell her everything I'd learned about how and why her father had died.

I didn't leave out anything relevant, although I glossed over the details of the actual murder. Annette didn't say anything for a long time when I'd finished. Just sipped her milk and ate a couple of bites of a chocolate eclair.

Finally, she turned to me and said, "You think my dad was sorry for what he did, huh—or didn't do, I mean?"

"I know he was," I replied.

She mulled that over a moment. "That's probably why he gave up music himself, and why he was so unhappy. He felt guilty about not trying to save the guy's life." She

scratched a scab off her knee, examined closely the dried blood under her fingernails for a moment, then rubbed it off on her shorts. Her mother opened her mouth to say something, shut it again.

"He didn't tell Fiona about Elli and he asked Elli not to see Fiona," Annette went on. "That must've been because he didn't want Fiona to find out what a rat her boyfriend was. Don't you think that's right, Peggy?"

I nodded.

"He wanted her to keep *her* illusions, at least. Don't you think?"

I nodded again, wondering what she was getting at.

"If he *had* told Fiona what a rat her lover was," she continued, her eyes narrowed in concentration, "Fiona wouldn't have killed him. Right?"

I hadn't thought of that. "Right," I said.

"Life is so weird," she said.

Butler materialized then and refilled her glass. She thanked him and told him how much she liked his eclairs. He deposited another on her plate.

She took a bite out of the end of it, chewed it and washed it down with milk, leaving a mustache.

"I suppose some people might think *I'm* to blame for Fiona murdering my dad," she went on, glaring around the room at each of us in turn, "because I told her about how he knew the Heimlich maneuver. But gol! How could I have known? I was just trying to tell her how sorry I was that the guy she loved died! I mean, if you have to worry about people murdering people every time you open your mouth to say something nice, you might as well not say anything nice at all!"

Nationally Bestselling Author

J·A·JANCE

The J.P. Beaumont Mysteries

Other Peggy O'Neill Mysteries by
M. D. Lake
from Avon Twilight

A MOTIVE FOR MURDER

"Thank you for coming, my dear," Dulcie said, patting my hand.

I got down to business. "The police have called your grandson's death an accident."

She made a disgusted noise. "The police . . . they're hopeless when faced with real crime. You remember Evan, of course," she said, "from my little Valentine's Day get-together."

I nodded. Her "little Valentine's Day get-together" had included a number of scantily dressed cherubs, a Cupid, a vulgar Dionysus, and a string quartet, as well as the more prominent people in town in evening dress. I had only a vague recollection of Evan Turner.

"And you met his wife, too," she added, her lips thinning in disapproval. "Marcy. They were still together in February." Her eyes glittered maliciously. "Although she was cheating on him at the time."

"I take it you think Evan was murdered," I said to Dulcie, "and that Marcy was responsible."

"I'm keeping an open mind about it," she replied virtuously, "but I'm not satisfied that Evan just fell off that cliff. I don't know of anybody who had a motive for wanting him dead beside Marcy."